The Beachcomber

ISBN: 978-0-9845926-1-6
Library of Congress Control Number: 2010929791
Published by Global Authors Publications

Filling the GAP in publishing

Edited by Barbara Sachs Sloan
Interior Design by KathleenWalls
Cover Design by Kathleen Walls

Printed in USA for Global Authors Publications

The Beachcomber
by
Walter P. Honsinger

Dedication:

To Tully.

Other books by Walter P. Honsinger:

The Cabin
The Blue Ocean's Peace

BEACHCOMBER

I stood on the Wildwood boardwalk watching white-tipped breakers crash on the beach. Piles of glistening foam, churned up by the waves, gathered along the water's edge. Great black backed gulls raced into the silvery surf as each wave receded.

An elderly man, his white hair windblown, crouched near the surf collecting something. I walked across the soft pale sand to the hard brown shoreline. A white bucket filled with huge walnut-colored clams sat nearby.

"You collecting surf clams?" I asked.

"Yeah, we had a storm last night that washed 'em ashore."

"I never heard of anyone eating them. I thought they were tough."

"Tough and sandy. The only thing worth eating is the hinge muscle. The rest is fish bait."

"Well, have a nice day," I said.

"You, too."

I walked back to the boardwalk and met Bruce.

"Do you know who he is?" I asked.

"Everyone just calls him the Beachcomber 'cause he's always gathering stuff."

TULLY

I never expected to spend the summer of 1975 at the beach; it just happened that way. One day Bruce called.

"Hey, you doing anything this weekend?" he asked.

"What's up?"

"I kinda rented a place in Wildwood, New Jersey, and I wondered if you wanted to go down."

"Kind of rented?"

"The deal went like this: A group of college guys rented a house for the summer. Some of them sold shares in the house for cash. I paid two hundred, and I can stay at the house during the summer."

"Okay," I replied.

Bruce, a tall brainy, blond kid, spent his high school years at Catholic school before going on to Villanova. He worked weeknights at a local supermarket bagging groceries.

That year the social and political turmoil we knew continued. The Vietnam War ended. The evening news showed Marines clinging to helicopters as they left Saigon. Gasoline shortages continued. We waited for hours in line only to have the gas station run out. A shortage of meat and other groceries began. Our political leaders warned us not to panic, but after Watergate no one trusted them. A few years before, assassins killed President Kennedy, his brother Bobby, Martin Luther King, Jr. and others. Everyone just wanted to forget everything that had happened. I just wanted to spend a summer away from the gas station.

I worked for a lecherous drunk who talked sex all day long. Blain stood about six foot even with grayish black hair that he combed straight back. He always wore a snow white work shirt that protruded over his ample belly. Blain not only talked sex all day long, he sold it. Eight millimeter porn movies showed on our wall most of the time. The films, magazines and sex novelties he sold to the freaks and perverts amounted to a sideline. Fixing cars, selling them and pumping gas paid our bills.

I started working at the gas station when I was twelve. I'd dealt with pissed-off customers who complained about the price of gas, the shortage of it and the oil companies that controlled it. I didn't want to waste another summer hanging around the gas station. Another summer watching everyone else enjoy themselves. I wanted a vacation. With my high school years coming to a close, I could take one. The beach sat waiting.

Bruce picked me up, and we drove to Wildwood, New Jersey. When we arrived I saw the house he'd described, a two-story wood sided saltbox with a balcony overlooking the street. From the noise emanating from the house, a full-blown party was underway.

"We'll have to sleep on the floor; the rooms are already full," Bruce said.

"That's fine with me. I expected that anyway." We walked in.

"It's only April, and the place is a pigsty already," Bruce said. Pyramids of empty beer cans rose from the floor, and bags of trash littered the yard.

"The original renters got tired of the constant parties and chaos; they sub-rented the place to anyone who was willing to fork over cash," Bruce said. "I have no idea how many guys have dibs on the house this summer."

"It's not a bad house; it's fairly new, and it's close to the beach and boardwalk."

The beaches at South Jersey sit on a series of barrier islands that protect the coastline. In the summer tourists from Philadelphia, Baltimore and New York City travel to the area to enjoy the warm blue waters of the Atlantic Ocean and the quiet back waters of the bays. It teems with wildlife, sea birds, dolphins and lots and lots of visitors. Huge schools of bluefish, tuna and trout gather off its shores. Flounder, kingfish, sea bass and crabs fill its back bays.

For us South Jersey really begins with Ocean City, a quiet town devoid of bars, liquor shops and clubs. A few motels sit on the island, but it's mainly dotted with duplexes and single-family homes. It sports its own boardwalk, but the beach is the main attraction.

Heading south from Ocean City you pass the even quieter towns of Sea Isle, Avalon and Stone Harbor. Avalon boasts that it's "Cooler by a mile" because of the evening thermals that blow cool ocean air over the island. Homes on this island sit nestled against green pine trees. A bird sanctuary covers its center.

At the southern tip of New Jersey sits Cape May, a Victorian village filled with colorful gingerbread homes. Bordered on the east by the Atlantic Ocean and by the Delaware Bay to the south, it's a quiet town filled with art galleries and unique shops.

Wildwood, the party capital of South Jersey, sits between Avalon and Cape May. Liquor stores and bars dot many corners. Quite a few motels line the streets of the town.

The beaches in Wildwood, the widest of any in South Jersey, sprawl long and flat. They offer room for everyone to stretch out. Unlike other beaches on the coast, they're free. The warm, greenish-blue water greets you.

Wildwood claims the longest boardwalk in South Jersey. It offers arcades, amusement rides and games of chance. As you walk it you'll see and smell caramel corn, salt water taffy and french fries. Freshly made pizza sits at each window.

On Sunday we drove back to Philadelphia to return to work. I dropped Bruce off and headed over to the gas station. I endured another week of work. That Friday I explained to my boss what I wanted to do.

"I'm thinking of quitting for the summer," I said. "If I did, could you find someone?"

"It's been kind of slow; we'll make out okay without you. You got something going?"

"I'm heading back to Wildwood; I have my car and three hundred dollars. The only other thing that I plan on doing this summer is taking a road trip out West."

"Well, you're welcome to work here if your money does run out." We shook hands and I went home to pack the few things I would need. I left that evening.

When I drove up to the beach house, I saw Bruce standing on the upper deck.

"We don't have to pay to stay down here, but I'm getting hit up for beer money all the time," he explained. "No matter how much beer anyone brings down, it seems that someone's always collecting money to get more."

"Well, at the rate we're downing beers, they're gonna have to keep collecting."

"I'm heading home first thing tomorrow," Bruce said.

"I'm gonna stay down and see what happens. If anyone wants me to leave, I will."

That night we slept where we passed out. For me it was an empty space behind a chair. At least no one bothered me there. I found a nail on the wall to hang my backpack.

The next morning I woke up to find Bruce had already left. I pulled my pack from the wall and headed for the boardwalk. The boardwalk is an elevated deck of tan-colored weathered boards that goes on block after block. A long flat beach leading out to the ocean sits east of the boardwalk. The town sits to the west. Games of chance, arcades, carnival acts, small shops and food vendors line the sides.

I walked on it barefoot oblivious to the signs saying shoes required. Exposed nails and splintered wood, fully capable of tearing your feet up, protruded from the weathered boards. The half-inch-thick calluses on my feet protected them. During the summer the cops would enforce the rules, but no one cared now. The boardwalk would become a madhouse from Memorial Day to Labor Day as people came down for the summer. Today few people walked it.

I passed a shop and smelled caramel corn being made. I resisted the impulse to buy it since all the food on the boardwalk is expensive. I needed to find something else to do.

Why not try fishing? I've got a spool of line, some hooks and a few sand sinkers in my pack. The salt air will help clear my head.

I found some surf clams still lying on the beach and smashed two together to open them. I baited my hook and cast into the surf. Almost immediately something big grabbed the line. It decided to fight out in the breaking waves. The line cut into my hands, but I pulled the struggling fish toward shore. A few moments later a large, silvery trout lay at the water's edge, its reddish gills opening and closing.

"That's a nice fish, son." I looked up and saw the Beachcomber standing next to me. "That fish would feed a family. Do you want me to cook it?"

"Sure." He took the fish and headed toward the boardwalk.

"That's my place," he said, pointing to a spot on the boardwalk.

I fished for almost an hour and then went to where he lived. Amid all the shops, restaurants, and arcades stood a plain black metal door. The door had no handle on it, only a key slot. I tapped on the door; it immediately swung open, and he invited me in. The darkness of the room surrounded me as I entered. It took time for my eyes to adjust. The room, a box-shaped structure, offered a kitchen at one end and a small-enclosed bedroom at the other. The neatness of his room struck me.

A place for everything and everything in its place, I guess you could say.

It contained a fully stocked fridge, all kinds of gear, and everything you would expect to find in a large home.

Well, he's not homeless, that's for sure.

"By the way, I'm Ethan," I said holding out my hand.

"Tully," he said, shaking it. "Some people just call me the Beachcomber; either's fine. I'll show you around, and then we can sit and eat."

"I can't hear any of the riotous noise from the boardwalk."

"I made false walls and filled them with twelve inches of insulation. Cuts out all the noise and keeps the heat out in the summer."

"Tully, how long have you lived here?"

"I grew up here, but I travel a lot."

Tully was probably in his sixties but could have been older. He had gray hair that he combed back, brownish leathery skin, a trimmed gray beard, and stood about five foot, six inches. He seemed to be constantly active.

We talked for a while, and then he brought a roasting pan over to the table with the trout in it. Peeled Irish potatoes surrounded the trout.

"Where I grew up, the words fish and fry were usually used together," I said. "If you ever caught fish, you had a fish fry."

"Steaming fish is a beach tradition. It's the way everyone used to cook 'em."

Tully and I ate the delicious trout and potatoes.

"You know trout ain't trout," he said.

"They're not?"

5

"They do kind of look like a trout, but they're not. They're really a kind of drum. We have all kinds of names for them here. Some people call them weakfish because they're mouths tear away from a hook easily. The locals call 'em trout 'cause it sounds better than weakfish."

"You learn something new every day."

"Come on outside," he said pouring a glass of iced tea. Rather than going out a door, we ascended a captain's ladder and climbed out a skylight to the roof. On top of the roof he'd arranged a wrought iron table and chairs. You could sit up there, look out over the ocean and imagine you were in one of the most expensive suites on the beach. We sat drinking iced tea and eating a blueberry cobbler.

"You okay?" he asked.

"My head was pounding earlier, but it feels better now."

"Beer will do that to you," he said.

How did he know about the beer last night? Maybe he smelled it on my breath?

"I saw you hand-lining on the beach; few people do that anymore," he said.

"When I was a child," I explained to him, "I often sat on the beach and watched people fish with giant surf poles. No fish would seem to bite, and they'd always complain about crabs stealing their bait. I already had some line, hooks and sinkers. That evening when everyone came out to fish, I went about a hundred yards down from them. I whirled the line around my head and threw it about twenty yards out into the surf. Almost immediately I started catching fish. That's how I learned about hand-lining."

"You're staying at that wood-sided house, aren't you?"

"Yeah, I am."

How would he know that? What are these vegetable plants doing on the roof?

"Is this your vegetable garden?"

"Just bedding plants."

"They look nice."

"Have you ever raised vegetables? Would you want to plant a garden with me tomorrow?"

"Sure."

"In the morning I'll show you my gardens," he said. We spent the next hour watching the sun, a fiery oval-shaped mass, setting in the west behind bluish white clouds.

JAMIE

I followed a line of wind-blown beer cans to our house. Two guys stood on the deck chugging beers and dropping the empties over the side. Someone handed me a Budweiser.

"Ethan, you doing anything tonight?" I turned to find a girl with shoulder-length brunette hair. Her mainline accent indicated money. I'd pumped enough gas to know.

How did she know my name?

"No, not really. And you are?"

"Jamie. Would you like to go to the Bongo Drum Room?" she asked.

"I'm spending money faster than I should, but, yeah, I'll go." She left the house and crossed the street.

An hour later she showed up back at our house all decked out in a new dress, jewelry, and shiny shoes. She brought three other girls, dressed the same, with her.

"Ready to go?" she asked.

We drove to the Bongo Drum Room, all squashed together in my Ford. I dropped the girls off at the door. By the time I'd parked, the girls were inside.

"They said you'd take care of their cover charges?" the woman at the door explained. I pulled out my wallet and paid her. As I entered, a cute barmaid with a blue flower behind one ear approached me.

"That'll be twelve dollars," she said. The girls held drinks in their hands.

"I'll pay for this round but no more," I explained.

"Yeah, that's what I guessed," the barmaid said. She bent her head to stare at me from below. I gave her a three dollar tip. She seemed satisfied and left. A few minutes later another barmaid, this one sporting a pink flower, came to collect. I searched and found Jamie.

"I'm not paying for any more drinks!" I declared. She shrugged and continued the conversation she was having. I ordered a beer for myself. I didn't see her again until closing time.

After we returned home, Jamie and her friends headed across the street to their house. About halfway across she turned around, came back, and planted a kiss on my cheek.

"I had a great time," she said.

"I'm glad someone did," I said.

I checked my wallet to find the date had cost sixty dollars.

"It looks like Jamie fleeced you!" a girl said. I turned to see a cute girl standing next to me, her long honey colored hair pulled over one shoulder.

"I'm Karen. You're the guy that sleeps in the corner right?"

"Yes, I'm Ethan."

"Well, Ethan let me give you a heads up. Jamie's heading back to Bryn Mawr tomorrow, so if you have any plans better do 'em now."

"No, getting burned once is enough. I'll call it a night."

"Suit yourself." The alcohol had kicked in by then, and I searched for a place to pass out. The spot behind the chair looked inviting.

At about eight the next morning Karen shook me awake.

"The Beachcomber's here for you," she said.

"You wanted to plant a vegetable garden?" he called.

"The rate I'm spending money I'd better plant something." I made a pot of coffee and sat drinking it. The coffee cleared my mind one layer at a time.

"Did you plan on sleeping on the floor last night, or is it just where you ended up?" he asked.

"I guess I ended up there."

He shook his head in disgust. A couple of the guys came into the kitchen, just getting in from the night before.

"This place is so dark, you'd think it was a cave," Tully remarked. Everyone rolled with laughter.

"Well, he found the perfect name for the house; it's the Cave," Karen said. I went with Tully to begin the long process of constructing a garden.

You need a sunny place for a garden with good drainage and soft soil. You till the ground with a rototiller or double dig it with a round shovel. You remove the rocks and carry them away. Once you plant your garden, you have to weed it, and protect it from bugs, rabbits and people.

Tully did things differently. His wagon held an assortment of bedding plants. It also held a flat spade, scissors, some empty milk jugs and a folded-up piece of used black plastic. Tully pulled his wagon down the street and into a backyard.

"I got permission from the owner to put a garden here," he explained. "He doesn't care what we plant."

"It's all crabgrass. How we gonna dig up the yard without a rototiller or a shovel?" I asked.

"We don't need 'em."

His method of planting was unlike anything I'd ever seen. He found a sunny spot in the sparse lawn and laid the black plastic on it. He then pushed the outer edges of the plastic into the sandy soil with his flat spade and put milk jugs full of water on the corners.

"After the first week the grass dies and the plastic will stick to the ground like glue," he said. "We need to cut x's into the plastic and plant the vegetables." That was it. No rototilling, no double digging, no raking out the rocks. The bedding plants would spread over the plastic, and no weeding was needed. Water would accumulate on the black plastic and drip down onto the plants' roots. Tully devised a work-free garden that took less than half an hour to set up and plant.

"I have gardens all over town. I grow tomatoes, honeydews, cantaloupes, sweet corn and watermelons. I also have potatoes, beans, peas, lettuce and yams. I time the crops so I have fresh vegetables to sell from May through December. The seeds can be bought for a dime a packet, and the used plastic comes from construction sites."

"You sell the vegetables?" I asked. He nodded.

"I have a garden down the street with ripe tomatoes. Started the plants in January."

"Ripe tomatoes already?" We walked down, and I saw red ripe tomatoes and other vegetables ready to pick.

We filled Tully's wagon and began walking back toward my place. On the way we would stop here or there and sell vegetables to one family or another. Tully worked one side of the street, I the other. We sold out in less than half an hour. I collected almost ten dollars, and Tully collected a little more. I tried to give him the money.

"You sold the vegetables, you keep the money," he insisted. "Besides, after all the money you spent on Jamie, I thought you'd be broke."

How did Tully know about Jamie? Is there anything he doesn't know about?

"Would you be interested in some work?" he asked. "Sometimes things come up, and I could use some help."

"Yes, I would. I have to head to Philadelphia for a few days, but I'll be back."

ASSATEAGUE

I drove back to Philadelphia to pack the rest of what I would need for the summer. I also bought some fruit, bread and other groceries. I stopped at the gas station and filled up.

"I could use you tonight if you're free," my boss said.

"I could use the money; I spent more than I should have."

"Let me guess, on a girl, right?" he asked.

"Yeah." Later that night I stood pumping gas into an old woman's car. I felt a tap on my shoulder. I turned to find a girl standing there.

"Godiva!" I lifted her up and twirled her around. Sadie appeared a moment later.

I'd met the two of them a few months before at Daytona Beach. Godiva was blond, beautiful and almost shy. I'd fallen in love with her at first sight. Sadie was tall, brunette, very pretty and easy to get along with. Together we traveled to concerts and took road trips. They didn't call themselves groupies, but everyone else did. The three of us could pool our thoughts, skills and natural strengths to overcome any obstacle we came across.

"When we're together, it's like three ships in a convoy," Sadie had stated. "Each ship has overlapping radar and ensures the safety of the other. Alone, we're vulnerable."

They showed up when I least expected it, and tonight was no exception.

"Where have you been?" I asked.

"We've been all over the place. Raleigh, Richmond, DC, Baltimore, Wilmington, New York."

"I can't believe you found me here. I've been living in Wildwood, New Jersey!"

"Really?" Sadie said. "We hoped you had a few free days. We wanted to visit Assateague Island."

"I have the entire summer free."

"I know it's late, but can we drive down tonight?" Godiva asked. "I really want to see the wild horses."

"You're lucky. I just packed my tent, gear and sleeping bags into my car."

I can smell stale beer," Godiva said. "You know how we feel about it."

"Ethan, you didn't pack any booze did you?" Sadie asked.

"Bruce spilled some in my car, but I don't have any with me."

"I'm just tired of dealing with drunks," Godiva said.

We left an hour later and arrived at Assateague around two in the morning. We set my tent up in the dark.

Assateague Island National Seashore begins in Maryland and continues on some thirty miles into Virginia. It is an area filled with stunted trees, beach dunes and grass-filled marshes. Somewhere back in time horses escaped and took over. They share the island with deer, foxes and lots of birds.

"Can we get up early to walk on the beach?" Sadie asked.

"Yes, but it'll be cold."

Once inside the tent Godiva zipped my two sleeping bags together so they would cover all three of us.

I woke up around dawn and pulled Godiva closer for warmth.

She looks as innocent as I remember. Sadie looks seductive no matter what. They asked to get up early, so should I wake them? No, I'll just let them sleep. I'll just fish on the beach until they get up.

I found more than enough sand crabs for bait. On my second cast I hooked a huge flounder.

That's more than enough for dinner, but I'll try again anyway.

I caught a few croakers before quitting. I put the fish in the cooler and walked back to the car. I found some leftover wood at the other sites and started a small fire. I made some coffee. Around nine Sadie got up, and then Godiva.

"The sun's already pretty high in the sky. Why didn't you wake us?" Godiva asked.

"I thought you could use the sleep. I have some oranges for breakfast. I also made coffee."

Godiva ate an orange. Sadie drank coffee.

"How far do we have to drive to find the horses?" Godiva asked.

"They roam all over the place. We could just take off walking and try to find some."

"And they're really wild?" Sadie asked.

"Yes. Once a year a fire company from Chincoteague comes and rounds up the young ones for sale. I don't know if they come this far north because that's like fifty miles south of here."

"Your fishing rod's out. Did you try your luck already?" Godiva asked.

"Yeah, I caught a nice flounder and some pan fish," I said.

"Maybe we could gather some clams or crabs and have a seaside dinner," Sadie said. "Bring the army shovel from your trunk."

We all dressed in jeans and pullovers, as the breeze was cold. I found two pairs of binoculars in my car. I also found a white bucket someone had thrown away. We headed south along the road until we could see the marshes leading up to the sound.

"How will we cross that to get to the water?" Sadie asked.

"We won't. I just thought this might be a good place to look for horses."

Godiva put the binoculars to her eyes and began staring out over the broad expanse of grass. Sadie did the same. A moment later Godiva put hers down.

"There's deer out there, but I've never seen anything like them," she said.

I took the binoculars and looked. A herd of spotted deer stood knee deep in water, munching on grass.

"Sika deer," I said. "Somebody brought them in from Japan a long time ago, and they're wild now."

We walked about a mile down the trail and came to an area filled with twisted, stunted trees. Paths led all through the area, and we walked in. The tree-lined path led out into another grass-filled marsh.

"It leads right up to the sound; let's walk down," Sadie said. Three horses walked out of the trees just as we got to the water's edge.

"Two pintos and a bay, they're so beautiful!" Godiva exclaimed. We walked toward them, unsure if they would run or allow us to approach.

"You're really not supposed to get too close; they kick and bite," I said. Godiva ignored me and walked forward to the larger pinto. The pinto allowed her to pet him, and she ran her hands over his shoulders and withers. Sadie walked forward and did the same. I started walking forward, but the horse seemed nervous.

"Ethan, will you please stay back? You're scaring him," Godiva called. I watched them pet the horses. After about ten minutes the horses decided to move on and disappeared into the stunted forest.

"You know, these are really ponies?" Godiva said. "I think they're Spanish."

"The legends say that a Spanish ship wrecked off here and that the horses swam ashore," I said. "Other accounts say the English grazed their horses here and some escaped."

We walked down and found a picnic table near the sound.

"I guess I expected to find more people here," Sadie said.

"It's pretty dead here until Memorial Day, and then it's crowded," I said.

"Come on; let's tread for clams," Godiva called. They slid out of their boots and jeans and walked into the cold water.

"This is freezing!" Sadie called. "Come on, Ethan. Don't be shy. We'll show you how to do this." I slid out of my boots and jeans and followed them in.

"I found one!" Godiva called. "Ethan, come here and feel with your toes." I walked over and she guided my foot to where she said a clam lay. I felt the smooth round form with my toes. She used my army shovel to scoop it into the white bucket.

"I found a couple of them!" Sadie called. As I was walking toward her I felt a few also and scooped them. We collected a bucketful of clams.

We sat at the picnic table drying off and warming ourselves in the bright sunlight.

"So you'll be around all summer?" Sadie asked. "We'd like to go to some concerts with you."

"I'll be living in Wildwood, so I'll have time to travel. Let's see what happens."

"Ethan, we're not trying to be pushy. We just want you to be happy," Sadie said.

"Well, it's working. I'm as content as I've ever been."

Late in the afternoon we walked back to the campground and found that it was still deserted.

"I have some rice in my pack," I said. "I also have my mess kit."

"We can wrap the fish and clams in foil to cook over the coals, but I'll need your pot for the rice," Sadie said. We made a nice fire and began cooking our meal.

"As usual your cooking smells terrific!" I said to Sadie. Steam rose from the foil pack signifying the meal was ready. We ate while watching the evening sky turn orange and pink.

"Let's shower off and get ready for the night," Godiva said. We walked over and got ready to shower.

"Wait let's try …," Sadie said pulling on several hot showers at once. We stood in the hot steam until our toes wrinkled. The next thing was a blur; Godiva and Sadie sprinted for the cold ocean. I ran behind them. Screaming, we dove in.

"The shock is a real rush!" Sadie said. We later walked back to the shower and washed all the saltwater off.

Sadie grasped my arm and pointed at a long scar.

"What happened?" she asked.

"It's an idiotic game. Two guys hold their arms side by side, and someone puts a lit cigarette between them. The first guy to pull away loses."

"And you allowed some fool to chide you into playing it? Haven't we taught you anything? Stupid pranks can get you killed; luckily you only got scarred." Sadie hugged me tightly. "We really care about you!"

"I'm sorry. What did you want to do tonight?"

"I wanted to go over to Ocean City," Sadie said.

"I'd like that."

We drove to the town and went out on the boardwalk.

"It's colder than I thought. I'm glad we brought our sweatshirts," Sadie said.

We walked along, bought a tub of fries and ended up in an arcade.

"Will you try and win a stuffed animal for me?" Godiva asked.

The vendor had a series of milk bottles that you knocked down with a baseball.

"Not that one," Sadie said. "Do the dart one instead."

"But they have the best teddy bears!" I said.

"You can't win at that stand; try the darts instead and take your time. The trick is to aim small, miss small." My first and second dart hit and popped the balloon. Sadie stopped me before I threw the last dart.

"Think of a grain of sand being in the middle of the balloon and aim at it," she said. I concentrated and hit the balloon. Godiva picked out a small purple monkey.

"What was wrong with the other stand?" I asked.

"The milk bottle on the bottom, center, is filled with lead. No baseball will knock it over," Sadie explained.

"How do you know?"

"I just know."

We played Skee ball for almost an hour, and Sadie won every time. A crowd gathered to watch. One group of guys couldn't take their eyes off Godiva. Another group seemed mesmerized by Sadie. Three girls stopped, looked at me, then at Godiva, rolled their eyes and stared. It didn't make me feel any better.

"It shouldn't bother me anymore," I said. "I just don't look like I belong with you two."

"Well, this will help," Godiva said. She came over, wrapped her arms around me and gave me a long kiss. The girls walked on. We headed back and stopped at a grocery store. Godiva bought a bag of apples and a scrub brush.

We returned to the campground late that night. I built a large fire, and we sat around staring into the flames.

"Can we sing songs or something?" Godiva asked. I thought about singing "Kum-bay-yah," but Sadie broke into "Good feeling to know."

"Sadie, you've got a beautiful voice," I said. She nudged Godiva, and she sang "Sweet Baby James." We all joined in.

"Your turn," Godiva said to me. We all sang "Ripple" and "Handyman."

"I'm tired. Why don't you two just sit up for a while?" Godiva asked. We sat staring at the fire for a long time, not saying anything. Sadie slid close and pulled my arm around her.

"You don't need to worry what others think about the three of us," Sadie said. "In fact, you don't need to worry at all!"

"I look like I don't belong with you two. It's not how I like it."

"I like things like this: soft, fuzzy … warm," she said.

"I like things … I don't know, mindless?"

"I think you mean like not a care in the world."

"Hun, you know I'm staying in Wildwood. I could keep both of you with me."

"And we'd love it, but it's not to be. If we stay in any one place too long, we'll get caught."

I wish I knew more about them ....

"Sadie I just wish…"

"Ethan, you're a really decent guy; you just don't know it. You need to go on to college! You could really make something of yourself if you did. You need to pull yourself up from the gutter and go on."

"You sound like the old guy I met."

"What old guy?"

"Tully. Most people just call him the Beachcomber."

"He might be just what you need." She pulled my arm tighter around herself and then relaxed.

"Sadie …." She was asleep already. I carried her in.

The next morning we tracked down another herd of horses.

"Look a colt!" Sadie said. I walked forward and saw three mares and a colt standing.

"Let me go forward," Godiva said. We watched as she went up, gave one mare an apple and watched it eat it. She pulled the scrub brush from her pocket, brushed the mare, and it seemed to enjoy it. I stepped forward; the mare threw her head and started to walk off.

"Ethan, stay back. You're scaring her," Godiva called. Sadie stood with me and didn't move. The mare returned, and Godiva fed it another apple. Finally the colt came forward, and Godiva fed it also.

"We're not supposed to feed the horses," I said. "We should head back to camp."

Later Sadie cooked chowder for us, using the remainder of the clams and my canned potatoes.

"Can you drop us off at the Foghat concert this afternoon?" Sadie asked.

"Where is it?" I asked.

"Wilmington," she replied.

"Yeah, it's on the way back to Wildwood." Two hours later we had packed everything and left.

At three-thirty I pulled up to the concert hall. Sadie and Godiva got their things out.

"Well, it looks like we're off again," Sadie said.

"I'll try and get down to Wildwood and visit," Godiva said. We hugged, and they headed in. I had all the usual misgivings watching them walk off. I wished I could keep and protect them. I headed down the road toward Wildwood.

CRABBING

The morning sky looked like a pearl, a pale slightly pinkish color. Herring gulls, their feathers blazing white contrasted against grey wings, dove, screamed and called among themselves. The heat and humidity of the summer had not yet arrived. The cool breeze blowing in off the ocean smelled almost sweet, a clean briny scent.

Mornings like this I'd make a pot of coffee and drink it alone on the deck. I'd sit and stare off into the distance. Sometimes hours would go by. *Why do I feel so guilty whenever I drop Sadie and Godiva off? I never know where they are, what they're doing or if they're okay. I know this isn't the way things are supposed to be, but it's the way things are. The only thing I can do is go forward.*

I heard cabinets closing and feet shuffling. A moment later Karen approached me.

"We're heading to Cape May for the day. Do you want to come? We could use an extra car."

"I need a break. I'd love to go." As it turned out, sixteen were going: ten girls and six guys.

"Can I drive with you?" she asked. "Tom and Jim asked me to drive with them but I'd rather not."

"Which ones are Tom and Jim?"

"The tall athletic guys."

"Both have short black hair and look like quarterbacks? I can't tell one from another. Why didn't you want to drive with them?"

"They're both a little hyper and argue all the time. So can I drive with you?"

"I'd love it."

Half an hour later my tires rolled along the highway as we headed south. A few minutes later we arrived.

"Cape May is a beautiful town full of Victorian houses, small shops and restaurants," she said. "Come on. Let's hit the shops." We shopped at several stores and got a bite to eat at a small cafe overlooking the ocean. Since I had driven, she bought lunch. Later we drove to Delaware Bay.

"Check this out!" she said. "During one of the wars, steel was scarce, so someone decided to make ships out of concrete. From what the billboard says, the ships worked out for a while but later became impractical to use." The ship laid beached a short way out from the shore. "Can you imagine living on a ship made of concrete?"

"No, I can't," I said. A pretty girl with curly brunette hair walked up.

"Do you know Connie?" Karen asked.

"No, I don't," I said. "I'm Ethan."

"Care if I join you?" she asked. We walked down the beach together. We came upon a guy glassing the beach with binoculars.

"You looking for birds?" I asked.

"Yes," the guy said.

"I noticed some strange shore birds poking their beaks into the mud," Connie said.

"They're Red Knots. This is a migration route," the birdwatcher explained. "The birds show up this time of year, but it seems that every year there's less of them. They need a quiet place on the beach to feed, and there's not much of that left."

We went further down the beach and found people digging, and sifting, the sand.

"What are you looking for?" Connie asked.

"Diamonds ...," the guy said.

"Diamonds?" Connie repeated. "You can find diamonds on the beach?" The man showed her a bag containing several white stones.

"They're called Cape May diamonds, but they're really quartz crystal," he explained. "The Lenape tribes that lived in the area thought highly of them. Jewelers in Cape May make rings and necklaces out of them. They say that these start as quartz rock up in the mountains and wash all the way down here." Connie turned and called to a dark-haired kid wearing a Steelers shirt.

"Ted, find me some diamonds," Connie called. He walked forward and joined her.

"Ethan, this is Ted," Connie said.

"There's diamonds here?" he asked. "Let's look for some!" We began digging in the sand, searching for them.

"I found one!" Karen screamed and ran it over to show us. Soon everyone had found a few.

"Look what I found; is this a wolf tooth?" Connie asked.

"Ancient shark tooth!" a guy said. "It's more valuable and rarer than the Cape May diamonds."

"Hey, let's grab some sandwiches and watch the sun go down!" Connie said. "We can watch it set over the water."

We all piled back into our cars and drove toward Cape May, stopping at a deli on the way.

"Come on," Connie called. "I know the way." She led us to a cluster of small cottages. Karen walked down to the beach, spread a blanket out, and everyone scooted together. We sat eating our sandwiches as the calm grayish waters of Delaware Bay seemed to swallow the fiery sun one layer at a time.

"What's this place called?" Ted asked.

"Sunset Beach," Connie replied. Later we drove back to the Cave and called it a night.

The next morning I drove down by the docks. I passed one of the marinas and noticed nearly a dozen tar-coated crab pots sitting off to the side.

"Who owns the crab pots?" I asked the dock master.

"Someone left them here last fall. I have to get rid of 'em before everyone brings their boats down for the summer. If you want 'em, take 'em, but take 'em all."

I looked them over and tried to decide if I could use them. Crab pots are normally set with the aid of a boat but could be set off docks also. Since I didn't have a boat, I'd have to set them off some of the private docks. I didn't know anyone who owned a dock like that, but the Beachcomber would.

I left the marina, drove down to Tully's place and parked. I walked up and was about to knock when the door opened.

"Come on in, son. What ya got?"

"I found some crab pots, but I don't know of any docks where I can put them."

"Crab pots? Can I see 'em?"

"If we caught crabs, would the fish shops buy them?"

"Oh, they'll buy them all right! But we could get a heck of a lot more if we sell them direct to people." We drove down to the marina.

He looked the crab pots over and decided that six of them were worth saving.

"We can fix these with bailing wire. The rest we'll smash down and throw out." We drove back to his place, picked up a roll of white rope, a large white bucket, bailing wire and some heavy lead weights. We stopped at a fish cleaning station for bait.

"I know more than enough docks to set these out," he explained as he fixed a crab pot.

To set a crab pots you simply filled the bait section with fish, attached a line to the trap and threw it into the deepest water you could find. The crabs, attracted by the bait, entered the trap. We drove one trap at a time to docks up and down the bay.

"Crabs need to be kept alive until sold," Tully explained. "You have to keep them out of the sun. The most common way of keeping crabs is to place them in bushel baskets. Since we don't have any, we need to stop by a fruit market where we can pick some up. It will be awhile until we get crabs by the bushel, but it doesn't hurt to think positive."

"Wouldn't it be better if we had a boat?"

"If we really want this crab thing to work, we need one."

"Where are we going to get a boat? They're expensive and lots of work."

"We don't need one with a motor; oars will do just fine. You'd be surprised what you can find around here if you keep your eye open." I tried to imagine rowing a boat all around the bays and inlets, against the wind, the tides, and in the face of drunken idiots driving speedboats. The thought of it was too much to bear.

"We have three days until we need to check the pots," Tully said. "I'll start taking orders for crabs from my produce customers. If we have anything extra after that, then we'll sell those to the fish dealers."

"I need to get home and change," I said. "Crabbing is messy work."

ELVIS AND SUNBURN

The month of May brings thundershowers to the beach. Intense storms form over the mainland and hit the beach with great ferocity. A storm lit up the beach last night. A lightning bolt hit the street below causing Karen to let out a scream. Everyone stayed up late. I got up around ten the next morning. Karen joined me on the deck. The mid-morning sunbeams glowed brighter than ever.

"The storm washed the air clean," Karen said. We sat on the deck until almost noon. Everyone was up by then.

"Tina, Connie, Ted and I are spending the afternoon on the beach. You gonna come, too?" Karen asked.

"Who's Tina?" I asked.

"You must be the only guy who hasn't noticed Tina," she explained. She nodded toward a short dark-haired girl in the kitchen.

Oh, I'd noticed her. I just didn't know her name. Too pretty, too well built, too well dressed and conceited as hell.

"Yeah, I'll come; I haven't spent much time at the beach." We gathered our towels, radios and sandals, and walked down. The smell of the washed sand struck us as we climbed down the steps.

"It's a beautiful sunny day, and the ocean looks great!" Connie said. "The water's clear with a greenish tint." We walked out into the cold water to get used to it. Ted started body surfing and swimming.

"Body surfing is all timing," he explained. "You swim out to where the breakers build and wait for just the right wave. Today the waves are coming in sets of seven, so the largest and most powerful wave is the seventh." When the wave began building, I could feel the ocean pull the sand out from under my feet. The trick was to be in front of the wave, swim like mad and stay on the crest.

"Sometimes there are sandbars just out from shore you can swim to," Karen said. "I think if we swim out past the breakers, we'll find one. It's fun to swim out to them and then ride a wave back into shore." We swam out, found one and stood beyond the breakers in knee-deep water. Ted swam out and joined us for a while.

"Connie and I are going to lie out and catch some rays," he said.

"Keep an eye on Connie," Karen warned. "She burns easily." Later we swam back in and decided to get something to eat.

"Ted, you'll watch Connie?" Karen asked.

"Yes, Mom," he said.

As we stepped onto the boardwalk a tall, brunette girl, wearing a tiny miniskirt, walked up.

"Oh, not now," Karen said under her breath.

"Karen?" the girl called.

"Ethan, you know Kathy, don't you?" Karen said. "She stays at the Cave from time to time."

"No, but nice meeting you," I said.

"Where's Ted?" she asked.

"I don't...," Karen started to say. I pointed down the beach.

"He's over there catching some rays with Connie," I said. "Why?"

"Oh I just wanted to say hello," Kathy said.

"We've got to move on," Karen said.

"Well, nice meeting you," I said. Kathy said nothing; she just walked off.

As we walked down the boardwalk I heard someone trying to play a guitar. He stood amid people singing and stomping their feet.

"Oh, that's Elvis," Karen explained. "How he got the name Elvis is beyond me because he looks nothing like him." We all walked forward to see a short, dark-haired man. "I don't know why, but he's always surrounded by teen-aged girls. He's certainly isn't the best-looking guy on the boardwalk, he obviously isn't rich, and his guitar playing is rudimentary at best. I don't mean to slight the guy, though, because he'll attempt to play and sing along to any song you pick." On this day Elvis's guitar only had three strings, but he did his best to strum out the tune "Tuesday's gone with the wind."

"Look out!" Tina shouted as a couple of rowdy guys pushed through the crowd.

"There's no place on the boardwalk for retards!" one of the guys screamed. He grabbed Elvis's guitar and smashed it on the boardwalk.

"You idiots!" Karen screamed and then walked off. Elvis stood, protected by some of the teen-aged girls. One of them hugged and comforted him. He stood; looking bewildered, and did not know what to say. A girl walked through the crowd and gave him her guitar. He looked at the new guitar, which had all six strings, as if he was looking at a long-lost friend. He began playing another song on the guitar, this time strumming out "Amie." Karen returned with a policeman and pointed out the guys who'd wrecked Elvis's guitar.

"He must lose a lot of guitars because he seems to have a different one every time I see him," Karen said later. "I think he's just slow, not handicapped. I sometimes see him riding his bike, a regular sidewalk coaster, either on the boardwalk or on the street. Where he sleeps or keeps his things is a mystery to me, but his clothes aren't dirty, and he doesn't look disheveled."

We walked farther down the boardwalk and came upon the game booths.

"Win a stuffed animal for me?" Tina asked.

"It takes a while to learn which of these booths you can win at and which ones are total rip-offs," I said. "The only game I feel comfortable with is the dart booth." You got three darts; if you break one balloon, they give you a ridiculous plastic toy. If you break two balloons, you have your choice of a small stuffed animal. If you break three balloons, you win a large stuffed animal. I broke two balloons, and Tina chose a small stuffed lamb, which she loved very much.

We went and bought soft pretzels at a shop before heading back toward Connie and Ted. When we arrived, we found Connie asleep on the beach.

"Connie!" Karen screamed. "You're burned to a crisp! I warned Ted to keep an eye on you! We have to get you home! Where is he?"

"I'll go find him, okay?" I said. I found Ted in a boardwalk bar with Kathy.

"What happened with Connie?" I asked.

"She seemed tired. I thought it was better if she just slept. She can't be burnt that bad."

I headed back toward the Cave where the normal nightly party was already going on. Karen and Connie, who lived across the street, headed over to her house. Connie's sunburn became painful as the evening unfolded.

"There's too much chaos going on at the Cave," I said. "I'm getting a shower and heading out." Just after I finished, Karen appeared, distraught.

"Do you know of any herbal medicine that would help Connie's sunburn?" she asked.

"No, I don't know anything about that, why?" I said.

"She thought you did."

"I've collected wild herbs and plants for people and have sold them from time to time, but I don't know how to use them."

"You've got to try something to help Connie; she's really hurting," Karen pleaded.

"Shouldn't Ted be the one to help her?"

"Ted? Tom and him left for New York City. Be back Monday."

"I guess I can try a few things I've heard of, but I can't promise anything."

I found some green tea bags in the cupboard and a bottle of aloe in the bathroom.

"Is that all you'll need?" Karen asked.

"No, I need plain yogurt also. Did you ever notice you can buy every flavor of yogurt in small containers except plain? Plain yogurt always comes in large or giant only." We walked to the corner store, bought the yogurt, and Karen left me in front of Connie's house.

I knocked on the door; no one answered. I opened the door, went in but could not find Connie.

"Is that you, Ethan? I'm down here," Connie called. I walked down the hall and found her sprawled out on a bed. I expected that her friends would be around, but they had all gone out for the night. I held my hand over her.

"Your sunburn's become redder since you left the beach," I said. "I can feel the heat streaming off you."

"What should I do?" she asked.

"I'm going to spread yogurt over the sunburn; it's supposed to pull the heat out."

I carefully spread the yogurt on her back and legs, making sure I didn't hurt her.

"I feel better already," Connie said.

"Tell me when the yogurt begins to make you feel chilly, because you'll have to climb into the shower," I explained.

After about five minutes she felt cold. We walked into the bathroom, and I ran the water in her shower until it was just warm enough.

"It's okay; you can get in," I said. While I was waiting, I noticed that Connie's room was neat and clean. I found some sheets and a comforter.

"The water feels really cold to me," she said.

"You only have to stay in long enough to wash off the yogurt." I heard the shower stop, and she reappeared. "Connie, your whole house is in good shape. One party or another has all but destroyed our house. You look better; your skin is less red."

"I can't feel the heat streaming off any longer either," she said.

"I need you to lie in bed. It seems a stupid way to help sunburn, but you dab the burned areas with the wetted tea bags."

"What's it supposed to do?" Connie asked.

"The tea bags contain tannin, and it's supposed to help the sunburn. I need to put aloe and a white sheet over you also. I don't know why, but you're cooler with a white sheet on than if you have no covers at all. You'll probably get chills in the night, so I have a comforter also."

"Please don't leave. Stay and talk to me?" Connie asked.

"I've got a pillow and a comforter; I guess I can just lay on the floor."

Karen appeared at the door about half an hour later.

"How you doing, Connie? It looks like the redness has faded already. I've got to run out. Ethan, can you stay and keep an eye on her while I'm gone?"

"Connie and I will just stay and talk; it's okay," I said.

Around one-thirty I woke up and found Connie shivering in bed. I covered her up with the comforter and tucked her in.

"I'm freezing," Connie said. I slid in next to her to keep her warm. Later I saw Karen reappear in the doorway.

"Looks like you made out okay," she said, and closed the door.

I usually got up around five-thirty in the morning, but that morning Connie shook me awake at eleven.

"I wanted to make you breakfast," she said.

"I can't remember the last time I had a regular breakfast."

"Look," Connie said, "my back's a light pink, and it doesn't hurt anymore."

"Don't go into the sun for a few days."

"Don't worry, I won't." We went into the kitchen, and Connie cut up a huge bowl of cantaloupe, strawberries and honeydew for breakfast.

"When you said breakfast, I expected pancakes or waffles or something. This is almost exactly the same thing I normally eat."

"How did you learn to treat sunburn?" Connie asked.

"A friend of mine got sunburned a few years ago, and this is what his sister did for him."

"I'm surprised you're living at the Cave. You seem so different from all the other guys. You keep to yourself. Do you think any of the other guys would have come to try and help last night?"

"I think some would have helped …."

"What do you think of Ted? Karen thinks he's a real jerk and that I should've dumped him a long time ago."

"He seems okay to me …."

"Yeah, but when I needed him, he was doing shots in the bar with …."

"He thought you needed to sleep."

"If I was your girlfriend, you wouldn't have left me to sunburn on the beach and run off with …?"

"Kathy? I think Ted simply saw a friend and walked off."

"Would you come over for dinner sometime?"

"I'd love to."

"Well, I'm still pissed off at Ted," Connie said giving me a slight hug. "Thanks for everything."

As I left the house I began to wonder how oblivious to relationships guys are. I had no idea Connie was even dating Ted; probably none of the guys at the Cave had any idea either. At the same time every girl on both sides of the street knew they were dating. Ted probably had no idea he had done anything wrong when he went over with Kathy. He met a friend and went to spend some time. As I said, guys can be oblivious to this stuff.

THE PROM

O ne morning I walked out onto the cold sand near the top of the beach and watched several Ruddy Turnstones picking at shell pieces. The heads of the birds held brilliant white feathers contrasted against black bands that wound across their eyes and bills. The flock walked just in front of me as I wandered the beach.

Early mornings are the best time to sort out things in your mind. I walked to the hard brown sand near the water. Tina and Karen walked up to me.

"I didn't expect you two to be up so early," I said.

"Early? We're just getting in from last night. What are you doing out here?"

"Trying to figure something out."

"Oh this sounds rich ...," Tina said.

"I'm thinking about going to my prom," I said. "I bought tickets last fall, but it just doesn't seem right now."

"You? The prom?" Tina said. "Who would you even take? Don't even joke about asking me!"

"I know it sounds stupid."

"It's not stupid," Karen said.

"I think you'd embarrass yourself by going!" Tina said. "Maybe we could find someone for you if you allowed my stylist to do your hair, and if we got you some real clothes."

"Let's just drop it, okay?" I asked. We left the beach and walked toward the Cave in silence. Karen stopped to look at something.

"The Beachcomber's coming up the street with his wagon," she said.

"I guess we have to pick and sell vegetables," I said.

"Well, we're hitting the sack and ... never mind," Karen said. I joined Tully, and we walked toward the gardens.

"My high school prom is next weekend. It seems stupid for me to drive home and go."

"Stupid? It would be stupid if you didn't go. Son, you end up regretting the things you don't do. Go and have a great time."

"Yeah, but who would I take?" I asked.

"That part I can't help you with. When I was a kid, if we didn't have a girlfriend, we took our cousins." We finished picking our produce and delivered it to his customers. I ended up back at the Cave around noon.

I could take Godiva. Aerosmith has a concert in the area and I know she'll be there. I'll just surprise her.

On Thursday I drove all the way to Passaic and found her. We sat together and watched the concert. I asked her about the prom.

"Could you do me a huge favor and take Sadie to your prom instead?" she asked.

"Sadie? Why not you?"

"She dreams of things like that. She never really attended school."

"You want me to take Sadie to the prom? Why not just ask me to take a Playboy Bunny!"

"You'll do fine. Just try and make the night special for her."

"Make the night special for her ... and someone's not going to pinch me and wake me up?"

"I know she intimidates guys, but just treat her nice."

"Tina says I should hire her stylist and get new clothes and ... she thinks I'll embarrass myself."

"Don't let her turn you into what she wants you to be. Be yourself. Wait until everyone at your school gets an eyeful of Sadie."

"You have to remember that I'm not liked around school. That area is about money and power. The girls could be nasty toward her."

"She'd actually love that," Godiva said. "I'll set it up. Meet her at your gas station at noon next Friday. Just make it a special night for her."

The day of the prom finally came, and Sadie met me as promised.

"I rented a hotel room for the weekend," I explained. "I want to make this perfect for you."

"It's been a dream of mine," she said. "And strangely you're the only one who can fulfill it."

"Some of the girls look down at me because I worked at the gas station, but they're the same ones who call me at three in the morning when their cars break down. They can't call their dads or boyfriends because they're not supposed to be out."

"They sound like nasty bitches," she said.

"They can be," I said. "And the football players get away with just about anything. They'll probably start something just to try and embarrass me in front of you."

"I'd love to see them try! I'll make complete asses of them. Did you rent a tux and gown already?"

"A friend of mine runs the rental shop. She promised to hold one my size. She has an entire rack that would fit you." We drove over and found she'd held a light blue tux for me. Sadie looked over the gowns and chose one she loved.

"You're wearing black to the prom?" I asked.

"I wouldn't have it any other way," she said. "Scarlet O'Hara wore black to the ball, didn't she?" Sadie's favorite color has always been black, so it shouldn't have shocked me. She went in the back to try it on. When she reappeared, she took my breath away.

26

"You look like a dream come true! Do you know how sheer that gown is?"

"And that's a bad thing? Feel it; it's like silk."

"Sadie, I still don't understand why you're here with me!"

"I'm here because I want to be with you. You're worried about making this night special for me, and that's cute! I want this night to be special for you also. Just love me, respect me and treat me nice. Let's get to the hotel, so we can finish getting ready."

We drove over, and I did feel a little nervous. I'd stayed in lots of rooms with Sadie, but Godiva had always been there. This would be our first night alone. I found our room and went inside. She stood in the hallway.

"Everything okay?" I asked. She smiled at me.

"Aren't you supposed to carry me in?" she asked. "No one's ever carried me in."

"Okay." Sadie slung her arms around me and gave me a kiss.

"Just relax, okay?"

I lifted her up and walked into the room.

"Don't put me down yet," she said. She pushed the door shut with her foot and then kicked both her shoes across the room. I set her down on the bed and showed her the corsage and flowers.

"You brought a purple corsage for me? It will match my dress."

"I don't know how to say it, but what do you really want?"

"Look, I understand guys are intimidated by me; it happens. You're relating to me one on one, and that's how I like it. Why don't we just nap a while? You need to relax."

Later we arrived at the prom and parked.

"Oh my God, look at her!" one of the girls muttered. "She's here with ... Ethan?"

"Ethan, can I sit with you?" Joe asked.

"Who's that?" Sadie asked.

"Joe. He just broke up with his girlfriend. He doesn't have a date."

"No, I want you next to me," Sadie said. She hooked her arm through Joe's, and we all walked in together. Everyone stopped to stare at her. We found our table and went to sit down. Joe went to sit across from us.

"No, over here, next to me," she called. Joe grinned ear to ear and sat down. I introduced her to everyone else at the table, and we began chatting.

"Sadie, you look beautiful," I said. She had styled her black hair in French curls that cascaded down her back. Her jet-black gown with its plunging neckline showed her nearly perfect figure.

"I think we made an impression when we entered. Now let's get them fired up," she said. She wrapped her arms around my neck and gave me a very long kiss.

"I don't know about them, but it worked for me," I said. She just giggled.

They served dinner and gave a few brief speeches. Sadie purposefully took forever with her dinner, stopping and feeding morsels to Joe or myself. I watched the football players fling spoonfuls of peas and mashed potatoes at the other tables. Our math teacher, Mr. Stevens, saw a wad of mashed potatoes head his way and dodged it.

"Make them stop!" a girl demanded, wiping them from her gown.

"I didn't see them do anything!" he lied.

"Look at that!" Joe said. "They promised us a trip to jail if we snuck booze into here, but the football players have bottles of vodka and scotch sitting on their table."

"Does that really surprise you?" Sadie asked.

The music began, and everyone went out to dance. Sadie pulled Joe out. As I suspected, she was an unreal dancer and danced rings around him.

"Oh my God!" a girl at our table called out. I turned and saw one of the football players lift the gown on a girl who was dancing. He stared back at his table, and it erupted in laughter.

About the time Joe was ready to sit down; the first notes of Freebird came waffling across the floor. Sadie loosely slung her arms around his neck and began swaying her hips back and forth. They slow danced until the pace changed; then she broke away and went nuts, wildly dancing and throwing her hair around.

"Thanks, I don't think I'll ever forget that," Joe said.

"Your turn," Sadie said pulling me up. We danced until my feet hurt.

Later we sat drinking Pepsi, trying to cool down. I looked over at the football players. They were all sitting by themselves; their girlfriends were out on the dance floor together.

"Did you see that moron lift the girl's gown?" she asked. "I've waited for this!"

"Waited for what?" I asked.

"This!" I noticed she was eyeing the football players with a look of contempt. "Hun, this is my show, okay?"

"Okay," I said, still not understanding. A moment later I noticed our prom queen coming over to talk. She brought her date, a fullback, with her.

"So, Ethan, who's your friend?" she asked, as if I didn't belong with her.

"This is Sadie," I explained.

"Is she like your relative or …."

"I'm one of his girlfriends," Sadie said. "Godiva and I share him."

"Share him as in …."

"You must be the girl who calls him at three in the morning? Your car broke down, and you don't want your boyfriend to know you're out?

28

You know what I mean about sharing him, don't you?"

"You mean you're really dating him?" the fullback asked.

"I'll do whatever he asks," Sadie said grinning. The two left red-faced. "Ethan, the fun is just beginning; wait until his drunken buds come over."

Joe and Sadie slow danced again. This time the football team was out on the floor with their dates. After the dance I saw a grin spread across her face. She put her lips to my ear.

"Don't do anything. He's mine!" she said.

"Who?" I asked.

"The fullback is going to ask me to dance with him, and I will."

"Why?"

"To teach him a lesson."

"About what?" I asked.

"You'll see," she said.

"Sadie, be careful," I said. She smiled another wicked smile. I didn't need to tell her to be careful as she can handle, and command, any situation that comes up. The song ended, and another slow song began. The prom queen and the fullback returned.

"Can we switch partners for this dance?" he asked. We agreed, walked out, and Oh Girl began playing. The prom queen laid her head on my shoulder, and we swayed to the music. I could just barely see them through the crowd, but I noticed his hands grasping Sadie's ass. I caught her eye, and she just shook her head.

"He's mine!" she mouthed. After the dance she walked him to our table, and they sat down.

"You were trying to find out what I'm wearing under this dress, weren't you?" Sadie asked.

"Ah, I ...," he replied.

"You could have asked, and I would have explained," she said. "You see, I don't have a stitch on under this dress. Do you want me to prove it to you?"

"Ah ... yeah," he said. Sadie got up, walked seductively all the way around the table and stopped at his chair. She turned toward him, placed her foot on him and exposed her entire thigh. She took his hand and placed it on her thigh.

"Go ahead and feel," she explained. A moment later I saw him squirm and realized Sadie's spike heel was digging into his crotch. She bent down, kissed the top of his head and increased the pressure on her foot. He couldn't get up or move. All he could do was take it.

"I'll move my foot if you want; just say up or down," she said. He had a look of absolute panic, and she pushed harder.

"Please ...?" he asked. I looked, and Joe seemed to be the only other person in the room that noticed. He looked sick.

"You know, in some ways you're lucky. Normally I'd leave you nude, tied taut to the four corners of a motel room bed. You'd be on your tummy, and a carnation would be sticking out of your ass. In most cases I'd leave a message for your mommy to come get you, but in your case it would be your coach I'd call or maybe, just maybe, his wife. The point would be the utter humiliation."

Sadie lifted her foot, and he ran toward the bathroom.

"Sadie!" I said.

"You think I overdid it, don't you?" she asked.

"Yes!" I said. Our prom queen walked over.

"Did you see Tommy?" she asked.

"I saw him head for the bathroom," Sadie said. I sat trying to catch my breath, waiting for whatever was coming.

"His girlfriend's beautiful?" Sadie asked. "And I warned him of exactly what I would do to him?"

"Yes."

"If I stopped him this very minute and asked him to dump his girlfriend and meet me at a motel, he would," she said. "That proves that he's an idiot and that I didn't overdo it." The music began again, and I tried to relax.

"Your table should head over to the photographer," a woman told us.

"Joe, come on!" Sadie called.

"No, I'm okay," he said.

"You don't want to get your picture taken with me?" she asked. They posed together, and it seemed like it would be a perfect picture to give to his family members. They took our photos also.

I lost track of Sadie for a moment. I spotted her standing by the football team's table. She pulled her hair to the side so the fullback could whisper to her and then she let out a long laugh.

"What did he say?" I asked later.

"He hasn't learned his lesson yet. He said something like 'I'll get you, bitch!'"

"Please be careful!"

"Hun, when the show's mine, I'm safe."

Joe and Sadie danced two dances, and we danced one. They announced it would be the last dance. Joe went to leave.

"I won't forget this, but I'm leaving before the fireworks start," Joe said.

Sadie and I danced slowly to Knights in White Satin. When I turned, I saw the fullback and three other football players waiting.

"We'll leave by the kitchen entrance," Sadie said. "We'll have a reception committee if we leave by the front."

"Okay," I said. The crowded dance floor hid us. Sadie led me into the kitchen. A moment later we drove away.

"Going to a prom has been a lifetime goal of mine, and this one was nearly perfect. The food, the dancing, nasty bitches, football players … my black dress. Thank you so much!"

"Well, this is an evening I'll never live down," I told Sadie.

"Will you be okay around town?" she asked. "Those football players could make your life hell."

"I'm living at the beach now, so it doesn't matter."

"Well, the sun's beginning to come up. Let's get some rest."

"Okay."

***

I woke up, and it was early evening. Sadie sat doing a crossword puzzle.

"I'd like to take you somewhere special for dinner, a French restaurant," I said.

"Can I wear my black dress?"

"I don't know why not." We drove downtown. They gave us a tiny room all to ourselves. Sadie ordered squab. I ordered lobster.

"I asked you to treat me like a queen, and you have," she said. Sadie ordered cherries jubilee for dessert, and the waitress lit it on fire.

"I still don't understand this. I mean, why me?"

"It's the caring. You really care about me. I asked for a perfect weekend, and you've given me one. You asked for nothing, expected nothing and worried only about me, and that's rare."

We returned to the room, and Sadie drifted off to sleep again. I just sat watching her. I had so many questions I wanted to ask her.

Where had she come from? What did she do? Why didn't she go to school? How did she meet Godiva? What about her mom and dad?

I had endless questions, and I realized that any of them could ruin the entire weekend. I decided it was better not to ask.

The next morning we returned my tux and her gown. We went to the art museum and caught a late dinner.

I woke up the next morning to find Sadie gone. A note lay on my dresser.

"I had a perfect weekend, and you couldn't have made it any better. I know how hard it is for you to let go, and this was the easiest way to do it. I will see you again soon. Love, Sadie."

I gathered my things, checked out and drove back to Wildwood. I had Sadie on my mind the entire way.

A BOAT

I walked west to Grassy Sound and found a deserted dock. I sat on the edge and stared into the water. Green striped minnows by the hundreds sat under it. A big crab, its claws wildly colored bright blue, red and stark white, stood trying to catch the minnows.

I'm trying to catch crabs, it's trying to catch minnows, and the minnows are trying to catch....

Grassy Sound separates Wildwood from the mainland. It's a shallow interconnected waterway with countless channels. Tall green spikes of grass grow along the water's edge. Thousands of yellow mussels lie partially exposed along the shoreline. Great blue herons wade the shallows looking for minnows and crabs. To the south, Grassy Sound connects to Richardson Sound. Docks line the edges of both.

I stared out over the water and watched black ducks flying just over the surface.

Why did Sadie have to go? Where is she and is she safe? God I hope I'm not falling in love with her. I just have to get busy with something and get her off my mind. I brought a hand line and a dip net in hopes of catching crabs for dinner.

Hand lining for crabs is easy; you throw out a series of lines baited with fish or a chicken neck, wait for a crab to grab the line, and net it. Watermen who catch crabs for a living have a disdain for this type of crabbing and call people who catch crabs this way "chicken-neckers." It's a fun way to catch crabs, as you are constantly running back and forth from line to line reeling up crabs and trying to net them. I noticed a partially submerged wooden boat near one of our crab pots, a sixteen-foot open skiff with the bow partially covered with wood.

It's old but not in too bad a shape. I don't see a motor around.

"Not much of a boat is it!"

I looked up and saw a man on the balcony drinking a beer.

"What happened to your boat?"

"My idiot tenant had a party, got drunk and fell off the dock. He put his foot right through the boat."

"Did the guy get hurt?"

"Not bad enough. Naw, he's okay, just embarrassed. I had to give a report to the insurance company on the whole fiasco. My insurance will cover the boat, but I have to get rid of it."

"Did you think about fixing the thing?"

"No, the boat's too old to mess with. You want it?"

"I don't know much about fixing boats, but I could give it a try."

"If you want the boat, it's yours, but don't bring the thing back. Wait, I'll write you a bill of sale and make it legal." The receipt he wrote said I was buying the boat in "as is" condition for the good and valuable sum of one dollar.

"I don't have a buck on me," I said. We both signed, the guy gave me a dollar and I gave it back to him.

"Just get it out of here, the sooner the better," the guy said.

I stopped to look at the boat. It had busted planks about a foot around. Other than the hole, the rest of it seemed okay. The old wooden skiff had seen many more years than I had. I needed to plug up the hole, bail the water out and float it to someplace where I could work on it.

I stopped at my car to see what tools I could find. I came up with a few screwdrivers, a pair of pliers and a Boy Scout hatchet. I went to look for a construction site.

I noticed a site with a pile of scrap wood out front. I searched it and found a piece of plywood, some canvas, nails and tar. I headed back to the boat, dragged the broken section onto the dock and inspected the damage. I nailed the canvas, coated with tar, over the jagged and rough hole. I fastened a square piece of plywood over the canvas.

I bailed out the water, and no more poured in. I noticed some life preservers, rope and oars stuck in the bow.

"Do the oars go with it?" I hollered up to the guy.

"Sure, take 'em and good riddance," he called down. "Bet you don't make it a hundred yards with that patch."

"It'll be fun, however it ends up."

"Well, good luck anyhow," he shouted.

I launched the boat, pulled on the oars and headed south. The boat floated, the incoming tide caught it and the current took me fast enough that I only had to paddle to steer. The patch held, and only a little water seeped in. Up ahead I could see the marina where I had found the crab pots. I decided to try to beach the boat near some broken concrete. Just when I thought I would miss the spot, the bow of the boat ran aground into the mud. I stepped out and pulled the boat as far ashore as I could, tying it fast to a piling.

I found a guy leaving the marina and rode with him back to Tully's place. I saw him sitting on his roof.

"I found a boat!" I called up. "It's got a big hole in it, but I patched it up."

"How much is it?" he asked.

"It was a dollar, sort of. It's not much of a boat, but it's free."

"Let's go see it. Don't worry, son, either we'll fix the thing or we'll drag it down to the beach and burn it for a clambake. Either way, we'll have fun with it."

We parked almost right at the boat. The tide was low, and the boat sat on dry land. Tully walked around the boat poking at it, feeling the gunwales and looking at the wood.

"Who told you about using canvas to fix the hole?" Tully asked. "Sailors have been fixing their boats in this fashion for centuries. We can fix this boat good as new, and it'll be close to perfect for our use."

I drove Tully home so he could pick up scrapers, sandpaper, tools and a very small saw. He also brought a roll of paper and some pencils. We drove back to the boat.

"We need to scrape the hole clean, cut away the broken wood and fashion boards to replace the broken planks," Tully explained.

Scraping a boat is very hard work. Barnacles covered the wood, and they were hard to chip off. It took us several hours to scrape the hull clean.

"I'll make a sketch of the planks, and then we need to go back to town."

Tully used the roll of paper to trace the damaged boards. We drove to a lumberyard to find the exact type of wood he needed. He examined board after board and finally chose one he liked. I drove him home.

"Can you pick me up at eight in the morning?" he asked.

"Sure."

I went back to the Cave, showered and changed. I sat down and turned the TV on. A short blond girl wearing a Steelers shirt for a nightgown walked up. She looked angry.

"What are you doing here?" she asked. "Why is the TV blaring?"

"I live here," I said.

"Ethan, that's not what I mean …."

"Have we met?"

"I'm Beth; we've spoken a couple of times, but I think you were too drunk to remember."

"Are you the girl that works from three in the morning until noon cleaning up a bar?"

"And tries to get some sleep during the afternoon?"

"I'm sorry."

"What I'm trying to say is that you're supposed to be eating dinner with Connie!"

"I didn't know she meant tonight!" I walked across the street and knocked. Connie answered the door and gave me a big hug.

"I hoped you hadn't forgotten about dinner," she said.

"Will Ted be eating with us?"

"No he's still away."

"What's for dinner?" I asked.

"I made a salad, spaghetti squash topped with tomato sauce, and flat bread. Where were you all weekend?"

"I took a friend to the prom."

"How was it?"

"Too perfect. I'm trying to get over how nice Sadie looked."

"Is she your girlfriend now?"

"No."

"Why not?"

"It's too complicated to describe, but she's not."

"Well, maybe you'll find someone here."

"Maybe it's better if I don't." We ate dinner, talked and had a good time.

***

I picked up Tully the next morning. He carried boards that he'd cut and shaped overnight.

"How'd you bend those boards?"

"I steamed 'em."

We drove up to the boat. Tully expertly fitted each board into place on it. He pushed tar-covered cotton into the seams. When finished, you couldn't even see a space where the wood joined.

"Come on, son." He led me to the marina dumpster.

"What are you looking for?"

"Cans of bottom paint." We found lots of partially filled cans and mixed them together.

"The paint will stop barnacles from growing and make the boat easier to row." We found some paintbrushes in the dumpster and soaked them in the paint to soften them.

"Bottom painting a boat's not difficult; you just slop it on and brush it out. The bright sunlight will dry it quickly."

"Won't the boat leak?"

"It will until the saltwater swells the boards, and then it will remain tight."

After lunch we pushed it out into the water. I sat in the back, Tully in the middle at the oars. When he pulled on the oars, the boat skimmed across the water like a feather.

"Can I try rowing?" I asked.

"Sure, the boat seems to respond well." We switched sides, and I found rowing the boat to be easier than I'd imagined.

"Turn in at that dock. I know the fella," he said. Tully went over to talk to the guy. They both returned a few minutes later.

"It's okay to keep your boat here," the guy said.

"We'll be crabbing out of here," Tully said.

"I don't use the dock myself, so just keep the place clean."

"It's Thursday, and we have to pull our crab pots anyway. You want some crabs?"

"I'd love some," the guy said.

"We'll be back in a couple of hours with your crabs," Tully promised.

Tully and I drove to another dock to pull in the first of our crab

35

pots.

"Let's see how many crabs we got," Tully said. "We'll sort and sell 'em." We drove to each dock and pulled in all six pots. We delivered most of the crabs to his customers netting twenty dollars each. We gave the dock owner three dozen crabs for letting us tie up our boat.

"Should we use the boat to set the crab pots out into deeper water?" I asked.

"No, we need supplies to stock the boat and more crab pots to set out. We'll get them Tuesday morning."

"Tuesday?" I asked Tully.

"Tuesday's the day to get our supplies."

"Yeah, but why Tuesday?"

"Because this is a holiday weekend," Tully said smiling. I had lost track of days. Memorial Day weekend, the weekend that begins the shore summer, was here.

WHERE DID I LEAVE MY CAR?

Memorial Day weekend brings the first crowds of the summer to the beach. Overloaded cars filled with kids and luggage. Bike racks bristling with spokes and wheels. On Friday night everyone will eat a quick dinner, jump in the car and head to the beach. Thousands of cars, each going nearly eighty miles an hour, will drive almost bumper to bumper. All hotels and motels will sell out. I didn't have to drive down this time, I was already there.

I showered and tried to relax. Karen walked up.

"We're all spending the evening on the boardwalk. You coming?"

"I'm kind of beat, but I'll go." We spent the night walking the boardwalk, playing games of chance and looking out over the ocean. I'd worked hard fixing the boat the last couple of days and felt exhausted.

"I'm heading home early," I said. I made it back, cracked open a beer and sat drinking it. I opened another. Later on I must have crawled to my corner. Sometime in the middle of the night two girls shook me awake.

They must be collecting beer money. I pointed at my jeans hanging on the wall. As it turned out they wanted my car.

I woke up late the next morning and stared at my dirty clothes. I decided to go to the laundromat, but I couldn't find my car keys. This wasn't a big problem as I keep several spare keys in my car. I couldn't find the car either. I spent over an hour walking around town looking for it. I'd parked and lost my car before, but this seemed weird.

I may as well go and do my wash.

I walked down to the laundromat and washed my clothes. As I crossed the street Bruce pulled up and gave me a ride back to the Cave. We drove up to find guys arriving for the holiday weekend. Several guys stood on the balcony holding cans of beer.

"This place is worse of a hellhole than I remembered," Bruce said.

"It's pretty bad. Tomorrow morning we'll have to step over the people passed out on the floor." Bruce looked at the damage done to the house.

"Someone's gonna have to pay for all this! I'm glad my name's not on the lease!"

"I'm glad my name's not on either!" I joked.

"Hey, let's go stay with my parents in Ocean City. You know, sleep in a bed, eat real meals, no drunks to roust ... sort of like a vacation."

"I'm on vacation!"

His parents' house had lots of extra beds since his brothers and sisters sometimes came down. Bruce's mom barbecued ribs for dinner.

"Ethan," Bruce's mom commented, "you look thinner than I remember."

"I'm living off the fish I catch and the vegetables from Tully's gardens."

After dinner we stopped by a place called the Sand Dunes, a massive club that offered several bands each night. I met a girl from Canada named Bev. Bruce met a girl he knew from college. After the bands finished their sets we all piled into his car to head over to the boardwalk.

"Yo, dude, that's your car," Bruce called. My car sat at the end of the parking lot. I got out and walked over, not believing my eyes.

"What's my car doing thirty miles from Wildwood?" I looked the car over, and everything seemed the same as when I had last seen it. The keys hung in the ignition, and it started right up. Bev and I followed them over to the boardwalk.

As it turned out, Tina and Kathy wanted to go out clubbing. I thought they wanted beer money. They'd come over, shook me half awake, and asked if they could take my car to the Sand Dunes. After they arrived Tina met someone she knew. She couldn't find Kathy, put the keys in the ignition and left. Later Kathy looked all over for Tina and thought she must have driven the car home. Kathy asked the guy she'd met to drive her back to Wildwood.

Bruce, the two girls and I met together at the Ocean City boardwalk. We walked out on the Fifth Street jetty, watching the night's waves. The surf sometimes covered the rocks, leaving white foam on them.

"Watch yourself," I called. "It's really slippery."

"I love the smell of the ocean," Bev said. "It's so fresh and clean." Around midnight we drove them back to the Sand Dunes before turning in for the night.

The next morning Bruce's dad greeted us at breakfast.

"I'm going out on the boat," he said. "You guys coming?"

"What are you going out for?"

"Flounder. We're drifting for 'em out in Rainbow inlet."

"Sure, I'd love to."

Fluke, or flounder as they're locally called, are caught while drifting. They lay buried in the sand and attack minnows as they pass by. Before the tide ran out we caught nine flounder and some small bluefish. We went back to Bruce's house, and his mom cooked them for dinner.

"I'm not used to sleeping in a real bed anymore or eating regular meals. I think you're spoiling me," I told Bruce's mom.

"Bruce says you've been sleeping on the floor?"

"Yeah, but it's free ...."

All too soon the weekend ended, and I hugged Bruce's mom good-bye. I headed back to the Cave. Bruce headed back to work.

When I returned to the Cave, I found a pigsty of trash, empty cups, beer cans and bottles. The stench of spilled beer filled the house.

"Will you help me clean up this mess?" Karen asked.

"If I don't, will anyone else?"

"No."

"Then I guess it's me." We finished and I passed out, exhausted from the weekend.

DUMPSTER DIVING

Memorial Day passed. Kids dressed for school recounting their weekend at the beach. Moms stared at piles of dirty wash. Husbands returned to work. I woke up with a start.

We're supposed to get supplies for the boat this morning.

I dressed in old clothes and drove over to Tully's place. He was up and waiting.

"I thought that you'd forget," he said.

"I did at first. Where do we need to go?"

"For a drive." We got into my car, and he explained the situation.

"Tourists come down for the holiday weekend and end up buying all kind of weird items that they can't use at home. Things like fishing rods, nets, coolers and household crab pots. A household crab pot is smaller than a professional one, and it's made of junk metal. It will work fine for us, though. They put 'em out in the trash when they leave."

"You mean we're going to have to find everything we need?"

"You already found a boat and some crab pots. We could spend a couple of grand putting this together, or we can try to find what we need. We need to cruise the neighborhoods before the trash guys come. Let's start with the homes near the docks."

The first two streets had nothing. On the third street we found a shiny new crab pot, a usable ice cooler and a minnow trap. We drove further and found two more crab pots and a water skiing rope. We drove our first load back to the Cave and returned.

On the next street we came across another cooler and a bicycle. I wouldn't have messed with the bicycle, but Tully thought it might come in handy sometime. We also found two more crab pots.

"We're doing better than I hoped," Tully said.

"We've found a pile of things, that's for sure."

"Stop, son, go back." We turned and drove up the street.

"That barrel ... there's your fishing rod, son!"

In the barrel there was an odd assortment of fishing rods, some with reels attached. Some of the rods were in good shape but missing rod guides. Two reels worked okay but had no line on them. We drove them to the Cave also.

Quite a collection of goods lay on the front yard. Crab pots would have to be painted black. Fishing rods, reels and nets needed repairs. A bicycle, coolers and a minnow trap sat on the grass.

"We need to make an anchor, son," Tully explained.

To make an anchor, he took two three-foot sections of concrete reinforcing rod and bent them into a w shape. He then laid one on top of another crosswise and laid the curved end in a coffee can. He tied the ski rope to the top of the v and filled the coffee can with concrete, all scavenged from construction sites.

We spent the day getting the equipment ready and transporting it to the boat. Tully constructed a floating wire cage to keep crabs alive until we could sell them.

"We need to stop by the fish cleaning station and get some fish heads for bait," Tully said. "Bring the minnow trap also; we'll put that out, too." We baited the minnow trap with bread and threw it out. Green striped minnows swarmed into it.

"Let's try out the boat. We can launch a few pots," Tully said. We waited until the last hour of high tide and pushed off with four of the crab pots on board, as it was all we could carry.

"Bait the traps with fish and attach new lines to them," Tully said. "At the end of each line, attach one of the empty laundry bottles that we painted purple."

"What about licenses and permits and ...?"

"Let me handle that, son."

"I assumed we would have to row the boat everywhere, but it seems the current is taking us right where you want us to go," I said. "Will it carry us to the upper reaches of the bay?"

"Yes, but this really isn't a bay, even though everyone calls it that. It's Grassy Sound."

"What's the difference?"

"I think a sound is shallower. Drop a pot over there, son, and one in that cove. The purple marker will show us where it's at."

At the upper reaches of the sound the boat seemed to be heading south one moment and north the next.

"How did you know exactly when the tide would change?" I asked.

"You get a feel for it, but it doesn't really matter; we've got time." All four of the crab pots were out, and the tide was now carrying us back toward the dock. As we got close, Tully gave a few pulls on the oars. I jumped onto the dock to pull us in.

"It doesn't always work perfect; sometimes the wind or current will goof with you, but we can always tie the boat up somewhere and walk off," Tully commented. "There are two high tides every day eleven and a half hours apart, so if it is high tide today at two o'clock, it will be high tide tomorrow around one or so."

That afternoon Tully showed me how to fix the fishing rods and reels. He removed the broken guides and added new ones. He took the reels apart, cleaned and oiled them before adding new fishing line.

"Good as new, son. Now you have a four-foot boat rod and a five-foot casting rod. I've already got a few, and now we're ready to start catching fish. If we head out at eleven in the morning, we should have two hours before the tide changes and about the same until the tide carries us back."

The way we found the boat and the gear to get the operation going might seem ridiculous to some, but it really made sense. A boat capable of running a professional crab operation would probably run five thousand dollars or more. To pay for the venture we would have to spend twelve hours a day fishing and many more on upkeep and repair. Instead of twelve hours a day on a boat, we might spend twelve hours a week. We had no commitments of time, money or responsibility in the operation. We had no overhead either. If we sold twenty dollars' worth of crabs, it was all gravy. The only thing we risked was time, and we had lots of it. When we went out, it wasn't drudgery but fun. A vacation.

CRABS, FLOUNDER AND EELS, OH MY!

I woke up, made my pot of coffee and sat on the deck drinking it alone. A girl wearing a long Steelers T-shirt came to the window, peered out and then joined me.

"I'm Ethan," I said. "You want some coffee?"

"That would be great!" she replied.

"And you are?"

"Beth? I'm the one who works nights and sleeps days? I didn't have to work last night." She seemed a little testy, and I figured she was just hung over.

"I'm guzzling a pot of coffee and heading out to catch crabs," I explained.

"Well, good luck."

I saw Tully walking up the street.

"I'm really sorry I forgot your name," I said. "I'm better with faces than names. I just haven't seen you around much."

"Well, have fun catching crabs."

I walked down and joined Tully.

We arrived at the dock with our fishing poles and loaded the boat with crab pots. I filled our floating minnow bucket before shoving off. We hung four fishing lines off the boat in hopes of hooking some flounder as we drifted along. As I threw the first crab pot out Tully hooked a flounder.

"We need the net, son," he called. I turned to get the net and saw fish pulling on our other two rods. I grabbed them.

"I'm trying to reel in two fish at once and keep the boat on course!" I said.

"Great day in the morning!" Tully called. "Talk about a wild time!" He grabbed the net, got his own fish in and then mine. By the time we had passed the second crab pot, we had three flounder and a kingfish in the cooler.

We drifted along setting out crab pots and catching fish as we went.

"I'm going to put the anchor out here until the tide changes," Tully said. "You know, the boat brings on a slew of opportunities I hadn't thought of before. Not only can we sell the crabs and fish to other boats but the minnows as well."

"How would we sell them?"

"The minnows are sold by the pint and quart."

"Suppose they don't have cash on board?"

"Most will have six packs of beer or soda to trade. I can't take any beer money, so you'll have to work that out."

43

"I guess I could do that." The tide finally turned, and Tully pulled the anchor in. We drifted back to the dock.

"I still have those frozen clams to sell, and we have fluke belly, minnows, and crab bait. Why don't you make up a sign? We could hang it from the side of the boat."

"Okay."

The next day our bait sign hung from the side when we shoved off. We hadn't gone a hundred yards when the first boat pulled alongside.

"What kind of bait do you got?" they asked.

"Almost every kind," Tully replied. He traded a pint of minnows for a six pack of Coke. I placed it in the cooler.

"You got squid?" the next fisherman asked. He traded a six pack of beer for it. I picked up a can to open it.

"You sure you want to do that?" Tully asked. "Drinking beer on the water makes you thirstier than when you started."

"I guess I could trade them for beer money at the Cave." We sold cold six packs of soda on the water, but Tully drew the line at trying to sell beer. He didn't care that it was on the boat, but he didn't want it drunk or sold.

"You know, son, there's no sense to drinkin', especially on the water. The idea is to have fun out here, not get drunk. And the idiots with the speed boats ...."

"Yeah, maybe we're doing 'em a favor by trading bait for it. We're doing well with the bait."

"At the far end of the sound we can catch shiners. They bring good money. The real money would be in live eels. We could catch those at tidal creeks. Striped-bass fishermen will pay a handsome price for those."

The next day Tully anchored the boat in a small creek.

"I brought some cut squid to catch the eels," he said. "I also brought a bucket of sand. It's easier to handle them that way."

"Sand?" A moment later my rod bent and I pulled one in.

"Eels are covered with slime. Wet your hand, cover it with sand and then grasp the eel. The sand will allow you to hold the eel long enough to unhook it." I tried it, and it seemed to work okay. We dumped the live eels into a wire basket that we hung off the side.

"The thing with eels is the smaller ones are the good ones and the big fat ones get thrown back." We caught more than we could use.

"We need to make a floating box at the dock to keep them in," Tully noted. "I guess I could fashion one if you help me."

"And bait dealers will buy them from us?"

"Yep."

The eels brought in a lot of money. Some of Tully's vegetable customers started ordering flounder or trout. Between the crabs, fish, bait and trading, I had to open a bank account.

"Tully, I'm on vacation, and instead of spending money, I'm earning it," I said.

44

OFFICER BUCKWHEAT

South Jersey is a ghost town during the winter. Few people remain, and many restaurants and businesses are closed. Signal lights are turned off, and stop signs replace them. The police work with a skeleton crew.

South Jersey hires a small army of police officers for the summer. Not only police but meter maids, fire crews and safety officers are brought onboard. Many are rookies looking for some first-hand experience. Lots of new faces arrive around Memorial Day.

One morning Tully and I went out very early to check our crab pots. I arrived back at the Cave exhausted. Karen stood in the kitchen.

"Beth and I are going down to the beach," she informed me. "You want to come?"

"I didn't sleep much; I think I'll crash in my corner." They left, and I passed out. Later that afternoon I heard a commotion on the street.

"Hey, is anyone in there?" Someone began pounding on the metal screen. A police officer stood at our door.

"We've received complaints about this house and about people coming and going. Your neighbors say drunks are pissing on their lawns. They also complain of loud music and car doors slamming. Who's on the lease here?"

"I don't know who's on the lease," I said. I didn't know what to say. Karen walked in a moment later.

"Why are the police here?" she asked.

"Something about guys pissing on lawns," I said. Beth walked up the stairs, and a big smile spread over her face.

"Buckwheat!" she shouted and gave the officer a big hug. Everyone stood back, not knowing what was going on. "This is Buckwheat. He's my friend."

"Look, you guys need to keep things civil. We can't have people calling us day and night complaining about the noise and problems. Could you try and keep things quiet, and for God's sake don't piss on Emma Henry's roses?"

I don't know whether to laugh or cry, but the mood's better.

"Guys are coming and going at all hours, and we have no idea how many people are supposed to be staying here," Karen explained. "There are four or five houses like ours around here, and maybe the neighbors are hearing them, too."

"I'll look in from time to time, but you need to keep a lid on things."

He returned to his squad car and left.

"Who was he?" Karen asked.

"We grew up together," Beth explained. "His last name is Bucksworth or something like that, but his nickname is Buckwheat. He played football at my high school, and we went on a couple of dates. He joined the Marines, and I lost track of him."

"Any of you guys pissing on Emma's roses?" Beth asked.

"I remember pissing outside but not on anyone's roses," Tom said.

Tina, Karen and I decided to go to Emma's house and talk with her. She showed us her beautiful roses.

"I love your roses," I said. "But who owns the dog?"

"Dog?" Emma asked. I showed her the dog's footprints.

"I know whose dog that is. I'll talk with her!" she said.

"Tully and I have been catching flounder," I said. "Could I bring you a few?"

"Are you the young man that's helping Tully?" she asked. "He attends church with me."

"We raise vegetables together. We also catch crabs and fish."

"Has the noise from our house been keeping you up at night?" Tina asked.

"No, at night I turn my hearing aid off. I don't hear a thing."

Emma Henry drove a monstrous Pontiac Catalina. Everyone knew to get out of the way when she came down the road. She would drive down either side of the street and would change back and forth for no particular reason. She always drove at the same speed, which was just above walking speed, about five mph.

"We'll try and make sure no one bothers you," I said. Karen hugged her good-bye. We walked back to the Cave, and Karen pointed at the metal sheds out back.

"Would you have any use for them?" she asked.

"I don't know." Later that day I checked the sheds and found they had electric outlets in them.

Maybe we could make them into some kind of a cooler to hold things. They're not in bad shape, and they have plywood floors.

I went over to Tully's place and told him about the sheds.

"I know a multi unit where we can get a couple of junk fridges," he said. "We can store crabs and vegetables in them. We can use the freezers for bait."

On Friday morning I waited as a van pulled up to the Cave. The door swung open, and I saw Tully in back. We unloaded four refrigerators from the van. We dragged these into the shed and plugged them in. They all seemed to work fine. Tully handed me a ten-dollar bill.

"What's this for?" I asked.

"They paid us twenty dollars to get rid of the refrigerators. The ten is your half."

We took the racks out like Tully suggested and loaded the freezer sections with bait.

"Well, the refrigerators work well, so what do we do now?"

"We need to get out on the boat, son." We kept the boat covered with a canvas tarp so it didn't fill up when it rained. I pulled the cover off. A few minutes later we drifted up to our first crab pot.

"You know, pulling in a crab pot is hard work," I said.

"Hard work does a body good. Sitting drinking doesn't. I really think every minute drinking takes an hour off your life."

"Well, I guess that's right because I'm having trouble pulling 'em up."

"Let the boat do the work. Grab the line, wrap it around a cleat, and the motion of the boat will lift it to the top." I tried Tully's method, and it worked great. It only took a minute or two to pull the pot in, dump the crabs, check the bait and throw it back in the water.

"I keep missing the bucket, and the crabs are getting loose," I said.

"We need to seal off the bow section and dump the crabs into it. We can sort them later. Crabs can give you a nasty nip, so it's best to use heavy gloves when you handle them." I found I needed gloves. Tully could reach in barehanded and grab them by their swimmer fins. Later we would size them and place them in bushel baskets.

The size of the crabs wasn't everything, though; the largest crabs, the Jimmies, were ranked by size and fatness. The size determined its worth, but some Jimmies could be twice as fat as others are and gave a lot more meat. Tully took orders from neighbors and sometimes restaurants for those fat Jimmies. On this day we caught two bushels of crabs, eight flounder and five trout. Tully had orders for all the flounder and trout and about half the crabs. The rest we sold to dealers.

"Why don't we get in on the soft shell crab market?" I asked. "The soft shells bring a fortune."

"The soft shells are a mess to keep, but we could make almost as much money on the shedder crab market. Fishermen will pay a fortune to have shedder crab for bait. Trout fishermen usually demand them."

"How do you know when a crab's going to lose its shell?"

"The color of the edge is different; it's kind of a white color." Tully made another cage to keep these crabs in until they were ready; then we froze them.

We usually went out to check our crab pots on Mondays, Wednesdays and Fridays, but there wasn't any set schedule. Friday was the day we had to go out and gather our crabs because chicken-neckers would rob them over the weekend. Most Mondays we would find the latches on our crab pots open, showing we'd been robbed.

"Some people just can't stand hard work. In an hour or two of hand lining these guys could catch more than enough crabs for dinner, but they have to hit us instead," Tully complained.

ALICE THE GOON

Early one morning I filled my thermos with coffee and went to Grassy Sound. I found a decrepit, deserted dock and began drinking my coffee. The sunlit water looked almost purple in the early light. I noticed a line of power boats heading south, white spray streaming off their bows. I watched them until they rode out of sight.

I walked back to the Cave and found Karen standing in the kitchen.

"I was thinking of having a …Why's a meter maid parking out front?" she asked. I looked out and saw a skinny brunette woman standing next to some kind of a golf cart. Her distorted features showed that she was furious about something. She spotted me and walked right up, handing me her card. I laid it on the counter.

"You're always double parked on the street," she yelled, "and you're always leaving your car running."

"He's not double parking cars or leaving it running!" Karen told the meter maid.

"It's not just him; it's everyone here!" the meter maid screamed. "I'm just going to have to start ticketing all your cars; then you'll learn."

Tina, Tim and Kathy came out to find out what the uproar was.

"Why's she so upset?" Tina asked.

"I've heard stories about what goes on in this house, and if I had my way, I'd run you all out of town," the meter maid said, stomping off.

She returned to her converted golf cart, glared at our house and produced a booklet. She wrote tickets for some of the cars and then left.

"I hope she knows that none of those cars are ours," Tina said. She picked up the card the woman had left and noticed the name, Officer Alice Gardner.

"They wrote that card wrong; her name should be Alice the Goon," Tina said. From then on this became the name we knew her by, "Alice the Goon." We would see her again that same day.

About an hour later an older woman came outside and saw the ticket on her car.

"Who ticketed my car?" she called up to us.

"Some crazy meter maid stopped and ticketed cars," Tim explained.

"I'll fix that!" the woman said. She knocked on a few doors and soon a crowd gathered.

"I called the cops; they're sending someone over to straighten

48

everything out," an older guy said.

A police cruiser pulled up, and Officer Buckwheat got out and began talking to the angry crowd.

"Everything will be okay. Go back to your houses," he said.

"Okay," Mrs. Henry said and headed to her house.

He walked up to us.

"This isn't some prank you guys pulled, is it?" he asked Tina.

"No, this crazy witch pulled up and just went off on us," she said. He got on his radio, called, and a few minutes later Alice the Goon pulled up in her golf cart.

"Let's watch from inside the house," Karen said. We all found windows to stare out of. Officer Buckwheat, Alice the Goon, and three neighbors had a heated discussion.

"It's all a mistake," Alice the Goon said, red-faced. She voided the tickets, seemed furious and kept staring at our house.

Eventually everyone returned home. Officer Buckwheat came over to talk to us.

"Look, the woman's the high-strung type; she could really make your life miserable. Could you try and not upset her? I think this is the last year she'll be down here." He returned to his cruiser and left.

"Before I was so rudely interrupted I was trying to ask if we could have a cook-out today?" Karen asked. "I'd like to grill chicken and sweet corn on the grill out back."

"I'd like that also. There's half a bag of charcoal in the shed. I have some old newspapers to light it with." We went out to the grill, twisted the newspapers and laid the charcoal on top of them. Karen lit the newspapers, and magically the whole thing caught.

"That worked better than I would've thought," she said.

"I'll go to the store and get the chicken and sweet corn for our barbeque," I said.

"I'll come also. We need to get enough for ten." We drove to the supermarket for the supplies. We returned later that afternoon.

"Someone was looking for you but left," Kathy said. "She said she'd be back later."

"Someone came looking for me?" I said.

"Yeah a ... Godiva?" Kathy said, annoyed.

"Godiva's here?" I asked.

"And she is ...?" Karen asked.

"Last winter, snowstorm after snowstorm pelted us. I couldn't take it anymore and headed to Florida. I met Godiva there, and she stayed the night. The next day she asked if her friend Sadie could stay with us also."

"You met her in Florida?" Karen asked.

"She traveled back to Pennsylvania with me and hung around for a while before beginning to travel again."

"So she just travels around ...?" Kathy asked.

"She goes to different concerts and …."

"You mean she's a groupie?" Karen asked.

"I wouldn't have called them groupies, but some might."

"Whatever …."

I went to take a shower, and Karen began pounding on the door.

"She's back!" she said.

I came out to find Godiva waiting in the kitchen, a backpack slung over her shoulder.

"Karen, this is Godiva."

Karen nodded and walked to her room.

"How did you know where I was staying?" I asked.

"I have my ways …. I've been following Foghat around. Can you get me into the Philly show?"

"Just you, or Sadie also?"

"Just me."

"Okay … how is Sadie?"

"She's fine; she's following AC/DC on their tour. She said you had a wild time at your prom?"

"It's something I'll never forget."

"You carried her into the room?"

"Yeah."

"You don't need to blush! She said she had fun with your football team?"

"I really haven't come to grips with it yet. She's sweet to me yet seems to go over the edge if she's upset with someone."

"You treat her nice, so she treats you nice. If someone's mean to her, then she'll retaliate."

"I feel that I'm always going to be torn between keeping you two, which I can't, and letting you go, which I must."

"That's the best we can do for now, okay?" *Godiva always looks so exotic, a contrast of wild beauty and innocence. I wonder what she sees in me?*

We cooked the chicken and ate on the deck. Tom called me away to talk for a moment. Godiva helped clean up, but Karen kept glaring at her anyway. I needed to break the tension.

"Let's go out on the boardwalk for a while," I said to Godiva. We walked down and found the boardwalk to be all but deserted.

"I don't have a bed at the Cave, so you'll have to crash on the floor with me."

"I kind of expected that anyway. I saw a stuffed bear at a booth. Will you try and win one for me?" We went back to the booth, a game where you threw a quarter into a shot glass. I won.

"A bear of your choice for the pretty lady!" the man called out, hoping to lure in fresh suckers. Godiva hugged her bear, and we sat down to watch the waves.

"How's your summer going?" I asked.

"It's going better than I expected. I've been traveling around a lot."

"I'm glad you're here. I've been working. I'm catching fish and crabs with an older guy."

"Is this the guy you told us about at Assateague, the Beachcomber?"

"Yes. We also raise vegetables and sell them."

"You live with some interesting people."

"Yeah, Tom already asked about you."

"What did you tell him?"

"That I had no holds on you."

"That's not true!"

"It's close to the truth. What did you want me to say?"

"You know how much I care about you!"

"Yes, but in a few days I'll have to let you go again and deal with everything …."

"No, you're right; explain it any way you wish."

We strolled back to the Cave. When we arrived, I found Karen waiting.

"Since it's so crowded here, I thought she might want to crash on Connie's sofa bed," she said.

"It's up to her," I said.

"I'd rather just stay with you," she said.

Later that evening I went to get a cup of coffee and found Karen in the kitchen.

"What are you to her?" Karen asked.

"I don't know. I never thought about it. I guess I'm just a friend."

"I asked her, and she said you were her boyfriend?"

"If she says I'm her boyfriend, then I guess I am," I said.

"What happens if any of the guys ask her out?"

"If she wants to go, she will."

"You won't be hurt?"

"She won't do anything to hurt me. Tom asked if she's available."

"And you told him …?"

"That he was free to take her anywhere she wanted to go, and that she especially liked concerts."

Godiva settled into the house with us. Karen and Tina seemed to accept her. All the guys went nuts over her. One evening we walked down to one of Tully's garden plots.

"Ted asked me to go with him to the Bongo Drum room," she said. "He said they have decent bands. Would that be okay? He said we'd be back early."

"That's fine with me," I said.

"There's something else, isn't there?" Godiva asked.

"It's about Connie …," I said.

"Karen told me all about it; it's okay."

"Told you about …?"

"About her getting sunburnt, about you putting her in the shower, rubbing yogurt and aloe all over her …."

"Ted's been dating Connie all summer, that's how she got sunburnt. He left her on the beach and took off with Kathy."

"Ted's dating Connie?"

"She gets off work at eleven."

"That explains why he wanted to be back so early. What a jerk, and he thinks she wouldn't know?"

"Karen would've told her in a minute."

"Hun, we've never hidden things from each other. What is Karen to you?"

"An acquaintance, a friend, I don't know. Why?"

"She's really protective of you …. I guess she doesn't want to see you hurt."

"I guess."

"I know what to do about Ted; let me handle this, okay? I'll come and crash with you again tonight, all right?" She kissed me good-bye and walked off into the night.

I returned to the Cave and began watching the ballgame on TV.

"Jim and I are collecting beer money," Tom said.

"I'll get a case out of the shed," I said.

During the bottom of the seventh inning Godiva returned.

"You okay?" I asked.

"Yeah, just hold me for a while, okay?" We snuggled together on the couch.

A little after eleven there was a big commotion outside. I looked out a window to see Connie throwing Ted's stuff out into the street.

"You're out, you Son of a Bitch!" Connie screamed down at Ted.

"I'm moving in across the street!" Ted screamed. Tom helped him pick up his things. They walked over and went into Tom's room.

"What happened?" I asked Godiva.

"I went over to Connie's bar and explained what happened. She said this was the last straw."

I thought the whole incident would have left Godiva in a bad way, but just the opposite happened. All the girls began asking her to go and do things with them. This worked out nice because she enjoyed their company, and it allowed her to see much of what Wildwood had to offer.

THE DELUGE

The bar scene at the beach sucked. You paid to get in the door, stood shoulder to shoulder, and the loud music made it impossible to talk to a girl, if you found one. The drinks cost a small fortune, the bartenders demanded tips just to sell you one, and the people acted nasty. Like I wanted that! If I wanted a beer I'd stay home.

One night the girls decided to all go out together because one of the boardwalk bars was having a Hawaiian night. They all put on sundresses and got ready to go.

"You're coming with us, aren't you?" Karen asked Godiva. "I have a sundress that will fit if you don't have one."

"No, I have one, and I'd love to go."

"It always amazes me that girls are always able to dress alike when the circumstances call for it," Jim said. "If us guys went out, none of us would be dressed alike. We would all have different types of T-shirts on that didn't match; some would wear jeans, some cutoffs, other maybe swimsuits or something, Oh my God … look at her …."

Godiva wore a white sundress made of a very light material. Knee length and backless, it tied around her neck and began again at her waist. She looked stunning with her waist-length blond hair lying against her tanned skin.

I gave her a twenty-dollar bill.

"Have a good time," I said.

"You'll come with the rest of the guys at eleven?" she asked.

"Yep."

After the girls left we sat down to watch TV. Thunderclouds formed in the night sky.

"I'm collecting beer money before the storm hits," Jim said. He returned with four cases, but by then the rain was coming down in buckets. An immense lightning storm ensued.

"Let's just sit out on the deck and watch the lightning," I said. For almost an hour the lightning lit up the night sky. The wind blew like mad and kept changing directions. Finally the storm moved on and bright stars appeared in the sky.

"It's getting late. We better go and meet the girls," Tom said. We walked down the main drag and found the road flooded with warm, clear water from the storm. We took our shoes off and waded through the water.

"Look, there's Karen!" Jim said. She walked forward wearing a stretched-out plastic Hawaiian lei.

"What happened to your lei?" Tom asked.

"They handed out leis to the guys so they could throw them to us. They'd only throw them if we showed off our boobs. A guy tossed one toward another girl, I grabbed it mid-air, and a tug of war began."

Tina walked up wearing three leis.

"Did you really show off your boobs to get the leis?" Jim asked.

"If you'd have been there, you'd know," she said.

"I wish I was!" Jim said. Beth, Kathy and Connie came walking up the street. Beth had two leis; Kathy and Connie had four each. Godiva came up last covered in them. She handed them out to anyone who wanted them.

"Did you have a good time?"

"I had a great time, we all did."

"I can see that."

"A really cute older guy with a beard came looking for you," she said. "Is he the Beachcomber?"

"His name's Tully, but how he knew you were staying at the Cave is beyond me," I said. We waded barefoot down the street through warm knee-deep water. It seemed like it was a night in a fantasyland, a night when anything could happen, and a night when nothing could go wrong.

"I should have gone with you to the bar," Jim said to Godiva. "I really love your dress."

"So it was my dress you wanted to see at the bar?"

"No, actually ...."

"Jim, I got it." As we turned to walk back I heard someone running through the water.

"It's the Beachcomber," Karen said. I turned to see Tully running up with a panicked look on his face.

"Tully, what's wrong?" I asked.

"We've got to get to the boats, son!"

"Are you worried about our boat, Tully?"

"The boats are sinking, and we have to save them."

What does he mean? The boat's indestructible. If it filled with water, it would lie on the surface until we bailed it out. If the thing sank to the bottom, it was only a few feet deep and we could pull it back up again.

"Please, son, we need to get to the boats before the rain starts up again," he replied.

If Tully says danger is brewing, then it is.

"Hun, I need to go with him and make sure everything's all right," I told Godiva. "Will you be okay? Do you need any money?" She held up the twenty-dollar bill I gave her earlier. She walked forward and hugged Tully.

"It will be okay," she explained to him. "You two do what you must." She kissed me good-bye.

"Jim, you'll make sure she gets home, okay?" I asked.

"Me, uh ... I'll stick with her like glue," he said.

Tully and I walked off and found my car. He guided us out of town onto a dirt driveway. A line of boats bobbed on the water.

"Our boat isn't here," I told Tully.

"These boats are sinking, and we have to save them." Another storm swept the area, and rain pelted down. I waited in the car as he pounded on the door of the dock master. A moment later he jumped back into the car.

"He's giving us access to all the boats and any tools we can scrounge up." The wind blew off the water so strong that it rocked my car. We carefully walked down the dock. I could see two open runabouts lying on the bottom of the sound already.

"Come on. We need to hurry," Tully said. "They're taking on water both from the rain and from the waves stirred up from the storm. The rainwater fills the boats and lowers them; then the waves break over the sides, and down they go. Boats with full canvas coverings and bilge pumps are fine. It's those without that we have to save."

"What should we do?"

"We need to begin bucket bailing the boats," Tully explained. "You start bailing, and I'll see if I can get some portable pumps working."

"Tully, these aren't our boats; we don't need to mess with this!" I saw the panicked look in Tully's eyes and realized he thought of boats in human terms. To him it was like saving lives. I began bailing and lost track of him.

"Son, I need your help; a sailboat is going under!"

"Sailboats can take anything; it will be all right!" A moment later a wind gust nearly knocked me into the water. Tully disappeared into the rain.

I walked down the dock to find him. He stood in front of a sailboat with its bow pointing up in the air and its transom underwater.

I can't imagine what caused the sailboat to take on water like that. Tully dove off the dock into the black water.

"Tully, where are you?! Tully!" Between the rain and the wind, I couldn't see him at all. Suddenly his head broke the surface near the dock.

"Get the hatchet from your car. I need it," he screamed. I ran down the dock, got the hatchet and ran back. I looked for him but could see nothing. A hand reached up from the water and I handed him the hatchet. I heard a chopping sound but couldn't see Tully.

"Tully, where are you!" The sailboat suddenly shot up out of the water and settled on the surface like a cork. Tully, exhausted, climbed out and lay on the dock, trying to catch his breath.

"One of the boat's lines got tangled on a piling. And once the tide and storm came in, it pulled it under. I swam out and cut the line." I went back to bailing out boats. He disappeared again.

"The dock master found six pumps for us to use," he explained sometime later. "Some of the boats have dead batteries, and their bilge pumps won't work. We need to jump-start them from boats close to them. Once the boats are running we'll leave them idling with their bilges pumping out water." We worked on into the night. The rain began to slow down.

When I looked at my watch, it was four in the morning. Of the forty or so boats in trouble, only five remained to be pumped out.

"Look east; the sky's turning pink," Tully said. "Well, no boats sank since we arrived; let's get the last few." I looked at my grease-covered clothes and arms. This certainly wasn't how I planned to spend the night.

"Tully, I just spent the last eight hours trying to stop boats, of people I didn't even know, from sinking. I've gotten filthy and ruined my last decent set of clothes. I just spent a miserable night in the pouring rain and wind. I'm sore and beat, and I have no idea why I did this. To me a boat is a tool, like a hammer or a drill; it takes me across the water when I need it to."

"No, son, a boat is a woman, and if you found a woman hurt or in trouble on the street, you'd help her, wouldn't you? You work with a boat, you love a boat and you fancy it up like you would a wife, adding bright paint and new sails. No, boats are alive, and you just can't let 'em die."

Dawn came late that morning. People arrived to see how their boats fared during the storm. The dock master greeted them as they got out of their cars.

"Tully, we have to get out of here. When the owners find the grease and messes we left on their boats, they're gonna freak out." Tully looked at me like I was crazy.

"No one's gonna be mad at us, son! Helping people is never wrong." A man wearing golf shorts and a knit sweater approached Tully.

"Are you the guys who saved my sloop?" he called out. I just stared dumbly as the guy hugged Tully and then shook my hand.

"I understand you dove into the water to free my sloop?" the man asked me, tears running down his face. I pointed over to Tully. The man and a much younger woman went aboard to check out the damage. As it turned out, some of the gear onboard had shifted around, but nothing was damaged.

"I can't repay you enough, but please take this at least," the man said holding out a hundred dollar bill.

Other boat owners arrived and handed out tens and twenties. Some offered cases of beer. Others could offer no more than attaboys, which we accepted.

"I'm tired, son," Tully finally said. "Let's head home." As we walked toward the car the dock master ran over to us.

"Can you stop back later?" he asked Tully. "I think the marina owners will want to give you something."

"We already got more than we can use," he replied.

"Please?"

"We'll be back around three; we need to get some rest."

I dropped Tully off and headed back to the Cave. When I arrived, I couldn't find Godiva. Tina stood in the kitchen.

"Looking for someone?" she asked. "Maybe you should look in Jim's room?" I didn't want to do that. I used dish soap to wash the grease off. I changed into shorts and a t-shirt.

Maybe Connie will let me sleep on her couch .... I walked across the street and found Connie in her kitchen.

"Connie, can I crash on your couch?"

"Go ahead," she said, giggling. When I went into the front room, I found Godiva sprawled on the sofa bed asleep. I joined her.

"How was your night?" she asked.

"Really rough. How was yours?"

"Really nice. Jim is really sweet."

"I half thought you might be with him, so I didn't go looking for you."

"Have I ever done that to you?"

"No."

"Then get some sleep."

I fell into a fitful sleep. The memories of the rain and driving wind were too much. Tully shook me awake in the early afternoon.

"Son, we promised we'd be at the marina around three."

"You two are not leaving until you have something to eat," Godiva said, rounding the corner of the kitchen. "I made some soup."

We ate and then drove over to the marina. The dock master greeted us when we arrived.

"I've got something you might be interested in," he told Tully. He led us into the shop area and showed us a Sears Gamefisher boat with a seven-horsepower engine.

"If you want it, it's yours," he said. The boat was large enough for the sounds we fished and had two built-in coolers.

"The engine will allow us to go places the tide can't carry us," Tully said.

"The boat's light enough to tie on top of my car," I said. "We could take it to Delaware Bay or just about anywhere else."

"I have something else for you, Tully," the dock master said. He led us to a tarp-draped item on the floor.

"Used to let the customers fool with this, but nobody has in years," he explained. He reached down and pulled the tarp off a small sailboat, resting on a pull cart. The sailboat was bright blue with a white deck and bow. The bow end was sealed, and there was a sunken depression where up to four people could sit at the back.

"I think most of the hardware is here, and the sail should be in good shape," the dock master explained. Tully walked around the boat with a look of disbelief, like a father when a doctor tells him he has a new baby.

"It's mine?" Tully said. The dock master nodded his head yes.

"You mean you're giving us the boat?" I asked.

"Yes, I thought Tully might enjoy it."

"We need to get this boat over to our sheds where we can look it over completely," Tully said.

"We can tie it on top of my car and drive it over," I said.

We put its cart, hardware and gadgets into the back. We lashed the boat to the top of my car. I carefully drove back to the Cave.

"Tully, I'm supposed to go out to dinner with Connie and Godiva. If you need parts, you can take the car to go get 'em." Tully didn't seem to hear; he was still in a state of shock over the sailboat. "Tully?"

"I'll just stay and decide what we need for our new boat."

Later Godiva, Connie and I walked to the boardwalk.

"Where do we want to eat?" Godiva asked.

"I'd really like a huge salad," Connie said. "I know a great Italian place that serves almost everything." Godiva and I ordered steak.

"You know you two should decide what you want to do," Connie said. "It's obvious that you both care for each other. I mean you can't just keep inviting her to visit and then telling her to leave."

"He never asks me to leave. It's hard to understand, but this is the best we can do right now," Godiva said. "It does pull at my heartstrings, though."

"She's right, though; at some point we ought to just take a couple of weeks off, just us two, and decide what we really mean to each other."

"And what do I mean to you right now?"

"A lot," I said, giving her a very long kiss.

We ended up back at the Cave after midnight. I noticed a light on out back. I found Tully working on the sailboat.

"You'd better get some sleep!"

"What time is it?"

"Twelve-thirty."

"Time flies when you're having fun."

I went back inside. Godiva and I settled into our usual spot.

Tully woke us up the next morning.

"Can you drive me to the hardware store? I need a few things for the boat," he said.

"Sure, but wouldn't it make more sense to go to a boat supply store for the parts?"

"We could buy the parts there, but they'd charge us four times as much. A hardware store will have what we need."

Tully purchased some stainless steel items, some fasteners and a large supply of marine line for the sailboat. By afternoon the sailboat was ready.

"Please, son, let's drag it down the beach and take it out!"

"I don't know; that's an awfully big ocean out there and ...."

"We'll be okay. We can launch it off the beach after the lifeguards leave." We towed the boat over to Tully's place on its little cart. The lifeguards left around five.

"It's now or never," Tully said. We pushed the little sailboat through the first set of breakers, grabbed our life jackets and paddled out. Tully set the mast into place, inserted the centerboard and pulled up the sail. The sail caught the wind with a loud boom, and the boat took off, skimming across the waves.

When the sail caught the wind, it jolted the boat so badly I almost fell overboard. I hung on for dear life and saw Tully, his long white hair streaming back, holding the tiller as spray from the ocean flew behind us.

"Feel the wind!" Tully screamed. "Get ready to tack!" I saw the boom fly back, almost hitting my head.

"Tully, be careful!"

We headed south for several miles before tacking again and heading north.

"I love the way the boat handles and how she cuts through the waves," Tully said.

"You're like a five year old at Christmas!" I said. "I think you'd rather sail than eat! You truly love the ocean!"

"The best time to sail is when the wind is up and the sea's foaming. That's when you can best feel what a boat can do for you and how she'll react." We sailed until the sun began to set; then Tully headed for home.

"We need to time things right when we reach shore," Tully stated. "You man the centerboard and pull it when I say." A moment later Tully beached the boat so gently I didn't feel it hit land. We dragged it ashore and wrapped it in a tarp under the boardwalk.

"It'll be safe there, and we can take it out whenever we need it," he said.

The next morning we went back to the marina to get the Gamefisher boat, motor and equipment.

"We need to figure out a way to make money using the sailboat out on the ocean," Tully said. "The sailboat opens opportunities for us. I just have to conjure up what they are."

He cut a twelve-inch round hole into the sealed bow and placed a watertight cover over the hole.

"We can store some fishing rods and gear in the hull. That way if we capsize the boat, which we probably will at some time, our gear won't be lost. I'll also make a wire basket that we can tie to a cleat. It'll hold any fish we catch."

"Why don't we try trolling a mile or two off the beach? Maybe we can pick up some blues or trout to sell," I said.

"I was hoping you'd say something like that. We'll try tomorrow morning before the lifeguards go on duty. I have some jigs and lures we can try. I'll bring some frozen clams also."

The next day, we trolled off shore and did well catching small bluefish.

"Bluefish are okay, but they're not worth much. We have to find a way to make a valuable catch," Tully said. "There's a wreck near here. Maybe we can catch some blackfish on those clams. If we can get a specialty market going we'd make out good."

We caught a few blackfish and several jumbo sea bass when a weird thing happened. Something heavy hit my line, but I couldn't see it. Tully peered into the clear water.

"Oh my gawd, it's a huge lobster!" A moment later it let go and sank into the darkness. That was all he needed to see.

"I can easily construct a couple of lobster pots. We'll haul 'em out here and drop 'em." Later that evening we pulled the boat in for the night.

"Will you need me at all? I promised Godiva I'd take her out tonight."

"No, I'm better off just puttering around. I'll figure out how to construct those lobster pots."

I arrived home to find Godiva in seventh heaven. Tonight Foghat played, and she lived for concerts.

"Is she always like this before a concert?" Jim asked.

"Like what?" I asked.

"So ... I don't know ... turned on?"

"It's kind of like a wave; there's a build up before the concert, a peak of a couple of days, and then a ...."

"A what?"

"Like a depression almost."

"Yeah, but she's so beautiful. How did you ever find her?"

"How I found her isn't the question; it's why she keeps coming back. I think it's because I support her after the wave crashes." Godiva and I drove to Philadelphia, watched the concert and returned home very late.

The next morning Godiva and I expected Tully to show up, but he never came.

"Hun, I hope Tully's all right. It's vegetable day, and he's always here."

"Let's go check on him," she said. We went to Tully's place, but he wasn't there. I checked under the boardwalk and saw the sailboat was gone.

"He must have sailed out by himself," I explained.

"We can handle the vegetables," Godiva said.

"I don't have the knack for selling that Tully has."

"It will be okay; we'll sell all of them. I'll help you." We went, and she insisted we pick twice as many as normal. We set bushel basket loads at the Cave.

"We'll never get rid of all these," I said.

"I think we will." We delivered what our customers ordered, but we still had two wagonloads left.

"Let's drag the rest to the street corner and sell them," she said.

"People will stop?"

"Yeah." Not only did people stop and buy the vegetables, but there was a near accident or two when guys spotted Godiva. We walked back to the Cave for lunch and found Tully waiting.

"I made three small lobster pots and set them out near wrecks," he said. "We'll wait a few days and then check them."

"Tully, we picked and sold all the vegetables that were ripe. I have your money."

"You two sold 'em, you keep the money, but we need to check the crab pots."

I gave all the money to Godiva. Tully and I left to head to the crab boat, which now had the motor on it.

"You know strange things happen," I said, "and this summer some of the weirdest have occurred. We started the summer with no boats, and now we own three, all basically given to us. I started the summer broke; now we're selling vegetables, crabs, fish, bait, cold sodas and hopefully lobsters."

"The Lord has been kind to us," Tully admitted. I baited the rods and hung four lines off the stern as we drifted from pot to pot. By the seventh pot we had a dozen flounder, four trout and a host of other fish on the boat. The front end of the boat bristled with crabs.

"We have more than enough to fill our orders," Tully noted. He started the motor, and we ran back to the dock.

I returned to the Cave. Jim sat on the couch looking dejected. Godiva sat next to him.

"Don't take it so hard," she said. She came and joined me in the kitchen.

"Did I miss something?" I asked.

"I think he misunderstood my feelings for him."

"Oh."

"Jim, we're heading out to get something to eat, wanna come?" she asked.

"Are you sure you still want me to come?"

"Yes, we want you to come!"

We headed to an Italian restaurant and waited to get a table. Godiva kept staring at Jim. I didn't know what to make of it.

"Jim, you know what I'm thinking?" she asked.

"No."

"I'm thinking about Connie sitting at home by herself. Why don't you call her and see if she wants to join us?" Jim blushed and shook his head no.

"You wouldn't mind if I invite her, would you?"

"No, I'd like that." Right about the time our table was ready, Connie appeared wearing a black cocktail dress.

"I didn't have time to change from work," she said.

"You look fantastic!" Jim said. We ate dinner together. They drank wine and talked long into the night.

"We have to get back," I said. "Godiva has to leave in the morning, but she'll probably be back again soon. She'll be heading to Baltimore." We arrived back at the Cave around two in the morning.

"Jim, could you stop over?" Connie asked. "I'd like to talk a while." Godiva and I headed inside.

"Well, this week I had more rest and fun than I've had in years," Godiva said.

"You've really tanned nicely, and your complexion is nearly perfect."

"Thank you. Let's get to sleep."

The next morning I stood waving good-bye to Godiva, never knowing if I would see her again or when.

A PARTY ON A BOAT?

I sat on the boardwalk and watched the spectacle of ring-billed gulls diving and cavorting. Someone threw a bucket of french fries onto the beach, and the gulls fought over the scraps. The stark whiteness of the gulls stood in contrast against the blue-colored water. Their cries and shrieks filled my ears.

Why did Godiva have to leave so soon? Where has she gone? Is she okay? Sadie and her have to keep moving, and I can't keep them. Letting go is hard. I need to keep busy or lose my mind.

I walked back to the Cave hoping to find something to do. Luckily Tully stopped by with a proposition.

"I've been talking with some of the party boat captains. One of 'em needs a couple of deck hands. His regular guys are away for a few days. He's got no one, and he's desperate. He'll pay us handsomely, and we can make nice tips filleting fish."

A party boat takes a large group of fishermen, sometimes over a hundred, out to a likely spot to try to catch fish.

"Tully, I've been on a lot of these boats. One out of every four guys will be smashed when they come aboard. I've seen guys wheel trash cans full of beer onboard and then head to the cabin to pass out. Some bring their wives, dressed in swimsuits, to go out fishing and it's cold out on the water. Those who should take Dramamine don't, and they're up sick all night."

"That can happen."

"The job of the deckhand is one of the worst. The captain's always calling on you to do some kind of work, the people fishing need help, and it's dangerous. Fishhooks and lead sinkers fly around, knives are always out. Sometimes these guys get into brawls. What would we be going out for?"

"Night blues."

"Night blues is the worst of all, and you're talking about a Friday night. The boat will be crowded with lots of drunks, and tempers will be high. Everyone will be fighting for the best spot on the boat; some guys will show up early and stake out their spots. Later, other guys will come, and there'll be trouble. Guys will be casting huge, heavy lures with giant hooks, and someone'll probably be hooked. Bluefish will run up and down the boat tangling everyone's lines. We'll have to settle the whole mess."

"We'll be okay, son."

"Will the captain at least let us winnow out the drunks and troublemakers before they get onboard?"

"I'm sure he will."

We arrived at the boat at five in the afternoon; it would depart at seven and arrive back at the dock around three in the morning.

"We need to clean the boat and make sure everything is onboard before we take off," Tully said. "We need to load bait, chum, fishing rods, tackle, drinks, food and supplies. Luckily, the captain has a checklist for us to follow."

"Okay, but I'm manning the gangplank," I told Tully. "I want to turn away the drunks. I'll try and warn everyone to bring warm clothes and take something for sea sickness."

We did the best we could to monitor who came aboard. At seven the captain blew the horn three times, and we steamed toward the bluefish grounds.

"Son, we need to grind the bunker into chum," Tully said. "We'll need two trash-can loads. You cut a section of their back and their tail out as bait, and I'll grind the rest up. Bunker is an oily fish, and the smell of it sticks to everything. We need to distribute bait to everyone on board."

When we arrived at the fishing spot, Tully began throwing chum overboard. The bluefish would follow the drifting chum line back to the boat. Bluefish are a strong, savage fish with very sharp teeth. They swim in large schools and will eat any fish they can. Our customers began catching fish immediately.

"Gaff!" several fishermen called at once.

"Just swing them aboard," the captain called down.

"Luckily, these fish are three to five pounds," Tully said. "They're small enough to be pulled in without gaffing. I think there's lots of fish also, which means everyone will catch some. We'll still have to run around and gaff a fish here or there, but it won't be so crazy." Tully and I got time to talk with fishermen and got tips for gaffing larger fish.

We made three stops during the night to try different areas. Some of the fishermen caught more fish than they wanted and gave them to us. Tully looked down into the water and saw fish swirling under the boat's lights.

"Captain," he called up, "we got trout, big trout!" The captain turned the floodlights on, and a school of large trout moved in.

"Nice going, Tully," the captain called. "Most fishermen would rather catch trout than bluefish."

Sometime after two in the morning the captain blew the horn three times, ending the fishing. He headed in. Tully and I began filleting our customers' fish. We charged a dollar a fish and made a lot of money.

About three in the morning we arrived back at the dock. We helped the fishermen off the boat and collected tips. I cleaned the boat and stowed away the extra gear. Tully sold the extra fish to onlookers.

"We did good on tips and filleting the fish. We made extra money on those we sold," Tully said. "The captain paid our regular wages and gave a bonus for a good trip. All total we made about two hundred each. I promised the captain we'd come back tomorrow night." We finished cleaning the boat and headed home.

I got home around seven in the morning and found Karen in the kitchen.

"Another long night with Godiva?" she asked.

"She left Thursday," I said.

"So you were out …?"

"I worked all night on a fishing boat."

"I'm sorry, I just …."

"What are you doing up so early?" I asked.

"Just thinking. I need to go and buy groceries."

"Here," I said, handing her five twenties.

"What's this?"

"Grocery money; you said you were going shopping? I've had a run of cash, but I don't know if it will keep up."

"Okay, thanks. You want to come?"

"I should sleep, but I'll take you." We walked down to my car.

"I like shopping early before the supermarkets get too crowded," Karen said. "You really didn't need to fork over this much."

"I'm putting most of the cash in the bank for fall tuition. The crabs, fish, vegetables and odd jobs have paid well. I don't have any rent to pay. I'm still being hit up for beer money, but fishermen often pay us with beer. I have eleven cases in the shed now."

"You know, we should work together. Sometimes I get ideas that might pay. Would you be interested?" she asked.

"Anything you come up with is fine. You don't even need to ask. And Godiva …."

"You miss her a lot, don't you?"

"It hurts just to talk about it, so let's not."

We arrived at the grocery store, and she chose what we needed. She took her time to look for deals. I wheeled the cart to the cash register, and she paid from the hundred I'd given.

"Here's your change," she said holding up two twenties and some ones.

"Just hold it in case you come up with some idea like you described." We drove home and unloaded the groceries.

"I'm going to my corner to crash. Could you please wake me up around three?" I asked.

"Sure. Do you need a hug?"

"I think I'll sleep better without one."

It seemed that I'd barely slept when Karen shook me awake.

"The Beachcomber's here," she said.

"What time is it?"

"Two-thirty in the afternoon," she said.

"Tully, you're early," I said.

"I promised the captain we'd pick up some supplies on the way. We're supposed to stop by the fish house for bunker and smelt."

"Okay."

We drove over, got the supplies and headed to the party boats.

"Tully, since you ground the chum yesterday, I'll switch with you. You can handle the drunks." Grinding chum is no picnic; the oily mess sticks to you like glue.

At seven the captain blew the horn and we were off to the same spot as yesterday. I hoped for an easy night, but giant bluefish awaited us. Tully and I ran up and down the deck gaffing fish as lines snapped and fishermen cursed. Each fish hooked caused a tangle in lines that we had to deal with. Fish broke lines just as we were ready to gaff them, and tempers boiled over.

"Just put up with everything; it'll calm down soon," Tully said. Sometime around midnight things did calm down. Smaller bluefish moved in, and everyone caught some. Later the captain blew the horn three times, and we headed in. Around three in the morning Tully tied the boat up to the dock. We helped everyone off the boat and began scrubbing it down.

"We made a lot of money again, son. The captain wants us on as regular hands, but I told him we couldn't. Do you want to keep things open in case he needs someone to fill in again?" I stared into the pinkness of dawn.

"Yeah, but not for a while. I need a break."

THE ROAD TRIP

I met Tully one morning, and we went to check our crab pots. "Tully, I've got a problem, and I don't know what to do."

"What is it?"

"Bobby and I had planned a trip all winter, and now it looks like it ain't happening. We planned to drive west and fish the Rockies. We'd camp along the way, living cheap and working at farms and ranches. The plan was a good one, but Bobby started dating Sara."

"And Sara said?"

"She says either he stays the summer with her or she'll walk. I really wanted to do this for years, and now it's melting before my eyes."

"Why don't you go then?" Tully said. "I told ya, son, you regret the things you didn't do."

"Who with? Could you come?"

"Me? No, actually I've got two weeks of work in Camden. I won't be around anyway. What about that blond girl?"

"Godiva? I can't see her climbing all over the Rockies, swatting flies and freezing to death at night. She's just too … feminine. The hiking and travel could be brutal."

"She's stronger and more resilient than you'd think."

That night I thought about Tully's advice.

Should I invite her to come on a road trip with me? We'd drive for days on end without sleep. We'd fish ice-cold streams, sleep in tents and walk on glaciers. Why not just ask her? She'll be at the Foghat concert. I can drive over and surprise her.

I found her, and we watched the concert together. I finally broached the subject.

"I've dreamed about a road trip out west for almost a year. I planned on living out of my car, camping as I went. I wanted to drive to the Canadian Rockies and fish my way south. I planned on working at ranches here and there if I needed extra cash. Could you come with me?"

"Sounds like the trip of a lifetime. I always wanted to go west and … oh my God, the horses! When would we leave?"

"Friday. You'd be safe out west?"

"I can't think of a safer place. Let's do it. I'll meet you in Wildwood." I drove home and went to Tully's. I found him waxing the sailboat.

"Godiva says she'll come," I said. "We leave on Friday just like you do. What do we do about our crab pots?"

"We let 'em soak. The crabs and, if we have any, lobsters will be fine."

Godiva arrived Friday morning. I'd packed my car the night before.

"I'm a little worried about my car," I said. "It has three hundred thousand miles on it, it's leaking oil, and the engine doesn't sound the best."

"If it gives out, we'll have to hitchhike. We've hitchhiked before."

I altered my Ford sometime back and transformed it into a kind of hatchback. The back was now a padded bed so someone could sleep while another drove. It had lots of space. I wanted to drive as far as I could before stopping to camp. We left Wildwood and headed west. The Alleghenies came and went. We had little trouble until we got to Chicago. As we passed the city and turned north, my exhaust system fell off the car. I pulled over and watched as a semi barreled down and flattened the thing.

"Well, that ends that!" I noted.

"Do we stop and buy a new one?"

"It wouldn't be worth it. The car will be loud and smoke a lot, but it should run okay."

We left, and it actually seemed like the car had more power.

"Let me use your CB. I can find if the road is clear ahead," she asked. She signed on using the handle "Blue Horse."

"The road's clear for at least a hundred miles," she said. We zoomed down the highway, drafting trucks and passing cars. We entered Minnesota, and Godiva slept in the back. I put on my headphones so I wouldn't wake her. I turned my Allman Brothers tape all the way up.

We continued on into South Dakota, a flat, dry state. We crossed the Platte River and continued west.

"You just can't keep driving and driving without sleep," Godiva said.

"I can stay awake for a long time," I replied.

"Oh my God, did you see that?" Godiva asked.

"See what?"

"Turn left up here and drive slowly." We turned off, came over a slight rise, and before us lay an unending field of yellow, orange and green. We got out of the car dumbstruck.

"What is it?" she asked.

"Field after field of sunflowers."

"It's like the field of poppies in the Wizard of Oz!" Godiva screamed, running through the flowers. I grabbed my pack and followed her. We came upon a slight hill, and for as far as we could see in all directions, it was nothing but yellow sunflowers. We sat and just stared for hours.

"Can we camp here tonight?" she asked.

"I really wanted to drive further before stopping, but this is perfect!"

"This is like living in a fairyland," she said. We sat on the rise watching a blazing red sun disappear into the yellow blooms. I got our gear, and we set up my backpacking tent and crawled in.

The next day we continued west and stopped at Wall Drug for ice water. Getting ice water seems stupid, but during the dust bowl migrant farmers considered it a blessing.

"Look, antelope!" Godiva screamed as we drove up the highway. The antelope looked almost painted onto the scene with brilliant white markings against light brown sides.

"They look so fragile!" I said. They pranced around on thin spindly legs. In a burst of speed they were off and disappeared across the prairie.

"Where will we stay tonight?" Godiva asked.

"We can camp for free close to Custer State Park and Mount Rushmore."

"I'd love that!"

I said the words before I really thought about it. I hadn't been planning on this being a touring vacation, but it might be fun.

We parked our car along a dusty road.

"This is perfect!" she said. "Ponds, green grass, and even a tiny creek." We set up our tent just beyond a butte that shielded us from the only road in the area. We had thousands of acres of rolling prairie to ourselves. Black Angus steers milled around us.

"There's more antelope!" Godiva called out. We watched a herd on a hillside. We also spotted a small herd of deer that bedded down in the creek bottom and came out at night. We found some dry brittle wood and made a small fire. We turned in early.

The next morning I couldn't find Godiva and wondered where she went. I began looking and found her in a tiny creek.

"What are you doing?" I asked.

"Panning for gold."

"Here?"

"The Black Hills are famous for gold. I found some gold dust. Look for yourself." She had my mess kit pan and sure enough, some gold dust lay on the edge.

"I'm glad you found it, but you've got to be careful; there are snakes all around here."

"Hun, I know about snakes. I grew up around rattlers, copperheads and cottonmouths."

"Where did you grow up?"

She smiled blankly and stared. "Not yet, okay?"

"Okay."

We packed up and drove through Custer State Park. We saw buffalo, big horn rams, elk and deer. Later we drove to Mount Rushmore and climbed up on top of the stone faces.

"This is incredible!" she said. "Those guys must have scaled up and down these, carving the presidents' faces in the rock."

Later that day we drove west to camp in Wyoming near the Custer Battlefield. After we set up our tent we drove to where we could see Devil's Tower.

"Can we stop at an Indian reservation sometime?" she asked.

"We should be at the Blackfoot Reservation tomorrow night."

I woke up in the middle of the night and stared at her.

My God, she's all but perfect with a beautiful heart-shaped face and a figure most girls would die for. She barely opened her eyes and stared.

"Hun, what are you doing here with me?" I asked. "I'm not good-looking; I have no money, a junk car ...."

She propped herself onto one her arm and stared. "You care for me, and I love you, that's why I'm here. It'll be dawn in a few hours; go back to sleep."

The next morning we continued our journey west. As we cleared a high hill she squealed out in delight.

"Look!" she screamed. I stared ahead and saw what looked like billowing clouds on the horizon. "It's the peaks of the Bighorns!" A moment later the grey rock sides of the mountains came into view, standing proudly against a blue sky.

"It's so beautiful!" We drove into Montana, continuing on as darkness fell.

The next morning we entered Glacier National Park from the east. We drove a short way in and saw a tiny creek cascading straight down a mountainside.

"Let's get out and walk," she suggested. We followed the cascading stream up into an alpine valley filled with tiny blue and pink wildflowers, contrasted against green grass. They led to a small snow-covered mountain pass that took us farther in. We followed an ice-choked stream back down to a road. I wasn't sure where we were or how far the car was. Godiva flagged down a woman in a jeep. The woman turned out to be a very young, very beautiful park ranger. She had her blond hair tied in pigtails.

"I'll give you a ride back to your car. It's further than you might think," she said. "Where are you staying?"

"We haven't decided yet," Godiva replied.

"You need to stay at Two Cabins; it's just up the road."

"Sounds good to me. We drove all night."

"I'll stop by to make sure you get in okay." In a strange show of affection, Godiva planted a kiss on the side of her head.

We found the campground, and it turned out it was on the Blackfoot Indian reservation. We set our tent up and napped.

"Do you really think that ranger will stop and check up on us?" I asked later.

"She'll be here."

"These mountains are having a weird effect on me. I'm not sure if I'm awake or dreaming."

The Beachcomber

About an hour before dusk the ranger drove up. We made a fire and sat talking. Her name was Darien, and she grew up in Montana.

"This place is so beautiful!" Godiva said.

"And we have the responsibility to keep it that way," she said. "When I first saw you two I wanted to do something really special, and tonight seemed the perfect time. Come on." She pulled a small bag from her truck and guided us down to where the stream entered the lake. She pointed at some flat rocks.

"Sit down and relax," she said. She pulled a small birch bark cone from her bag and coughed into it. Across the lake a moose bellowed back. She practiced one call after another. Long after the sky had totally darkened, she stood up and howled. A pack of wolves returned her howl.

"This really is a special night, but I've got to get home to my husband and baby," she said. "Thank you for sharing this with me."

Late that night Godiva and I lay in our tent dumbfounded.

"You're right; these mountains are a powerful place," Godiva said. "I can't believe she spent the evening with us."

"We're new here; it will take some time."

When I woke up in the morning, Godiva wasn't in the tent. I found her standing in the creek catching minnows.

"This should be a good place to catch fish. The creek enters the lake here."

"How do you know so much about catching fish?" She just stared. "Yeah, I know, your secret. I'll get my fishing rod."

I drifted a minnow in the current, and almost immediately a nice cutthroat trout followed the bait but didn't take it. I tried several times without getting a bite.

"Can I try?" Rather than fishing the pool in the creek she let the current wash the minnow out into the lake. A few minutes later the line began jerking, and it was obvious she had a fish on. I took the rod from her.

"The way it's pulling, it's got to be big," I said.

"If we were in South Carolina, I'd swear you had a big blue catfish," she said. I let the fish run all over the lake before it turned into the shallows. I handed her the rod and waded out to grab it.

"What is it?" she asked.

"It's a lake trout; I think they call them tongue here."

"It's more than enough for breakfast," she said.

"And dinner," I added. "Hun, did you grow up in South Carolina?"

"Yes."

"Do you want to talk about it?"

"No."

"Okay."

We fried part of the lake trout for breakfast and put what was left in our cooler. We packed up to head into Canada. Godiva seemed nervous.

"Have you ever been into Canada before?" I asked.

"No."

"You have ID?"

"Yes."

"Canada's really relaxed; don't worry about it."

She smiled and seemed to calm down.

We entered without any difficulty, followed the road north to Calgary and then turned west. We camped in the mountains.

"This area is so beautiful!" Godiva said. "Snowcapped peaks, tumbling waterfalls and frozen lakes." We set up camp and tried to settle in. Around dusk a couple stopped and asked if we were going to attend the lecture.

"Lecture?" I asked.

"The park ranger gives a talk at the pavilion; it's really informative."

"I'd like to go," Godiva said. We walked down. They had a nice fire going and made tea.

"I love his accent," she said after the lecture. "It's kind of like a strong British accent with some Scottish thrown in."

"Do you fish?" he asked us.

"Yes."

"If you follow the creek up from the campground, you'll find a lake. It's loaded with Grayling."

"Are there any grizzlies up there?" Godiva asked.

"They're actually above that, but you could run into one."

After the lecture we headed back to our tent. A chill had set in, and I wondered if we would have frost.

"Could we hike up there in the morning?" she asked.

"I thought about it, but I didn't know if you were strong enough."

"We'll see."

The next morning she made oatmeal for breakfast. I packed what I thought we would need. The trail looked rough, and it seemed to head straight up. Godiva went ahead and quickly outpaced me. I found her standing by the trail with a perplexed look on her face.

"Do you think the water washed the rock away, or did an earthquake cause this?"

"Cause what?"

"This." Almost at her feet lay a chasm some fifty feet deep. It was less than a foot wide in some spots and seemed to go almost straight downhill. At the bottom of the chasm a small creek roared through the rock walls.

"I've never seen anything like it," I said.

She took off again and quickly walked out of sight. I climbed over a steep ridge and found her sitting on a rock next to a perfect alpine lake. I noticed her eyes were misty, and it looked like she had been crying.

"Are you okay?" I asked.

"This is the most beautiful place I've ever seen," she said. Skinny grayish spruce surrounded the lake, green grass grew along the bank, and the water stood crystal clear.

"I've never seen anything like it, either."

"I didn't mean to cause any friction back there, but I'm stronger than you imagine."

"I think I learned that today."

"What do you think these grayling will eat? What bait would be best?" she asked.

"Why don't you try streamers on the fly rod?" I showed her how to hold the fly rod and make casts. It didn't take her long to catch on.

"I got one!" she screamed.

"Take your time," I said. A few moments later the fish was at her feet. I gently lifted it and showed her its dorsal fin.

"It almost looks like a mini sailfish with its fin up," she said. "You're going to let it go, aren't you?"

"Yes, that's why I lifted it so gently."

"Your turn," she said, handing me the rod. I tried, but I couldn't get the motion right. I caught nothing.

"Once the streamer's in the water you have to give tiny jerks on the line," she said. She took the rod and almost immediately caught another fish. I tried but had no luck. She caught four before I got my first fish.

"We'd better begin heading back. It'll get dark fast once the sun sets against these mountains," she said. We headed down, and this time she walked with me. About halfway down we came across a mountain sheep. A small herd appeared a moment later.

"They are so beautiful; their coats look like soft cotton," she said.

"I always wanted to see one of those."

"We'd better keep moving; it's dusk already."

Night fell fast and darkness enveloped us, but we found our tent. We ate what was left of the lake trout for dinner. Exhausted and sore, we fell asleep to the sounds of wolves howling in the distance.

Over the next few days we fished the area's streams and lakes. We hiked across mountains into alpine pastures. We walked through towering forests and crossed raging creeks. It was nearly perfect. On Friday we again headed west.

As we came out of the mountains a large, long valley appeared. A large building stood in it.

"Oh my God, that's the Banff Hotel!" she screamed.

"The what?"

"The Banff Hotel--please let's stop! Please let me get some tea?"

"We haven't splurged much; let's eat dinner." We parked and went inside. From our table we watched skiers enjoying the last of the snow on the mountain.

A man wearing a kilt and white gloves served us. We sat across from two men who also wore kilts. I ordered steak. She ordered lamb.

"I've always wanted to come here! I saw the hotel in a brochure years ago, and I said to myself, "I've got to get there someday!" Sadie would be freaking out if she were here. I've got to buy her something ...." Her sentence was cut short as she listened intently to two of the men across from us. They talked quietly in a language I couldn't understand. Godiva suddenly smiled, and a look of absolute mirth came across her face. She turned and softly spoke to the two men who turned red-faced, grabbed their check, and left.

"What happened?" I asked.

"They were talking about me ... they liked my boobs. The one wondered how soft they were. I asked them to lift their kilts so I could see how soft their asses were."

"What language was that?"

"An Irish dialect ...."

"You know Irish?"

"Sort of. Please, no more, okay? Let's just enjoy the meal." Two bites later Godiva cracked up laughing, and I ended up laughing also.

"The look on the older guy's face!" I said.

"I thought the one guy would piss himself," she admitted. "I know what I'm going to get Sadie. I'll get her a doll of a guy wearing a kilt."

We finished our meal and bought the doll.

"I want to drive to Jasper National Park tonight," I said. "It's as far north as I want to go."

"Let's do it." We drove and late that evening we set the tent up in the dark.

I awoke the next morning to find her standing just outside the tent. I joined her.

"The peaks are unbelievable here; the snow is so white, so delicate," she said.

"It's got to be the wildest place I've ever been in." We drove north through the park along an ice ridge.

"What are those?" she asked pointing toward the edge of the ice shelf. I got the binoculars and stared.

"I think they're elk, but they don't look quite right," I replied.

"No, I think they're caribou!" she said, staring through the glasses.

"You're right! I can see their distinctive antlers!"

We returned to our tent. I found wood for a fire.

"We drove all night; let's take a nap," she said. We slid into our sleeping bags.

"I'm really glad I came with you," she said. "There's something about these mountains that clears your head, puts things into perspective."

"Like what?"

"I've been thinking about everything. I mean do you think we're doing right?"

"I think we're doing the best we can."

"No, I mean Sadie and me."

"I really don't know what you're doing. I don't know where you're from; I really don't know what you do. I don't know if either of you have families. I do know that at some point I won't be able to let you go."

"What should we do?" she asked tearfully.

"I'm not even sure what's going on, but you need to stop someplace and take root. It would be better if you just told me about yourselves."

"I can't …."

I didn't know what else to do so I started rubbing her back. "If you ever want to talk about all this, I'll be here."

"I know. I wanted to say something else: This old guy …."

"Tully?"

"Yeah. He's been a godsend to you. You seem stable, happy, industrious, like you have a purpose in life. For a while it seemed you were just drifting."

"He's unlike anyone I've ever met. He's really special; I don't know what I would've done this summer without him."

"Well, learn what you can from him. I'm also happy that you've respected my feelings about booze on this trip."

"I know you can't stand drunks or the smell of booze."

"Enough of that. Why don't we see if we can catch something for dinner."

"We still have oodles and oodles of groceries if we don't," I said. We found a clear creek that ran into a lake. We decided to fish it using red and white spoons. I handed her a rod and rigged up my own.

"You first," I said. She cast out in a long ark and began retrieving her line. I did the same. About halfway back she hooked a fish.

"That's a pickerel, isn't it?" she asked.

"No, it's a medium-sized pike, but they're pretty good over a campfire." Three casts later I hooked something that swam to the bottom and fought viciously. A few minutes later I had it at the shore.

"What is it?" she asked.

"Whitefish, and those are about the best eating fish of all." We had enough for dinner and headed back. After dinner I sat hugging her from behind.

"Well, from here it's straight south, stopping wherever you wish," I said.

"I'd like to stop at Glacier on the way back," she admitted. "I'd like to spend some time studying the Native American culture."

We left the next morning and drove straight through. About ten miles from the U.S. border something strange happened.

"Pull over," she said. "Look down into the valley. What's going on?"

"It looks like the highway just ends in a sea of mud. I can see cars stuck everywhere."

"What should we do?" she asked.

"Just drive through it, I guess." We drove up to a scene right out of a horror movie. The road ended, and a sea of mud began. The mud went on for something like half a mile before the road began again. Cars, trucks and even jeeps were stuck everywhere.

"I think this is a mud slide or flood. I think the road is still underneath. We just have to stay on the road and not stop," I said. We backed up and drove into the mess at full speed, fishtailing this way and that. We passed a jeep stuck in mud up to its windshield.

"Don't stop and I think we'll make it through," she said. We passed three mud-coated girls sitting on top of their Volkswagen.

"Please stop and help us!" one called. Right about the time I thought we'd never make it, my Ford caught the pavement. We slipped out.

"You are going to help them, aren't you?" Godiva asked.

"Yes, I have a rope in back." I tied one end to my car and waded through knee-deep mud to them. I tied the rope to the frame on their car.

"You're going to have to walk out. I can only pull the car," I said. A few moments later their car was free of the mud.

"Do we owe you anything?" one asked.

"No," Godiva said.

We crossed the border without incident. We found a local campground near Kalispell. We entered Glacier National Park from the west. We stopped to look at the road sign. "GOING TO THE SUN ROAD," it read.

"What a neat name!" she said. We drove it until we came to a beaver pond. We caught brook trout until our arms tired.

"Are we getting low on cash yet?" she asked. "I might be able to find a few days of work around here."

"We're okay, but we ought to look around." A few minutes later a jeep pulled up. It was Darien, the ranger we met earlier.

"I thought you two left?" she asked.

"We drove all the way up to Jasper, fishing and hiking as we went," Godiva said. "We were just wondering if there was any work around here, you know just a few days' worth."

"No, we have a long waiting list at the park, but I'll contact you if I hear anything. Where are you staying?"

"The campground right up the road," Godiva said.

We drove back to our campground.

"We've spent a lot of nights cramped up in your backpacking tent. Can we set up the big tent tonight?"

"Sure, I'd like that."

"I think we're going to have a storm tonight," she said. "Make sure everything is either stored away or covered."

"I don't think it'll rain, but I'll cover everything." The downpour began around ten and continued on into the night. Around eleven we saw the headlights of a car and then heard girls talking in the darkness.

"Do we have a tent to set up?" one called.

"A tent to set up? As drunk as you are, you couldn't tie your shoes!"

"Whose idea was it to do shots anyway?"

"I'm getting soaked!"

"We've got a plastic sheet, right?"

"Hun, they don't have a tent, and they're freezing out there," Godiva said.

"Who?"

"The girls you pulled out of the mud."

"How do you know?" I asked.

"I just know, okay?"

"What do you want me to do?"

"Let me invite them in. We have extra sleeping bags and towels and ...."

"Okay." A few moments later Godiva appeared through the tent flap followed by three girls, one dressed only in soaking wet underwear.

"Here's some towels. I'll get you some dry clothes," she said. "Ethan and I can share one sleeping bag; you'll have to share the other two." A moment later the storm intensified, and it began to hail.

"God, I'm glad we're not out there now, hiding under that piece of plastic! Thanks for saving our asses again," one said.

"Can I get a hug? I'm freezing!" one asked.

Godiva sat up and looked around.

"Screw it, let's just get into one big pile," she said. She spread our sleeping bag on the ground. All of us lay like sardines on it. We pulled the other unzipped bags over top.

"Were you drinking Southern Comfort?" she asked one girl.

"Yeah, way too much! Why?"

"I can't stand the smell," Godiva said. "You go on the other side of Ethan."

A buxom red-haired girl arose, slid behind me and hugged me from behind for warmth.

"Everyone warm now?" Godiva asked.

"I am!" I said.

"Yeah, I know," Godiva replied.

"Since we're sleeping together, can I at least get your names?" I asked.

"I'm Denise," one called out.

"Wendy," the other said.

"I'm Carla," the one hugging me added.

"Well, goodnight!"

The next morning broke bright and sunny. Everyone felt better. The girls dried out their gear and salvaged what they could. I helped Denise, a tall thin girl with droopy blond hair, hang her sleeping bag. Godiva helped

Wendy, the pudgy brunette, do the same.

"We need to set up our tent!" Denise said.

"We could've set it up last night if we hadn't been doing shots at the bar," Carla, the buxom redhead, said.

"Doing shots at the bar?" Denise said. "You showed up with a white t-shirt and no bra? I'm surprised the guys didn't send over booze by the bottle!"

"Is it my fault that most of my clothes were muddy? You drove the car into the mess!"

"They did cover our table with booze," Wendy admitted. "Ethan, what do you think?"

"About Carla, the shots or what?"

"About setting up our tent!"

"You have a tent?' I asked. "I can help you set it up." Their tent, as it turned out, was an old canvas Boy Scout type with high walls and support poles.

"I just saw that the campground has a washer and a dryer," Carla said. "I'll drag all our soaked gear over and get it started. Ethan, can you help me?"

"I'll give you a hand," Godiva said.

"Ethan, maybe you can help me make lunch?" Wendy said. I helped her set up their portable stove. She made franks and beans. Godiva and Carla started their wash and then joined us for lunch.

"Ethan, will you help me with my sleeping bag?" Carla asked.

"I will," Godiva volunteered. By early afternoon all their gear was dry and stored in their tent. Just about the time we had a chance to relax, a jeep pulled up.

"Ethan, it's Darien!" Godiva called out. Darien slid out of her jeep and walked up.

"You won't believe what happened," she said. "It looks like a family of bears moved into the area around Red Indian Lake. We need two people to hike into there and make a full report. It pays thirty-five dollars a day."

"You mean they'll pay us to hike into there and camp?" Godiva asked.

"Yes," Darien replied. "We'll give you a portable radio to report back to us with. You'll have to be careful not to upset any bears in the area."

"When do they want us to go in?" I asked.

"Tomorrow morning," she said, climbing back into her jeep. We watched as she drove off.

That evening the five of us sat around a blazing fire.

"You two are really going to hike into bear country?" Wendy asked.

"We're camping in bear country right now," Godiva said. "I bet we're within walking distance of a grizzly right now."

"What do we do if they come to our tent?" Carla asked.

"Pray," I said.

"Ethan, if a bear comes for me tonight, you'll protect me, right?" Carla asked.

"Protect you?" Wendy said. "God help the bear!"

"I didn't sleep much last night. I'm heading to bed, bears or not," I said.

The next morning we left at daybreak and drove to the ranger's station. They gave us a radio and read us the riot act about disturbing the bears.

"Report to us twice a day," the ranger ordered. "Do not attempt to chase any bears away. Explain any movement you see." We parked the car and hiked the ten miles in to Red Indian Lake.

"Do you think we have enough supplies?" Godiva asked.

"We have two weeks' worth of freeze-dried food, but I hope to catch trout while we're there."

"What about the bears?" she asked.

"I think Carla just had us jumpy about them. I really don't expect to see any."

"Carla? Between her and the bears, I'd be more fearful of her. With her flaming red hair and boobs she'd make a good stripper."

"I hadn't really noticed," I said.

"Yeah, right!"

"Well, about the bears, if we leave them alone, they'll leave us alone," I said.

"Maybe you should use the same approach with Carla."

We arrived around one in the afternoon. The blue lake greeted us. A grass-covered hillside rose toward black craggy peaks.

"That's where I'd expect to see bears if any are around," I said.

We set up my backpacking tent near the lake and made a small campsite. I untied my fishing rod and attached a yellow rooster tail to the line. I cast in and caught a small brook trout, one of nearly a dozen we caught that afternoon.

"There's the bears!" Godiva called out. They strolled right past our campsite on their way into the thick forest. "It's a sow and two cubs, isn't it?"

"Yes, we'd better call it in because they walked right past the tent. A sow with cubs is dangerous, especially around a campsite."

Godiva picked up the radio and tried to get the office. She got no one. I tried and couldn't get anyone either.

"I think it's the valley we're in; tomorrow we'll hike up to Triple Divide pass and see if we can get better reception."

We ate dinner and had a quiet night.

"Is everything okay?" I asked.

"Yes, I'm a little worried about having those grizzlies so close, but

...”

"But what?"

"But this is their lake, and we're the ones intruding!"

The next morning we hiked toward Triple Divide, a rocky, snow-covered peak surrounded by stunted spruces.

"The scenery is unreal," Godiva said.

"I think most of the water runs west from here and it's drier to the east."

Near the peak I tried the radio and found it worked.

"We spotted a large sow with two cubs; they walked right into camp," I reported.

"They walked right into your camp?" the voice asked.

"Yes." We could hear people talking excitedly but did not know what was going on.

"You need to break camp immediately and head back," the voice said.

"Did something happen?"

"Yes, one of our volunteers saw two cubs and tried to push them together for a photograph. The sow charged her and ripped her up really bad. We're putting your area off limits for at least two weeks."

"We're not at the camp; we couldn't get reception so we hiked to Triple Divide."

"Head back as soon as possible!"

By the time we hiked back it was dark. We spent another night at the lake.

"Do you think it's safe?" she asked.

"As opposed to hiking those cliffs in the dark?"

"You're right. Let's try and get some sleep."

Sometime during the middle of the night she shook me awake.

"Listen ...," she said quietly. I heard snuffling sounds and realized a bear was right outside our tent. "What do we do?"

"Call Carla."

"No really, I'm scared! What can we do?"

"Nothing."

The next morning we broke camp at dawn. We didn't eat breakfast.

"We can eat lunch at our campground," she said as we hiked. The hike out seemed easier than the journey in. We drove to the ranger station and made a full report.

When we arrived back at our campground, Denise, Wendy and Carla were still there.

"We're heading to a bar up the road tonight. Will you join us?" Wendy asked.

"We'd love to!" Godiva responded. "We're going fishing for a while, but then we'll join you."

"Can we come fishing with you?" Carla asked. "Ethan could teach me how."

"I'm sure he will!" Godiva said.

We all headed over to the Flathead River and found a long deep pool. I tried red and white spoons and even diving plugs but caught nothing. The girls walked the banks, threw stones into the river and goofed around on the shore.

"Try this!" Godiva said, handing me a hunk of meat.

"What is it?

"It's a piece of road-killed squirrel."

"A trout wouldn't eat that!"

"Please try it?" she asked.

I tied a hook on, baited it with the squirrel and cast out. A few minutes later something grabbed my line. I pulled in a huge trout.

"What is it?" I asked.

"It's a Bull trout!" Denise explained. We released it and two more before heading back.

That night we all piled into our cars and headed south. The bar as it turned out was right up the road. About fifty miles up.

"You'll love this band!" Denise said. "They play Southern rock and country."

The band played Pure Prairie League, Blackfoot and Skynyrd songs. All the girls wanted Godiva to dance with them, but, as usual, she refused.

"You dance with them!" she said grinning. I did, and we danced until I was too tired to go on. Late in the evening they finally asked for requests from the girls.

"Play 'Willing,'" Denise told them. They played the request, closed for the night, and we headed toward our cars.

"Please drive with us!" Wendy asked Godiva.

"I will as long as Carla comes also," she said. Denise rode with me.

Denise drank about five shots too many at the bar and kept passing out against me. When we arrived at our campground, Godiva helped me carry her into their tent.

The next morning Darien drove into the campground.

"I have your checks," she said.

"Can we cash them around here?" Godiva asked. "We're heading south today."

"The bank in Kalispell will accept them," Darien said.

We said goodbye to Carla and her friends and went to find the bank. The car began making strange noises.

"I'm sorry, the Ford is acting up. I changed the plugs, but it's still running rough."

"It doesn't sound very good."

"When we lost the exhaust system, it began burning up what was left of the valves."

"Besides that, we're using a quart of oil every fifty miles now," she said.

"It won't hold up much longer. We'll probably be walking in a few days," I predicted.

"Well, I can't wait to see Yellowstone, by car or by thumb," she said.

"There's also a range with wild horses on the way. I'd like to take some pictures."

"Wild horses?" she asked.

"I remembered you loved horses from when we were on Assateague. The area here is a huge Bureau of Land Management section. The horses are supposed to live in the canyons."

We drove some eight hours before entering the area.

"How do we find the horses?" Godiva asked.

"I guess we just drive around until we see tracks and follow them," I replied.

We drove and found horse tracks, but none seemed fresh.

"Those tracks aren't from wild horses," she said.

"How do you know?" I asked.

"Because they're shod?" We drove down dusty trails for almost an hour before she spotted some unshod tracks.

"Let's just take the backpacking tent and follow the tracks," she said.

"Sounds good to me. Let's go before the sun sets too low." She found an old scrub brush and a screwdriver in my trunk. She put them in my pack.

We followed the tracks as the herd meandered across the rolling prairie. The trail led to a sagebrush-filled valley. We hiked to a small ridge to camp for the night.

"Can we just sit and watch the sun set?" she asked. The sagebrush, backlit by the setting sun, glowed a fiery orange against the sky.

The next morning we followed the tracks out onto a prairie filled with gullies. Godiva spotted a small herd of horses near a tiny creek.

"They're so beautiful!" she said. "Let's get closer." We walked downwind of them and came up from behind.

"Look at the pinto. He's not a wild horse. He's tame!" Godiva said. "He's so beautiful!"

"How do you know he's tame?" I asked.

"What I'm trying to say is that someone owned him. I think he was set free."

"How do you know that?" I asked.

"He's a gelding?" she said.

"Oh."

"Give me your rope and stay here. Don't follow me, or he'll bolt."

She took a rope from my backpack and walked out. Talking to the pinto, she slowly crept forward. About ten feet shy of the horse she stopped but kept talking. The horse walked to her. She tied the rope around the horse's neck and looped it over his nose.

"Get the brush and screwdriver from your pack and leave them on the ground," she said. I put them down and walked away. She led the horse forward until she could grasp the brush and screwdriver. She curried the horse, talking to him and feeling his muscles.

"They love this," she said, brushing him deeply from nose to tail. "They also love having their hooves cleaned." She scraped the rocks and thorns from the V on his hooves.

"Let's see how he runs!" she said, pulling him along by the rope. The two of them ran at full speed through the sagebrush and seemed to enjoy each other. Finally she stopped to catch her breath and began rubbing him down again. What she did next happened so quickly it stunned me. She grabbed hold of his mane, made an arching jump and landed on his back. The horse twirled slightly as if unsure what to do, but seemed okay having her on.

"You know how to ride?" I asked. "How are you sitting on him?" She had landed far forward on him, almost on his neck. She sat in a position I'd never seen. Her knees were drawn forward against the horse's neck, and her feet were almost crisscrossed on his back like she was squatting on him.

"Won't you fall off like that?" I asked. "You've got no saddle, no reins ...." She shook her head no, leaned all the way forward so her head was next to his, and spoke something. The pinto took off running at full speed.

"Godiva, be careful!" I screamed. She didn't bounce around on his back like I would have but rode like she was glued on.

She's riding like she's lying down on the horse. Her face near the horse's eye, her long blond hair blowing back, her curves and the pinto's intermingled.

I waited for a long time, but they did not reappear.

I hope she's okay ... if she fell off, she might be unconscious out there! I'd better make camp. Where will I find wood? Where could she have gone to? How will she find her way back? I found some dry wood, set up the tent and began making dinner. I looked west and saw them slowly walking toward the campsite. She stayed on the horse, looming over me at the campsite.

"I've never seen anyone ride like that! How do you control the horse?" I asked.

"Knee pressure," she explained. "You press against his neck the way you want to go."

"I thought for sure you'd fall off. Where did you learn to ride like that?"

"My secret."

"Well, you're an expert rider, that's for sure. Is it my turn now?"

"I don't think he'll let you on, but you can try if you want." I went to hold the tether but he whirled away, bucked twice but never came close to dislodging her.

"No, you're right," I said. She slid off and took the rope from his neck. "Why would someone let him go?"

"I think he hurt his leg at one time but it's healed now." She slapped him on the flank, and he bolted away.

"I love horses; would you buy me one someday?" she asked.

"A horse?"

"Oh God, listen to me! I can't even tell you where I learned to ride a horse, and I'm asking you to buy me one. Hun, what do you really think of me?"

"The world."

"Come and sit down. It's just us two, isn't it." She hugged me tightly and stared toward the horizon.

"I don't want to say too much, but you need to know a few things. I grew up in a very sheltered community. A place where everyone is interrelated and no one is allowed to leave. What I'm trying to say is that relatives are probably looking for me, and if they catch me, they'll drag me back."

"Do you mean something like a cult or radical group or something?"

"Something like that, but please no more, okay?"

"And they love horses?"

"Yes, they love horses and dream of open spaces like this. Thank you for understanding. Can we just call it a day?"

"I'd like that. Let's just eat and then get some rest."

The next morning we hiked back to the car and resumed our journey. West Yellowstone lay a few hours ahead.

"Do you want to camp in a rural area or someplace touristy?" I asked.

"Why don't we find a touristy place and then hike in for a few days."

We found a campground with a pool just outside the park.

"Why don't we just hit the pool today?" I asked.

"I'd like that. Let's just take it easy." She changed into her white bikini and I into my swim trunks. I sat staring, mesmerized.

"You okay?" she asked.

"You've got an unbelievable figure," I said.

"I think I've dropped a couple of pounds, probably from all the hiking."

"Hun, I don't know I ...."

"You're jealous? Now you know how I felt about Carla. Don't worry about the guys at the pool; I'll be here for you, okay?"

"It's hard to describe."

"Your heart's aching, isn't it?"

"I've been in a strange mood for days now. Seeing you riding that horse with your hair flying free really hit me hard. It's almost like I don't know you at all."

"You know me better than anyone else ever has."

"I feel lost."

"You need to clear your mind. Let's just swim, take in some sun and relax. "

We swam and, like I thought, Godiva was the center of attention at the pool. It didn't bother me that all the guys drooled over her; it was the strange, strained relationship we had. Sometime in the next few days I would have to say good-bye and she would have to go. I wouldn't know where she was or if she was okay or not. It didn't make sense; neither of us liked it, but it was the reality of the situation. It sucked!

I fell asleep on a lawn chair. Late in the day Godiva woke me up.

"Can we go into Yellowstone tomorrow?" she asked.

"I'd love it."

The next morning we entered Yellowstone National Park from the west.

"I found your camera. I'm taking pictures of everything," Godiva said. We didn't drive far before we came upon a herd of elk.

"Stop, let's get all the shots we can," she said. She took picture after picture. We saw Old Faithful, the Fire Hole River and several hot springs. Late in the day we pulled into the ranger's office to get back-country passes.

"We're going to hike back in for a few days," Godiva explained. "We want to hike along Yellowstone Lake and camp some ten miles in."

"You need to study the map on the wall; it lists the trails and difficulty," the ranger explained. "Then you need to fill out the forms, and we'll give you the passes you need."

The next morning we broke camp early and headed to the trail that would take us back in.

"This is marked as a horse trail, but it's much shorter than the hiking trail," I said. "If a horse can walk it, I can."

"Wouldn't it be better if we stayed on the established hiking trails?" she asked.

"It seems to be a shortcut to where we want to go."

"Do you think we'll run into any bears? I have bells to wear. They'll hear their tinkle and know we're coming."

"Can't hurt."

We began hiking the rough trail. That afternoon we walked through an area that had recently burned in a forest fire. We stopped to soak our feet in the ash-filled pool.

"These pine forests seem to go on forever," she said. "Yellowstone Lake is one of the most beautiful things I've ever seen." She viewed the lake while I scouted ahead. I walked back and explained what I saw.

"The trail disappears up ahead. It appears to be a narrow muddy ditch that goes on forever."

"Really? You'll have to show me."

I walked her to the spot.

"What happened?" I asked.

"The horse's hooves cut the trail away. We'll just have to hike on through the mud."

We hiked ahead through the narrow ditch. The ankle-deep mud didn't help, and the ditch made me claustrophobic. We finally emerged onto rocky ground.

"At least we're out of that!"

"How much further is the campsite?" Godiva asked.

"About a mile. I'll be glad to get there; we only have about an hour before the sun drops behind those hills."

Godiva walked ahead and suddenly stopped.

"Something smells dead!" she said.

"I smell it, too!" We walked on and saw a reddish brown flash run through the brush.

"What was that?" Godiva asked.

"I think it was a deer," I said.

"Let me get my camera out. I'd love to get a picture of it," she said. She fumbled with her pack as I stepped forward. I walked around the brush and came face to face with a huge grizzly.

"Bear!" I said softly.

"It's a what?" she asked loudly. The bear reared, made popping sounds and galloped right at us.

"BEAR!" I screamed. We dropped our packs, ran through the woods and scrambled up the first big tree we could find. Godiva climbed right over top of me. The bear swiped at my boot but didn't catch it. We climbed higher.

"What do we do now?" she asked.

"Wait." After a few minutes the bear seemed bored and left. We waited until dark before climbing down. We grabbed our packs and headed back the way we'd come. We camped about a mile down from the bear encounter, setting up our tent right on the edge of the lake.

"Do you think he'll follow us?" Godiva asked.

"I don't think so, but if he does, we can swim out into the lake." We didn't get a lot of sleep.

The next morning I scouted around the camp, but the bear was gone. I decided to try fishing the lake. Godiva emerged from the tent looking exhausted. I cast a red and white spoon out into the water.

"I got one!" I reeled in a Yellowstone cutthroat.

"Can I try?" She cast out and caught a large trout on her first cast also.

"We have more than enough for breakfast," she said. "Let's eat and then take a nap." She fried the trout for breakfast. We got up again around noon.

"Should we head back now?" I asked.

"No, let's confront our fears. We hike to where we were supposed to camp and spend the night there," Godiva said.

"Are you sure?"

"Yes, I know about being afraid." We packed everything and hiked up the trail. About a mile further we came upon a strange sight. Something lay dead on the forest floor. Something huge.

"What is it?" I asked, looking at the half-eaten carcass.

"It's a mule," Godiva said. "Probably from one of the pack trains. That's why the bear charged us; he was defending the mule carcass."

"I can't imagine that the bear killed the mule," I said. We entered a valley filled with breathtaking scenery.

"This is gorgeous!" she said. We set up camp and settled in. Around four we heard the sound of hooves on rocks.

"It's a pack train," Godiva said. She walked forward to talk to the wrangler.

"We lost a mule on the way in," he explained. "It stumbled and fell on a dead stump; it pierced its lung."

"We saw it on the trail," Godiva said. "Be careful; a bear was guarding the carcass."

"A bear, a big one?" he asked.

"Yeah, it chased us up a tree last night," she said. The pack train went on, and we fished the lake. We caught several trout for dinner.

The next morning we hiked back to our car.

"Where to now?" Godiva asked.

"Colorado," I said.

"Do we have enough money, or should we try and find some work?"

"I'm okay, why?"

"I'd like it if you got home with as much cash as you left with. I would think I wasn't a burden to you. Some of these ranches need tractor drivers."

"You're not a burden. Do you know how to drive a tractor?"

"It's not that hard," she said.

We left Yellowstone by the east entrance and drove through Cody.

"You hungry?" I asked.

"I filled up on trout this morning."

"Then let's wait until dinnertime to stop."

As we traveled east, the country seemed to turn from lush mountains to dry prairie. Large herds of antelope appeared, and they all seemed to be heading east.

"The antelope look beautiful!" she said.

"They sure do." Our gas gauge showed low.

"I should've filled up with gas in Cody, but I didn't. What's the next town?"

"Meeteetse." When we pulled into town, the gas stations had closed for the night.

"We'd better camp here for the night," Godiva said. "In the morning we can get gas and go on." We found a free camping spot at the edge of town.

"Let's get something to eat first and set up camp later," I said.

"I saw a bar that served food," she said. We drove back, parked and went in.

"You arrived on the right night," a girl told us. "Tonight's five-cent beers and ten-cent hot dogs."

"I don't care about the beer, but the hot dogs sound great!" Godiva said. I bought a couple and noticed that a pool table sat in back.

"How much is it to play pool?" I asked.

"Free," the bartender replied.

"Here's why," Godiva said, holding up a cut-off broomstick.

"Well, there's not much else to do, so let's play." We played, ate hotdogs and talked with a couple of locals.

"The only other place I saw one of those was in Louisiana!" she said, pointing. The bar had a drive-up window where you could order a shot or a beer. We watched as people pulled up and ordered their booze.

"Look, they sell pizza also!" Godiva said. "I wonder how much it is." A moment later the unthinkable happened. A girl rode up to the pickup window on a horse.

"I want two hot dogs," the girl said. She dismounted to pick them up. As she stepped down, her horse stuck his head into the bar, grabbed a whole pizza and shook it. Pizza sauce, cheese and pepperoni flew all across the bar.

"Tammy, get in here and clean up this mess!" the bartender called out. A moment later the girl appeared at the door and attempted to lead her horse into the bar.

"Tie it outside!" the guy yelled at her. She found a rail, tied it and then came in. He handed her a bucket and a mop. Later Godiva called Tammy over. She was cute with frizzy blond hair.

"Well, I can see I'm not the only little gal in this town tonight," Tammy said.

"You have a beautiful horse! Where do you keep him?" Godiva asked.

"I board him for free at the stable. I work there, and they don't mind. You staying at the motel?"

"No, we're going to camp down the road a ways."

"It's not safe to camp around here; some of the guys are real Neanderthals. Why don't you stay with me at the stable? I've got a room up there."

"I'd like that!" Godiva said. "I love to be around horses."

"Tomorrow's auction day. There's work if you want it."

"Really, doing what?" Godiva asked.

"As pretty as you are, you could be a receptionist," Tammy said. "He'll have to help unload cattle. If we're gonna do it, we better get to bed now. We'll be up at three-thirty."

She guided us to her place. We climbed the steps to a small room with four bunks. Tammy's bed lay off to the side. The first thing I noticed was the smell of fresh hay.

"This is perfect," Godiva said.

"The bathroom's off to the side. I have a tiny kitchen also. This is used as a bunkhouse a couple of months a year."

The next morning Godiva and Tammy sat side-by-side taking buyers' names and handing out auction cards. I unloaded steers and forced them into small corrals.

I guess there's worse jobs, but I can't think of one right now. The dust tastes alkaline; the sun's hot and the steers are ornery. One of the buyers invited Godiva and Tammy to lunch. I walked over to the bar and ordered hot dogs again. On my way back I saw a guy wearing a Stetson open a door for Godiva. She walked over to me.

"Tammy said there's some road work around here also if we want it," she said.

"Road work?" I asked.

"You know, holding stop signs and directing traffic."

"Sounds okay ...."

"Are you all right?" she asked.

"The steers are awful. I got bumped by their horns a few times, knocked around and ...."

"Are you jealous that I was invited to lunch?"

"I guess so. Unloading steers isn't any fun." She shook her head.

"Come on," she said. I followed her to the corral. "Steers aren't that hard if you follow a few rules." She walked up to one, held her arms in the air and guided it back against a fence. "They're more frightened of you than you should be of them. If you have real trouble with one, twist his tail and push; he'll go where you want."

"I'm sorry, I saw you go to lunch with that buyer and ...."

"It's you I'll be with tonight, isn't it?"

Late in the day we got paid, and she made ten dollars more than I did.

"They have no lack of bums to help handle steers, but pretty receptionists are hard to come by," Tammy explained. "It's kinda like that with the road work also. Hey it's not that late; would you two like to go riding'?"

"I'd love that!" Godiva said. I said nothing.

"He seems kinda down?" Tammy asked.

"He's a little jealous," Godiva said.

"Well, he's got the prettiest girl in this part of Wyoming," Tammy said. "I think it's cute that he's jealous."

"It's a little more than that, but riding will be fun," I said.

"Well, Godiva and I need to change first," Tammy said. "Why don't you be a dear and start the rice and beans?"

After we'd eaten she took us into the stable.

"Pick out a good horse for yourself and for him," Tammy said. Godiva found a beautiful Palomino for herself and a huge white horse for me.

"Do you know how to saddle him?" she asked.

"Not really."

"I'll help you." Half an hour later we rode out onto a huge ranch. It seemed to go on forever. We rode down a long creek bank and came out onto a flat wash.

"We need to be careful here, lots of prairie dogs around," Tammy said. "Watch out for their holes." We stopped and walked the horses until we came upon a herd of Herefords.

"It's okay from here on," Tammy said. She and Godiva rode off, but I decided to keep walking. I looked back and saw prairie dogs popping out of holes and looking around. I also spotted some kind of weasel chasing one. I got back on my horse and caught up to the two.

"I saw some kind of weasel chasing the prairie dogs around," I said.

"It's probably a black-footed ferret. Lots of biologists are around here looking for 'em," Tammy said. "They thought they was done for and then found some here. I'll report it."

We rode to a hill and watched the sun set in the west. The sky glowed red, pink and dark blue all at once.

"We better head back," Tammy said. When we returned, we helped her brush down the horses and clean the stalls. I dragged several wheelbarrow loads of manure outside.

"Thanks, I've been putting off doing that," Tammy said.

The next morning Tammy dressed in a tight t-shirt and jeans. Godiva did the same.

"If you look pretty, they'll let you hold the signs," she explained. "If not, then you're down in the ditch with the rest." She wasn't kidding; she and Godiva held signs and talked with drivers. I spent the day shoveling. We made a lot of money, but the work was brutal.

The next morning we made breakfast for Tammy.

"We need to move on," Godiva said.

"Well, you take care of yourselves then," Tammy said. Godiva hugged her good-bye, and we drove south.

"I'd like to see Colorado and then call it quits," I said.

"I've really loved the time we spent together, but I'd like to get back also. I'd like to spend some time with Sadie. Her tour ended last week."

"Do you know anything about her? I mean where did she come from? She's incredibly intelligent yet never really went to school."

"Pull over," she asked. I pulled off the road onto a parking lot. She seemed torn and unsure of what to say.

"Hun?" I asked.

"Would it be right if I told her your secrets or for you to tell her mine? What I'm saying is to just ask her and I think she'll tell you. She might not tell everything, but she'll at least tell you enough so you'd understand, okay?"

"Okay."

We crossed into Colorado and drove to Estes National Park. We found a good site and set up camp. Godiva seemed troubled.

"Are you okay?" I asked.

"No."

"What's the problem?"

"You're the problem ...."

"Did I do something wrong?" I asked.

"No, you did everything right."

"I don't understand?"

"You're the most dangerous thing in my life, and that worries me."

"I'm dangerous?"

"You're stable, you live in a town. If someone wants to find me they can follow you to me. Sadie and I are on the move all the time, never staying long anywhere. We're hard to track down and can leave quickly if something comes up."

"You're worried that someone will track you down and drag you back to ...?"

"Yes."

"To where?"

"Just back."

"And they want you for ... sex, money, what?"

Godiva just stared at me. "I would list it as honor, children, money and then sex."

"Hun, I'm not going to let someone grab you and drag you away, okay?"

"I'm sorry. I shouldn't have said as much as I did. We need to drop this now!"

"Okay."

"Just one more thing you need to know," she said.

"What?"

"You're the only boyfriend I've ever had."

"The only boyfriend?"

"You really don't want me to explain, okay?"

Estes National Park contained huge snow-covered peaks, lush valleys and clear tumbling rivers. We caught trout in the creeks and hiked to the summits. We stayed two days before heading toward Boulder.

The car lost power on the highway. We drove down a long flat stretch and barely made fifty.

"Does the car need to be tuned up again?" Godiva asked.

"No, I think the valves are all but shot. I hope we make it into Boulder."

We limped along losing speed by the mile. Since we'd driven so long, we decided to get a room for the night. The room included a small kitchen.

"I want to roast a chicken and stuff it, and make sweet potatoes and …," Godiva said. We drove out to a supermarket and stocked up on groceries. The car would only do around ten miles an hour in town.

She made an unreal dinner, and we spent the evening loafing around the room.

"I'm really the only boyfriend you've had?" I asked.

"Yes, but let's not go there. Please don't ask me to go there. Let's go swimming." We headed to the pool and swam for almost an hour in the cool water.

In the morning we decided to drive out of town and see the countryside. A long hill led out of town, and the car couldn't make it up. It drove slower and slower until it died. We sat by the side of the road trying to decide what to do.

"Look, if the car's history, it's okay. We can go on," Godiva said. "I've hiked all over the place. We'll get home or wherever you want to go." I got the car started, but the engine was really weak. We turned and slowly drove downhill back into Boulder.

"I'll help you if you want to try and fix it," Godiva said.

"No, it's shot. The best thing we can do is sell it to a junkyard."

"I saw a place; it was called Oyster Street Salvage," she said. I drove down and found the place. I sold the car for thirty-five dollars. We hitchhiked back to the motel. She tried to cheer me up.

"We'll be okay! We've got the room, and this is Fourth of July weekend," she said.

"I drove that car and covered most of the country," I said.

"I know." We slept until it was dark.

"No one's outside, and everything's really quiet," she said. "Let's go for a dip."

We snuck down and swam in the cool water. After about ten minutes the entire pool lit up.

"What the hell?" I said.

Godiva and I pressed ourselves against the side of the pool. A moment later the motel owner appeared alongside the pool.

"I would have turned the lights on sooner if I knew you were going swimming," she said.

"Oh, it's okay; we just wanted to take a dip," Godiva said. The woman walked back to her office and left us alone. We snuck back to our room.

"Thank you for helping me get over this," I said.

"When do you want to leave for home?" she asked.

"Sunday morning."

"Okay, we need to rest tomorrow anyway. It'll be a long hike home," she said.

"I'm thinking it would be easier if we took the bus. They have a deal where you can go anywhere for fifty bucks."

"Okay."

The next afternoon I bought tickets to take the bus home.

"Today's the Fourth of July!" Godiva said. "Let's just tour the town and watch the parade." We walked downtown and found a community picnic underway.

"They're barbecuing an entire side of beef over there; let's get some," she said.

"I hope they have corn on the cob also," I said. We loaded our plates with fantastic food.

"They're going to have sack races; let's get in on it," she said. We stepped into burlap bags and hopped like bunnies across a field. We also did a three-legged race and a contest where she shot whipped cream off my face with a squirt gun.

"We need to head back to the room soon," she said.

"Aren't we going to stay for the fireworks?" I asked.

"Oh, I think we'll see them all right."

"What do you have in mind?"

"You'll see," she said. We went back to our room and rested. We got up at sundown.

"Come on," she said. "It's cool outside; wear your jeans." We began climbing the hill behind the motel. We climbed higher, and the hillside changed from lush forest into grass and then cactus-covered desert. The top of the ridge lay just above us, and I used the last of my strength to reach it.

"What are we doing here?" I asked.

"Watching the fireworks," she said. We stared out over a vast plain. Almost a hundred miles east a town set off their fireworks.

"They're unreal!" I said. Other towns began setting theirs off. They lit up the sky.

"Look!" she said pointing down. I saw something I never expected. Planes flew below us. Ten or more spread across the vast plain. Billowy white clouds slowly moved along below us.

Boulder set off their fireworks. Later the town began to sing the National Anthem, and we joined in. The finale of a perfect night.

"Hun, I'm really glad you came with me. I wouldn't have missed this for the world."

"I know I'll never forget any of this," she said. "We climbed the Rockies, hiked across glaciers and fished everywhere possible. We met really nice people, rested when we wanted to, and worked as we wished. We saw elk, moose, mountain sheep; we even got treed by a grizzly! It's been a life-changing thing."

We arrived back at our room around two in the morning. Exhausted, we collapsed into bed. I expected we would sleep until late the next morning, but I was wrong.

Around four in the morning I heard the sobbing sound of Godiva having a nightmare. I hugged her and gently tried to wake her up. I felt her shivering. She awoke with a start.

"Don't let them take me!" she screamed at me. "Don't, don't let them take me!"

"Who?" I asked.

"The guys in the limo," she said.

"Hun, it's just a nightmare, and I won't let anyone take you, okay?" She finally calmed down enough to fall back asleep. We got up around nine because the bus left at noon. We packed our things to walk down.

"Hun, it's today," she said as we walked.

"What's today?" I asked.

"We're going to be on the bus, it will pull over, a black limo will be waiting. I saw it!"

"A nightmare, that's all it was," I said.

"No, it's real and it's waiting." We arrived at the station and found our seats on the bus. I stashed our backpacks in the luggage holder.

"We're supposed to sit there," she said, pointing to a seat.

"Why there?" I asked.

"Because that's how it was in my dream," she said. "Promise me again that you won't let them take me, okay?"

"I promise, but please tell me what you think you saw?" I asked.

"It's in a deserted place. A limo is beside the road. The bus stops. I struggled in the limo as guys held me down."

"Why would the bus stop in the middle of nowhere? It makes no sense. We'll be all right, okay?" Godiva said nothing, and the bus pulled out.

About an hour into the trip she finally relaxed. I felt her breathing slow, and I knew she was asleep. I pulled my sleeping bag down and covered her. I began reading. She awoke with a start.

"We're here!" she said.

"Where? There's nothing here?" We were driving through the middle of an empty prairie. I looked ahead and saw a black limo sitting by the side of the road. The bus slowed and pulled over. I felt fingernails dig into my arm.

"Don't let them take me!" she pleaded. She pulled my sleeping bag over her head. The limo's trunk lid popped open. A man dressed in a suit emerged from the limo. He began unloading luggage and placing it in the bus's storage section.

"What the hell's going on in that car!" a woman screamed. Godiva slid the sleeping bag off her head to stare. The car door opened. Four men wearing suits dragged a kicking and screaming girl out of the limo. The bus door opened, and the girl was thrown onto our bus. The men ran to the limo, piled in and sped off. The girl got up off the floor and wiped tears from her face. She slowly walked to the back of the bus and found a seat. The girl looked strangely like Godiva. Our bus resumed its journey. Godiva clung to me and sobbed for the next two hours.

Around midnight Godiva composed herself and washed her face.

"Get my sleeping bag down; yours is wet from my tears," she said. She walked to the back, hugged the mystery girl and sat caressing her. She covered both of them with her sleeping bag and settled in for the night. I didn't see her again until the bus stopped for breakfast.

"Are you okay?" I asked.

"No and neither is she. Yesterday she didn't believe that a group of men could drag her from her home and throw her on a bus, but they did."

"You saw her in your dream? You thought it was yourself?" I asked.

"Yes."

"What happened to her?" I asked.

"She's Mormon."

"And ...?"

"She's not really sure, but she thinks she failed some kind of test or thing or ... it really doesn't matter. Yesterday her church elders showed up, explained that they annulled her marriage, she couldn't see her husband, and they were sending her home."

"Home?"

"They literally dragged her out of her kitchen, grabbed a few of her things and drove her to the bus station. If she returns, they'll have her committed."

"Committed, they can do that?"

"Yes, they can; it's a small town. The police are all church members. There's no one she can go to. She leaves, or they'll lock her away as if she's crazy or something. I thought I explained this to you already? If they don't want her to leave, they can keep her; if they want her to go, then she must."

"Can't she ...?"

"No, she has no option now except to head to her nearest relative, an aunt in Zanesville, Ohio. She doesn't have any idea what she did wrong!

Her husband and her weren't fighting."

"That really sucks!" I said.

"Come eat breakfast with us," Godiva asked. "Help cheer her up."

The girls name was Clair, and she seemed really nice. Godiva took time to brush Clair's hair. We played cards together to pass the time. She seemed to soften a little as the day wore on.

"Ethan, do I seem okay to you?" Clair asked.

"Yes, why?"

"You keep staring at me funny."

"It's hot, I'm sweaty, and you're wearing long johns under your dress," I said.

"Ethan ...," Godiva said.

"You're not supposed to be looking at what I wear," she said. "They're not long johns, and I have to wear them no matter what!"

"I'm sorry," I said.

"No, it's okay, I thought you disliked me because I'm no longer ...," she said. I went to ask, but Godiva shook her head no. Later Clair fell asleep, and Godiva slid over.

"She thinks she's damaged goods because she's no longer a virgin," she whispered.

We finally arrived at Zanesville and hugged Clair good-bye.

"You two are so in love. I hope you have a lot of children," she said.

"Clair, can I have your address? I'd like to write," I said.

"I'd like that, too," she said. She wrote the address on a slip of paper. I stashed it in my pocket. We watched as she walked away. I stood on the sidewalk stunned.

"What was all that about children?" I asked.

"I told her we were married," Godiva explained.

"Married? Children?" I asked.

"Yes, it's impossible, isn't it?" Godiva asked, wiping away tears.

I sat on the bus trying to comprehend what Clair and Godiva had said.

"Hun, did I say something wrong?" I asked.

"No, you did everything right. It isn't you; it's me."

"She said we were so in love; are we?" I asked.

"I know I love you and that you love me, but that doesn't mean we're in love!"

The bus continued on through the mountains. We would be home soon.

"You'll stay with me tonight, won't you?" I asked.

"No, the sooner you let go, the better you'll be." The bus pulled into the station, and we retrieved our packs.

"Let's make this short and sweet," she said.

"Short? Sweet? Why?" I asked.

"Because I'm going to be hurting enough as it is," she said. We kissed, hugged, and she shouldered her pack to leave.

"You'll stop by soon?" I asked.

"Yes, but please don't watch me walk off, okay?"

"Okay." I turned and fought back tears. I felt a tap on my shoulder. I turned again and saw her standing.

"Hun, Clair wasn't damaged goods. I am!" she said. Godiva disappeared into the crowd. I walked away alone, again.

CORN AND CRABS

I need to get over this fast and get back to Wildwood. Here I am stuck in Philadelphia again! Why did everything end so badly? Well, I need a car; my boss at the gas station will have one. I can take the subway and buses over.

I found Blain standing in his usual spot, a glass of Jim Beam in his hand.

"What do you have in the way of junk?" I asked.

"You lose your car?" he asked.

"It's sitting in Boulder, Colorado," I said.

"I've got a couple of beat up Dodges, a Corvair; I just sold a Lincoln and got a Pinto in the trade."

"A Pinto? At least I know them." He showed me the car, a red '72 model. It needed some work but ran okay.

"Take two hundred?" I asked.

"Two-fifty," he said.

"Okay." I paid him and got to work on the car. It needed a tune up and two tires. Rather than buy the tires, I found them in his scrap pile. They'd last until winter at least. The car ran smoother after the tune up.

"You seem kinda down; some girl do you in?" he asked.

"I don't want to talk about it; I need to get going."

"You driving back to Wildwood tonight?" he asked.

"Yeah, I need to get back. I promised Tully I'd meet him tomorrow morning." My boss held up the fifth of Bourbon.

"Well, at least have a shot or two!" he said.

"I really can't. I've got miles to cover." I drove back that evening and found the Cave deserted. I settled into my corner and stretched out. A moment later Karen walked in the door.

"How was your trip?" she asked.

"The trip? Fantastic! But Godiva left really upset."

"Do you want to talk about it?"

"No."

"Well, it's good to have you back." I fell asleep almost immediately and slept later than I should have.

"Ethan, you need to get up. The Beachcomber's here!" Tina said. I woke up to see Tully standing in the kitchen.

"How was your trip?" he asked.

"Too good to be true," I said. "How was Camden?

"Camden, oh, I didn't stay there. Spent the time sailing," he said.

"Sailing?"

"Yeah, but now I got another deal going. We can make a lot of money picking sweet corn."

"What about our crabs?"

"They can wait a little longer."

"Picking sweet corn all day in the hot sun doesn't thrill me. Well, it can't be that bad. Maybe it'll take my mind off of Godiva."

We stopped at the local supermarket. Tully picked up a stack of brown paper bags and two large boxes.

"What do we need the bags for?" I asked.

"They'll come in handy; the field's not far," Tully said. "Everything okay between you and that girl?"

"Godiva? Everything went well until the very end."

"Well, you two spent a lot of time together; let her be for a while. Give her a chance to think. She seems really nice to me."

As we drove up I saw a migrant crew picking sweet corn. The farmer showed us where to pick. We walked into the fields and began pulling ears of corn.

"This is at least as bad as I imagined," I said. You had to twist each ear of sweet corn off, fill the sacks and drag them to a tally area.

The air became hot and humid. I lost sight of Tully.

After about three hours of picking, I spotted him.

"Do we get paid by the hour or by the sack?" I asked.

"You don't get paid at all," the farmer chimed in.

"I'll explain it to you later," Tully said and walked off.

After hours of brutal picking, the field was done. A truck hauled the corn away. The migrant crew climbed onto a bus and left.

"How do we get paid?" I asked Tully.

"Way the deal works," Tully explained, "is we get to keep and sell any corn left in the field."

"It sounds like a rotten deal to me!"

"Let's start picking again," Tully said.

We reentered the field and began picking. We filled the boxes with corn. The field held more unpicked corn than I imagined. We dragged it to the roadside, dumped it and picked again. We soon had a large pile of sweet corn next to the road.

"What now?" I asked.

"Just watch," Tully said. He made a sign out of one of the boxes that read, "JUST PICKED SWEET CORN." He stood next to the pile and smiled at the drivers. Cars pulled over, and he started selling it. He did a brisk business selling corn and talking to customers.

"I'm tired of picking corn. Can I try selling it for a while?" I asked.

"Sure. The corn's two dollars a dozen from the fresh pile or five dollars for all you can fill into a bag from the picked-over pile," Tully explained. After about fifteen minutes I called out to Tully.

"I'll go back to picking. I don't have the skill you do for luring customers."

Traffic on the road got heavier. Tully's knack for luring customers worked; nine cars sat by the side of the road.

Late in the afternoon we loaded all the remaining corn into my car. The cold shed at the Cave could store it. We drove back to the Cave.

"I'm crashing on the hammock," I said to Karen. "I'm so tired and sore now, I can hardly function."

"Rest?" Tully said. "We have to go out and empty our crab pots. Since we haven't emptied them for so long, they're sure to be full."

"Can I take some of the corn?" Karen asked. "We could cook some for dinner?"

"Take all you can eat and all you can use," Tully remarked.

Tully and I found more crabs in our pots than we could sell. We made the rounds emptying the pots and filling up bushel baskets with the crabs. We sold all we could to the fish houses and had a lot left over.

"We can easily sell the rest of these to our customers tomorrow," Tully said. "Let's store them in the cold shed."

When we returned we found a large pile of corn shucks outside the door. Karen and Tina cooked the corn in a huge canning pot. A group of the guys sat at the picnic table eating. I unloaded the crabs.

"Great now we have crabs also," Karen said.

"Enjoy them," Tully said. He chuckled and left.

"Karen, we sell the crabs and corn to our customers, I don't know...."

"I've been charging five dollars per person for all the corn you can eat and all the beer you can drink. But since we have crabs also, I'm raising the price to ten dollars," she said.

"My beer from the shed?" I asked.

"I'll keep your cut for you," she said. "I sent Kathy to ask for more canning pots. We have kegs of beer on the way also."

"I'm heading to my corner. Just let me sleep awhile, okay?" I pushed through the crowd and pulled my sleeping bag over my head. A moment later I felt a hand brush through my hair.

"You okay?" Karen asked.

"Just exhausted."

"Okay." If anyone in the noisy crowd stepped on me that night, I didn't know it. I was dead to the world. Sometime around midnight I woke just long enough to look around. The Cave was full of people and not just the usual college kids, either.

"Who are all these people?" I asked.

"College kids, some of our neighbors, people off the street, I don't know," Jim said.

I passed out again and didn't wake up until the first light of dawn. The Cave looked worse than I remembered. People slept wherever they could. A sixty-year-old guy sat passed out on the easy chair. I didn't know most of the people in the room, but that wasn't unusual. I saw a guy pumping beer out of the keg in the yard. I made a pot of coffee, sat down, and drank it.

The corn and crab pots still sat on the stove. I drained the water out of them and dragged them outside. Three empty beer kegs lay in the yard. We now had six picnic tables out back, probably taken from the neighbors. I found a massive pile of picked crab shells, corn cobs and paper plates. I checked the cold shed, and all the crabs, corn and beer were gone. I noticed Tully walking down the street.

"I want to take the sailboat out and check the lobster pots," he said.

"Okay, let's go before the lifeguards go on duty. Tully, I think all the corn and crabs are gone."

"We made out fine; we cleared over two hundred yesterday."

"Karen might have come out okay. She was charging for the corn, crabs and beer. If she has any cash for us, I'll give you half."

"You're gonna have to figure out how to separate the beer money; you know I can't take it," Tully said.

An hour later he steered the little sailboat northeast into the waves.

"We're nearing a wreck where I set a pot," he said.

"I thought lobsters are a New England thing. If it hadn't been for almost reeling one up from the bottom, I wouldn't have believed it."

"The ocean's always surprising you." With his unerring sense of direction we came upon a bleach bottle that marked the lobster pot.

"I can't pull it up," I said, "What did you weigh it down with?"

"Let the motion of the boat pull it to the surface." The lobster pot, which Tully had fashioned like a giant crab pot, held jumbo-sized sea bass and blackfish. "So far I've set out six lobster pots," he said. As we pulled them we found sea bass, blackfish and other bottom fish in them. The last one held something different.

"This one has a nice lobster," Tully said. "We'll have it for dinner. Why don't you come over at four?"

"Okay."

"I've been asked to go out on a nighttime charter boat; you want in on it?"

"Yeah, why not." We iced down the fish and sold them to a fish store. I ended up back at the Cave.

"Ethan, can you help me return the empty kegs and tap back to the beer store?" Karen asked. We drove over and got her deposit money back.

"We had a great party last night." She handed me a roll of cash.

"I can't take that much," I said. "Keep some for yourself."

"I already kept two hundred!" she said. "You supplied the corn and crabs, and a lot of the beer. Together, the sky's the limit!" She gave me a big hug and a kiss. I didn't know what to say.

"Karen, what do you mean?" She went inside. I went in, but she was nowhere to be found.

"A policeman stopped by last night. He asked about you," Tina called from the table.

"The police came last night?" I asked.

"Yeah, first Alice the Goon showed up and went through the roof. Later this guy showed up. He got really pissed off. Everyone told him this was your party. We couldn't find you last night, and it really made him mad!"

"Officer Buckwheat?" I asked.

"No," she said, handing me a card. "It was an Officer O'Neil. You're supposed to call him as soon as possible."

"Great, just what I need." I went to a pay phone, called the number and got a recording. I stopped by the bank and deposited most of the money I'd made.

When I returned to the Cave I found it still crowded with strangers. I heard a guy describe some kind of deal he cooked up. The girls seemed excited.

"I wanted to talk to Karen. Did you see her?" I asked Tina.

"What do you want her for?" Kathy asked. "Wasn't that blond enough for you?"

"Godiva? No, I think Karen had a business deal, but I didn't understand what she meant."

"Well, is the blond your girlfriend or not?" Tina asked.

"I don't know ...."

"You don't know?" Kathy said. "Look, maybe if you cut your hair or got some decent clothes, then you'd know. You look like a beach bum!"

"I guess you're right."

Later that afternoon I smelled chicken and pork barbecuing.

"Is someone cooking?" I asked.

"It's the guy next door," Beth said. "A party."

"We need to make a good impression," Kathy said. "Where's my resume?"

"Is that why you're all dressed up?" I asked.

"Are you coming to the party tonight?" Beth asked. "Karen will be there."

"No, Tully's making lobster, and we have a night charter to do."

I met Tully for dinner. We enjoyed a fantastic lobster meal including fresh sweet corn and clams. We ate, and then headed out to the night charter.

"What are we going out for?" I asked the captain.

"Our charter is nine guys fishing for trout under the lights," the captain said. "This should be a relaxed trip."

When we arrived offshore the captain turned the lights on at the back of the boat.

"Trout off the back, big trout!" Tully hollered. I saw them swimming in the light. The fishermen on the boat caught some huge trout. Later, schools of squid appeared in the light, and we could see large fish chasing them.

"I've got a shark," one fisherman called out. We pulled a mako aboard. I turned to see a fisherman nearly get pulled overboard.

"What's that?" I screamed.

"I think it's a big tuna!" Tully hollered back. The fisherman fought the fish long and hard.

"It is a tuna; get the gaff, son!" Tully hollered. During the night we caught five more. Everyone caught fish, a good trip. I arrived back at the Cave around dawn.

"Someone had one hell of a party!" I said aloud. Empty beer kegs lay scattered on the lawn. Trash cans full of chicken and pork bones sat nearby. The two charcoal pits still smoldered. Meat, wrapped in aluminum foil, lay on top.

I may as well have some.

I took a wrapped piece of chicken and ate at the picnic table. I found the floor of the Cave covered with people sleeping. I decided to crash on the hammock.

"Ethan!" someone called in a nasty voice. "Ethan, get up!" Someone jabbed me with a nightstick. I twisted in the hammock and landed face first in the dirt. A police officer stood over me talking a mile a minute.

"I thought I made it clear that there would be no more loud parties," he said. "I specifically warned you about kegs of beer." I looked at the name badge. Officer O'Neil.

"I worked all night on a charter boat," I said. "I don't throw parties." Some of the neighbors came by to see what was going on. Officer O'Neil walked over and grabbed the beer tap. Swinging the beer tap like a baseball bat, he smashed it against the brick wall.

"What the hell did you do to my beer tap?" a man screamed. A white-haired gentleman walked up.

"We got another report of a wild party here last night," Officer O'Neil said.

"A wild party? We had our annual Kiwanis cookout last night. Even the mayor was here!"

"We got a report it was his," Officer O'Neil said.

"His?" the neighbor asked. "He wasn't even here last night. I paid some of the girls to help serve at the party. It was a good deal for them since they could hand out resumes to business leaders."

"Well, it was a mistake then," Officer O'Neil said

"Mistake! You just busted my beer tap! Who's gonna pay for that?" I noticed Karen waving me into the Cave. The argument over who owed for the busted beer tap continued. I snuck into the Cave.

"We're gonna be on that cop's list for a while," she said. "We need to keep things sane and quiet."

"I haven't been having the parties," I said. "Actually I've been working my ass off. I'm not gonna get a break because Tully will be here soon to check his lobster pots again." I poured a mug of coffee and sat down.

"I'm sorry," Karen said. "I wanted to talk anyway and … someone's coming up the steps. It's the Beachcomber."

"What's O'Neil so upset about?" Tully asked.

"It's a long story. I'll tell you while we're out."

We sailed just offshore and trolled lead-headed jigs. We caught some bluefish. We checked the lobster pots again. More fish and small lobsters. We sailed in and sold our fish. I could hardly keep awake.

"I thought of a vacation of sorts. We could take the sailboat and sail up into the Chesapeake," Tully said.

"Sounds good, but let me think about it for a while. What I really need is one decent night's sleep." I went home and collapsed.

SASHIMI

Iawoke to find a Chinese girl in a black miniskirt looming over me. I couldn't understand a word she said.

Does she want beer money?

"My money's in my jeans." I must have fallen back asleep again. She rocked me awake with her foot.

"What do you want?" I asked.

"Fish ... restaurant ... food?"

She must be hungry.

"Sit at the table," I said. I made some coffee. "Are you hungry?" I offered her some toast.

"No," she said.

I dated a Chinese girl some months back, and I had no problem understanding her, but this was different.

"You my sharpie?" she asked. I guzzled some coffee. I heard footsteps, and Tully stepped in.

"What are you doing here, Tully?" I asked.

"I came to see if you'd go to church with me," Tully replied.

"Church?"

"Who's your friend?" He began talking to the girl in a language I couldn't understand. They talked for several minutes.

"Do you know Chinese?" I asked Tully.

"She's not Chinese; she's Japanese," Tully said. "She wants us to supply her with live or very fresh fish and seafood. She sells it to restaurants." Her words began to make sense to me. She silenced them at the end, making them hard to understand.

"She's been traveling up and down the coast trying to find dealers who will supply either live or extremely fresh seafood. She wants us to call her Sashimi, since that and sushi are the result of what she supplies."

"Does she live here?"

"She's a foreign exchange student who began supplying seafood to restaurants. The business grew, and, even though she has some suppliers, she's always looking for more. The local fish markets won't supply the freshness she demands. They sent her to us."

The caffeine began to work its magic, and my head cleared.

"What does she want us to supply her with?"

"She wants certain species of live or perfectly kept fresh fish on

Tuesday and Friday mornings. She wants large fat eels, large live sea bass, tuna, albacore and even blowfish. She also wants large razor clams, tautog, butterfish and porgies. She'll take flounder and trout also, but only in perfect condition. She's offering top dollar for everything she buys from us."

"Can we do that?" I asked.

"We'll have to take the sailboat out into the ocean to get most of the fish. Tuna and albacore can't be kept alive, and they're hard to catch. We'll have to build a pen to keep the fish alive in."

Sashimi seemed happy enough and left.

"Have you decided what you want to do yet?" Tully asked.

"I guess we can catch fish for her," I said.

"No, I mean about church."

"I don't have anything to wear."

"What you have on is fine."

We walked to his church. When we arrived, I noticed Elvis sitting in the back surrounded by youths.

I've attended church before but nothing like this. Everyone's friendly and nice. Several people stopped to talk. I felt relaxed during the service. At a set time, a guy would wail on the organ and we'd sing.

Afterwards, my curiosity got the better of me. "Tully, where did you learn Japanese?"

"I learned it during the war but mostly from my wife," he said.

"You were married?"

"Still am," he said. "My wife's from Okinawa and wants to stay there."

CAN YOU HELP ME FIND ELVIS?

I made grilling an art at the beach. I took six black charcoal briquettes, wrapped them in newspaper and placed them in my hibachi grill. I struck a wooden match and lit the corner of the newspaper. I relaxed in the hammock until the charcoal fully caught. Ten minutes later a bluefish fillet sputtered over the coals. I sat at the picnic table alone enjoying my meal.

After lunch I headed toward the boardwalk. A strange thing happened when I came upon it.

"Do you know Elvis?" a woman called. I turned to see a well-dressed woman with flaming red hair sitting in a new gold Mercedes.

"Yes."

"Can you take me to him?"

"I guess."

The woman parked at a fireplug.

"They'll ticket you there!"

"I really don't care anymore!"

"I can see you've been crying. Are you okay? Where do you know Elvis from?" She didn't answer. "Are you Elvis's sister?" Again no answer. "What do you want Elvis for?"

"He's the only person that can make any sense of my miserable life!"

Elvis? She started crying again.

"Why don't you have a seat? We'll talk."

"Just get me to Elvis," she said.

"He usually sits near the pizza joint, where all the park benches are placed together."

As we rounded the corner I noticed Elvis sitting with a few teen-aged girls.

"Carrot-top!" he called. The woman ran down, hugged him, and they walked off to talk. One of the teen-aged girls came forward.

"I saw you at church with Tully," she said. "Are you the guy that fishes with him?"

"Yeah. I can't believe she walked off with Elvis."

"She needed to talk."

"Elvis nods more than talks, stutters a lot, and suddenly stops and stares at the ground. I can't imagine they'll have much of a conversation.

Where would she know him from?"

"Her real name is Carrie; she's from a rich family. When she was a teen-ager she used to hang around a lot. Three years ago she married some rich guy from college. Now her marriage is going down the tubes."

"Why not get a marriage counselor or a psychiatrist or something?"

"She tried all that, and it didn't work ... she spent a fortune. The difference between a counselor and Elvis is that he listens. He's better at figuring out life than most."

"I guess I totally underestimated him." I returned to the Cave and rested.

Later that evening Tina, Karen and Connie got ready to go out.

"Can we borrow your car?" Karen asked.

"Can we have some cash also?" Tina asked. "I'm a little tapped out." I pulled out two twenties and gave them to her. She thanked me and left. A moment later Karen reappeared.

"Why did you give that money to Tina?"

"She said she was broke. Do you need some cash?"

"You should have given the money to me. Who means more to you, me or her?" Karen stomped off.

Now what did I do? I'd better get back to sleep!

In the morning Tully stopped by.

"We need to check our crab pots," he said. We got to the boat, baited the rods and cast off. I dropped the lines overboard as we began drifting from pot to pot. We emptied them and made a good haul.

"We caught quite a few flounder today, but trout seemed to have vanished," Tully said.

"I wanted to talk about Sashimi's offer," I said. "What does she sell?"

"Remember, she just wants us to call her Sashimi? Sashimi is fresh fish that is sliced, marinated in lime juice or soy sauce, and served alone. Sushi can contain a slice of Sashimi or shrimp, clam or lobster and is served wrapped around pickled rice. Since either dish is served raw, the quality of the fish has to be perfect. Live fish are preferred but difficult to get. Extremely fresh fish are next in line. Not all of what we will supply will be used for sashimi or sushi. Some will be used for other dishes. The type of fish sought is critical also."

"What kinds of fish?"

"All types of fish can be used if fresh enough, but some types are valued above others. Tuna and albacore are widely used. Eel, sea bass and blackfish are popular also. She even mentioned blowfish which, if you do it wrong, is poisonous. In Japan a sushi chef goes to school to learn all this. We'll only be able to supply a few of the fish she wants. We could catch and probably keep alive sea bass and blackfish. We're already catching eels. We'll have to trade for tuna and albacore. They're impossible to keep alive; we'll have to ice 'em down. We'll use the sailboat to do a lot of this; we'll be paid top dollar."

We decided to tell Sashimi that we would try it. Tully built a pen to keep the fish alive until we sold them. I found a hanging wire basket and plastic tub to hold the fish until we could get them to the pen.

"Let's try it out," Tully said one evening. "We'll check our lobster pots first."

"You know, Tully, we don't catch a lot of lobster in those pots, but we catch some giant sea bass in 'em. Maybe if we baited 'em with surf clams, we could catch a lot of sea bass."

We stopped at a clam bar to collect the big clams. Surf clams are large sandy clams that are hardly ever used for food but make good fish bait. After collecting some thirty clams, we headed out to Tully's first lobster pot, which was now going to become a sea bass pot. We traveled to all the pots and changed the baits from fish heads to clams.

"Let's stop at a lump and drift for sea bass," he said. "She only wants the largest, those with the blue hump on their head." Tully hit the area on his first guesstimate, and we filled the live well with giant sea bass.

"On the way home we can troll feathered jigs," Tully said. We caught several small bluefish that way.

"We need to run the inlet to get our fish in," Tully said next. "We can't haul the live well across the beach."

An inlet by its nature is hazardous. The incoming ocean clashes with the water released by outgoing tides from the sound. Giant breaking waves can form at any time. Add giant cabin cruisers, idiots in speedboats and giant fishing boats to the mix and imagine our tiny sailboat trying to navigate it. It's not for the faint-hearted.

Tully sailed into the inlet at full speed. We hit a ten-foot wave that popped up out of nowhere. We cleared the wave to see a party boat right on top of us. Its wake spun us around. I didn't breathe until we cleared the inlet.

"I'm going to have nightmares about that," I said to Tully.

"We made it in; are the fish still okay?"

"I'm surprised; almost all the fish made it home alive. How will we supply tuna? Catching them is hit or miss."

"Setting up a tuna market isn't going to be easy," Tully said. "We'll have better luck buying them from fishermen."

"How will we keep them?" I asked.

"We'll lay the extra fridges down in the shed, take the shelves out and fill 'em with ice. The ice will keep the fish, and if we're lucky the fridges might even run like that." In this arrangement, we were able to keep the tuna in near perfect condition until Sashimi bought them.

The next day Tully steered our crab boat into a creek mouth.

"We catching eels?" I asked, as we usually caught them there.

"We've been catching and selling eels as live bait all summer. The fishermen who bought them wanted the smaller eels, so we always had to throw back the larger ones. Sashimi wants the largest, fattest eels, so we no longer have to throw those back."

Sashimi stopped at the Cave at five in the morning on Friday. A couple of the guys were still partying from the night before. They tried to pick her up.

"Leave me alone!" she screamed. I woke up, heard her voice and went running out the door.

"Guys, she's here to buy fish from me," I said. "You don't have to act like drunken animals all the time." The guys muttered a few choice words and went inside.

"Come on in. I didn't expect you here so early."

"I must get fish to customers early for weekend," she explained. As we talked, I realized just how pretty she was. About five-foot-ten-inches and thin, she had long black shiny hair that sparkled whenever she moved. She had black almond-shaped eyes and snow-white teeth. When she talked, she had a way of keeping her head bowed but always still stared into your eyes. I guess that was part of the allure, like a child who looked up at you.

"Do you want coffee, tea …?" I asked.

"Just the fish …."

I took her out back to the sheds and showed her the tuna we'd iced down.

"These are good … I need more oil?" she said, rubbing her fingers. "More oil pay more? Also color?"

We loaded the tuna and albacore into a refrigerated section of her truck

"I'll drive you over to the live fish," I said.

"No. I follow you in truck." When we arrived at the boat, I was surprised to see Tully waiting. We netted the live sea bass, blowfish and eels. She chose the ones she wanted and placed them into her live well.

"I only use twenty blowfish. Keep rest alive until next week? Maybe take all then?"

Sashimi wrote a receipt for the fish. "I bring check next week?" she said.

"Son, she's promising us a small fortune," Tully explained. "Those blowfish are a specialty item; that's why she couldn't take 'em all."

Sashimi left before 7:00 AM, but we had crabs and flounder to supply to our regular customers. Tully started the boat. I baited the rods.

"Tully, she said if the tuna were covered in oil they would be worth more. Also something about the color?"

"No, what she meant was that a tuna having high oil content is worth more than one without it. In Japan a hole is cut into a tuna's tail so you can feel the oil on your fingers. The color of the meat is important, too. We'll just have to accept any that we get."

"We're getting larger crabs but less of 'em. Maybe we should concentrate on the ocean for a while?"

"It might be possible to put this motor on the sailboat. It would make it easier to get in and out of the inlet."

That afternoon I tried to take a nap. The weekend crew would filter in soon, and a madhouse would ensue.

A few hours later Karen shook me awake.

"Can we talk?" I got up, took a shower and tried to find some clean clothes to put on. She sat at the table. She seemed upset.

"Look, I'm sorry about last night, but this has been confusing ...," she said.

"Last night?"

"About you giving your money to Tina?"

"Do you want to go for a walk?" I asked. We left and headed up the street.

"You don't give me credit for the things I do," she said. "You give in too easily to Tina and Kathy, and your eyes light up whenever you see them."

"Karen, I give you a lot of credit. I've had more than enough cash this summer. I don't mind sharing it with whoever is tapped out. Do you really think I'm trying to buy Tina's love?"

"What about Godiva?"

"She comes and goes as she pleases. I'm glad to see her come and don't question her when it's time to go."

"I wish you'd involve me more in your life. We could do a lot together. We could hang around as friends."

"I thought that's what we've been doing all summer. Can't we just enjoy each other's company?"

"You just don't get it!"

"What don't I get?"

"It's like a pecking order, and now I'm on the bottom. I'm trying to help you, and you don't see it."

"See what?"

"You need someone to look out for you, and I'm really the only one here who will."

"Okay. Anything else?"

"Yes, you look like hell. Maybe we could take a trip. Relax somewhere?" Karen gave me a nip on the cheek and walked into Connie's house. I went inside the Cave and looked at myself in the mirror. I did look like hell. I needed a break from my vacation. I headed back to bed.

THE MOUNTAINS

The heat and humidity of the summer baked the shoreline. Lawns, green all summer, turned brown and withered. The ocean warmed until it felt like bathwater. Tully and I stayed out of the midday sun and fished and crabbed in the early morning hours.

Karen joined me on the balcony one morning as I drank my pot of coffee.

"I talked with Connie and Mickey. We thought we could take a trip. She can borrow some camping gear."

"Mickey?"

"Tall guy with brown hair and a beard, been hanging out at our place with Tom?"

"And Jim won't mind him going with us and Connie?"

"It's not that kind of a trip; she's going with me, he's going with you. We want to go to the mountains."

"The mountains? I know a good spot. I have a sleeping bag and some camping gear. I'll need to talk to Tully. We have a lot to do before we go."

"Can I help with any of it?"

"If you really want to start working together, you could help me with the vegetables. Anything you sell is yours." We walked to one of the backyard gardens. We filled the wagon with honeydews, tomatoes, cantaloupes and peppers.

"Godiva just stood on the corner with the wagon, but you can do it any way you want," I described.

"Anything else?" she asked. "Could I help you two with the crabs?"

"Do you know where our boat is?"

"Yes."

"Meet us there around ten."

I found Tully near the arcade.

"I'm heading up to the mountains for a few days; will you be okay?"

"I'll be fine. You should get away for a couple of days."

We drove over to the crab boat and went out. When we returned to the dock, Karen was waiting.

"She's gonna try and sell what crabs she can," I said. "I figure she'll make out better than we would with the locals."

"Works for me," Tully said. We loaded two bushels of crabs on the wagon for Karen and placed the rest in my car.

"I'll see you at the Cave," I said to Karen. "You packed?"

"I'm ready to go," Karen said.

That evening we loaded Connie's gear into my car.

"Where we heading?" Mickey asked.

"A part of Hickory Run State Park," I said. "It'll be dark when we get there, but I've camped there many times."

"How long will it take to drive there?" Connie asked.

"About three hours." We stopped and loaded up on groceries. Mickey loaded up on beer.

Several hours later I had Mickey get out and lift a cable that blocked off a jeep trail.

"Bruce and I found out long ago that you could lift the cable and drive right under it. We've camped here many times." We set Connie's tent up first, a large cabin tent. I set up my tiny backpacking tent.

"What do we do if bears come to visit?" Karen asked.

"The bears in this area are shy; they'll leave us alone."

After setting up camp, mostly by flashlight, we lit a fire and settled in for the night. Later we grilled steaks and sweet corn over the coals.

"After dinner can we make s'mores?" Karen asked. Mickey fished in the grocery bag and found chocolate, marshmallows and graham crackers. Later we sang songs around the fire. Complete darkness settled in over the mountains.

"Let's use our flashlights and see if we can spot any deer on the trail," Karen said. "You can easily spot deer; their eyes glow in the light." We spotted the first deer, a doe with a fawn. Up the trail a little further, we spotted two does together and then a large buck with velvet antlers.

"Why do its antlers look so weird?" Connie asked.

"A buck loses its antlers every year and begins growing a new set. The antlers have a fuzzy covering that's later rubbed off by the deer," I explained.

"It's getting late; let's get back to camp," Karen said.

"It'll be a little tricky finding the trail in the dark," Mickey explained.

We made it back okay.

"What happens if an ax murderer or chainsaw freak shows up in the middle of the night?" Connie asked. "We're in the middle of nowhere, and there's no one we can call for help." They insisted on being armed and took a hatchet and a tire iron into the tent with them.

I woke up late the next morning and started a fire, since it was a little chilly.

It's so peaceful sitting by the fire in the morning. I had forgotten how quiet the mountains are. I heard a rustle, and Connie came walking out, trying to wipe the sleep from her eyes. Karen came next, still clutching the hatchet. Mickey still slept in my tent so Karen woke him up. He looked dead to the world.

"Can you get the sausage and eggs out of the cooler so we can cook them for breakfast?" Karen asked. "Can you also get the bananas for Connie? Where did you want to go today?"

"I thought we could head over to Little Falls on the Bushkill. It's an out of the way spot near a Boy Scout camp."

Later, we all sat around the fire eating.

"How should we dress for this?" Connie asked.

"It'll be cooler, so you're dressed fine."

We piled into my car and drove to Little Falls.

"I'm glad there's still some sections of these mountains that haven't been commercialized. Those falls are really spectacular," Mickey said.

"I'll show you another section near our camp," I said. "A river runs right down a mountainside." We drove to see a series of waterfalls on Black Creek, which ended at a large pool. The creek and the waterfalls were awesome to look at, and the water was clear.

"It's starting to get hot. Could we go back to camp for lunch, change into our suits and swim here?" Connie asked.

"The water's really cold, but I'd like that," Karen said.

We arrived back at camp. Mickey cooked hot dogs and beans for lunch. Connie had vegetable soup.

"I think I'm going to sack out for a while," I said. "I really didn't sleep much last night."

"I saw a bush loaded with blueberries on the way in," Connie said. "Karen, will you help me pick some?" They walked up the trail together. I slept. Mickey sat on the car drinking beer. The sound of screaming woke me up. When I looked out of the tent, I saw Connie and Karen running up the trail.

"You said there'd be no bears!" Karen screamed. "We started picking berries and saw a huge black bear picking berries on the other side of the bush!"

"Did it run away?" I asked.

"I don't know!" Connie said.

"Let's go look." We walked back up the trail, but Connie and Karen seemed terrified and hung back.

"Was it around here?" I asked.

"Here's their bucket," Mickey said. "There's a lot of blueberries on the vines."

"There's the bear!" I said. The bear sat on the other side of the clump. It licked blueberries off its paws.

"It's beautiful!" Mickey said. "Watch the sunlight glisten off its fur!"

"Can't we just go now?" Connie asked.

"No, the bear doesn't want to harm us. Walk up slowly and look."

"It's really beautiful," Karen said. The bear walked about fifty feet away and began licking its paws again. It walked off into the woods.

"Let's get changed and go swimming," Connie said. We walked back to the tent, changed, and piled into the car to head back to Black Creek.

"It's harder climbing on the rocks than I remembered," Karen said. We walked up to the rock pool.

"You go in first!" Karen said. I waded into the water and began swimming.

Connie stood on the rock and jumped in.

"Oh my God, it's cold as ice!" she screamed. We plunged into the cold water, got out and rested on the warm rocks.

"Let's get back to the car," Connie said. "My teeth are chattering now."

We drove down one of the back trails and were about a mile from camp when we came upon Fourth Run Creek. This creek is a small babbling brook with a few beaver dams on it.

"Look! I think that's a beaver!" Mickey said.

"It's a beaver, and it's towing a branch."

"Let's get back to camp and eat dinner; I'm starved," Karen said. We swerved to miss a rock in the trail and got stuck in the mud. We tried pushing the car out, but it wouldn't budge.

"We need to jack the car up and get it out of the mud," Mickey said. We tried, but the car sank in further.

"It's getting dark already. We need to hike to our campsite before the sunlight's gone," I said. "We don't even have a flashlight with us; they're in the tent."

We walked the mile or so back to camp in pitch-blackness, holding hands so we wouldn't get lost.

"I think this is the spot, but our tents are a hundred yards back in off the trail," I said.

"How are we going to find our tents? It's so dark we can't see a thing," Connie said. "And I'm freezing; my bathing suit's still wet!"

"Karen and I can head one way, and you and Mickey can go the other," I said. "Just don't get separated." We headed into the blackness of the night, calling back and forth to each other. When nothing could get any worse, it did.

"Karen, I lost Mickey. Come and get me!" Connie hollered.

"Mickey, where are you?" Karen cried out.

"He's screaming that he's caught in quicksand or something!" Connie called back. A moment later I tripped over something and went flying head over heels.

"Ethan, where are you!" Karen screamed.

"I tripped over my backpacking tent. Stay put. I'll find my

flashlight." A moment later the flashlight settled on Karen's face. I guided her to the tent. She found a huge spotlight and shined it across the woods.

"Connie, we're over here," she called.

"I can see your spotlight!" Connie shouted. A few moments later she walked up to the tent. We went into our tents, got warm clothes on and came out

"We need to find Mickey," I said. "He's still out there in his swim suit!"

"Karen and I can start a big fire; maybe he'll see the blaze and walk back to camp."

"There's a swamp back in there," I said.

"He said he was in quicksand or something," Connie said. I grabbed a flashlight and went to find Mickey.

The swamp looked eerie with trees growing out of the water. The water shone like black ice under the flashlight. Green moss covered the hummocks in the swamp.

"I'm over here," Mickey called. I found him covered in mud on a little island.

We headed back toward camp, and the flashlight slid out of my hand into the knee-deep black water. Mickey reached all around in the black water but could feel nothing.

"That's weird; the flashlight must have died as soon as it hit the water," he said.

"I think I remember the way," I said. Mickey spotted the campfire. We found our way into camp.

"I made some stew for dinner," Karen said.

"Just the fact that I'm out of the swamp is enough to down a few beers," Mickey said. He changed and cracked open a beer.

"Well, let's eat and get to bed."

Early the next morning Mickey shook me awake.

"While I was drinking last night I thought of a way to get the car out of the mud. All the weight of the car is with the engine in front. The back tires of the car are stuck in the mud. We need to find a thick pole and lift the car up. We can place rocks under the back wheels."

We walked to the car and found a downed tree to use as a pole. Mickey stood on the pole and jumped, lifting the back end of the car out of the mud. Each time he jumped up, I piled rocks under the tires.

"You try driving, and I'll try pushing," I said. The car broke free of the mud, and I ran up and jumped in. Mickey drove right past our campsite.

"You forgot to stop!" I said.

"I didn't forget; we're out of beer. We need to stock up." We found a little town with a beer distributor. Mickey bought two cases and a dozen doughnuts.

When we got back to camp, we found Karen and Connie still passed out from the night before.

"They've got the right idea; let's crash also," Mickey said.

Sometime after noon I awoke to find Karen and Connie eating our doughnuts.

"We came up with an idea; it's kind of fun and dangerous," Karen said. "We want to buy blow-up air mattresses and ride them down the Lehigh River. We could ride the rafts to wherever we wanted and hitchhike back to the car."

The Lehigh River is shallow and rocky. The route we chose took us away from any roads for quite a distance. During the spring rains it swells with water providing a wild ride. In midsummer the current is slow. We wanted to relax.

We bought four air mattresses at the dollar store and blew them up.

"I found a good spot on the river to launch them," Connie said. "Put the car keys on top of the driver's side front tire so Karen and I can find them."

We pushed the rafts in, and the current took us downstream.

"Connie, the sun's bright. I'm worried about you getting sunburnt again," I said.

"It's okay; I put on sunscreen." We drifted downstream enjoying the river, the sunlight and the scenery. A couple of times we got stuck on rocks or sandbars and had to shove off.

"I see a deep pool ahead; can we stop and just swim awhile?" Karen asked. We found that someone had tied a rope swing at the spot. The swing took you way out over the pool so you could dive in. Later we continued on and covered many miles. Green hemlocks and red oaks crowded the river's banks.

"We're pretty far down; can we find the way back?" I asked.

"We need to find a spot where we can hitchhike to the car," Karen said. Mickey found a spot where we could walk up to a back road. Connie and Karen flagged down two guys in a Volkswagen.

"We'll try and be back before dark," Karen said before climbing in with Connie.

Mickey and I waited, and it did get dark.

"I wish I'd brought the beer from camp," Mickey said.

"I wish I was at camp!"

We waited and waited, but no one came. Somewhere around ten he noticed a pair of headlights heading up the road.

"It isn't my car," I said. The car was the Volkswagen they'd left in. Karen was driving, and Connie sat next to her.

"When we got in we found that the guys were smashed. They drove around forever and ended up at some backwoods cabin," Connie said. "They were so drunk that they passed out. Karen spotted their keys on the table, and we borrowed their car."

Mickey and I piled into the back seat. Karen sped off trying to find the way out. We passed the cabin twice. All roads seemed to bring us back to where we started.

"I thought I saw another trail, but it looked like we'd have to drive through someone's backyard to get there," Mickey said.

"At this point I'll try anything," Karen said. Mickey directed her to the trail. It was a utility easement, and we did drive through someone's backyard. It took almost an hour to get back to my car.

"We need to return that Volkswagen before they call the cops," Connie said.

"Does anyone remember the way back?" I asked.

"I do," Mickey said. "But I'm not going till I've had a beer." We stopped and picked up a quart of Bud for him. I drove my car and Karen the Volkswagen. Mickey guided us back to the cabin. Karen quietly pulled up, left the keys in the ignition and climbed into my car.

"You backwoods hicks!" Connie screamed hanging out my window. A figure appeared at the cabin's door.

"Let's get out of here; he's got a shotgun," Mickey said. We drove off with Connie still screaming.

"Let's find a place to eat; do you know where we can get something late?" Karen asked.

"I know a bar that serves food," I said.

"Works for me," Mickey said. I drove to the bar. We all went inside and changed in the bathrooms.

"Can we still get dinner?" Karen asked the bartender.

"I don't know why the hell not!" he said.

"Okay, then just keep the beer, burgers and fries coming," Mickey said. Two guys walked up to Karen and Connie.

"Will you play pool with us?" they asked. As it turned out Karen and Connie knew how to play billiards well and began beating the guy's game after game.

"Hello, Ethan, will you play Bochi ball with me?" a girl asked. I turned to see a thin girl with long blond hair. I thought I knew her.

"You're Sherri's friend Sunshine aren't you?" I asked. "Do you still sing with a group?"

"Not much anymore." We played Bochi for a while. She knew the game better than I did and won almost every set.

"Will you drive me home?" she asked.

"Yeah, let me tell Karen."

I assumed that Sunshine still lived in the area, but as it turned out she now lived about twenty minutes away.

"What you been up to?" I asked. "I haven't seen you in a year."

"I've been living with a guy; he can be hard to handle at times. I'm not sure I'm going to stay with him." We talked in the car for a few minutes before she had to leave. I returned right before closing time. Karen gave me a nasty look. We headed back to the campsite.

"You staying up?" Karen asked.

"No, I'm beat; we rafted, borrowed cars, dealt with backwoods idiots and got lost more times than I care to know."

"We need to talk," she said. "Why didn't you spend more time with me today?"

"I spent the entire day with you! The only time I didn't was when you went off with the two bozos in the Volkswagen or when you played pool. Did you want me to knock your admirers aside and play pool with you, too?"

"You were gone like two hours with that blond you picked up."

"I didn't pick up Sunshine. I know her. She used to live around the corner from that bar, and I thought she still did. As it turned out she lives over near Lake Harmony, like an hour's round trip."

"I'm constantly confused over what we're doing and never know where to stand."

"Join the crowd."

"To tell you the truth, I only carried on with the guys in the bar to try and make you jealous, and it didn't work."

"You will attract guys wherever you go, and it doesn't bother me. Cute girls attract guys, period. Where do we go from here?"

"It just seems disrespectful to me if you're carrying on with some girl while I'm there."

"So to summarize, I should let you talk to other guys but not talk to other girls if you're around. We're not dating, but I should tell you where I'm going but not ask where you're going?"

"Exactly!" she said smiling through her tears.

"I think most guys would tell you to shove it where the sun doesn't shine, but the sun's coming up and I'm too tired to care."

That afternoon we packed up to head home. We got back to the Cave late that night. I passed out almost as soon as I hit the floor. I heard someone ask Karen and Tina if they wanted to go to a club.

SASHIMI AND KAREN

I woke up around five in the morning, made a pot of coffee and sat drinking it at the table. I heard a van pull up outside and realized it was probably Sashimi coming for her fish. I went to greet her.

I wonder if Tully caught any fish or traded for any tuna while I was gone.

"Sashimi, I have some green tea. Please have a cup while I check the shed." I found four good-sized tuna and an albacore in the coolers. A moment later all hell broke loose in the Cave. I ran in to find Karen crying, Tina shouting at Sashimi, Sashimi shouting at Tina, and Connie glaring at me.

"Did she spend the night?" Connie asked.

"Why does she keep calling you her sharpie?" Tina demanded.

"She's here to buy fish, and I don't know what sharpie means." Sashimi and I walked outside to load the tuna into her truck.

"Which one girlfriend?" Sashimi asked in her broken English.

"None of them."

"Americans all crazy!" she said. I went inside to get my car keys. Karen stood glaring at me.

"Enough with the girls okay?" she asked. "I mean look at her. She's gorgeous!"

"Karen, she's buying fish!" I went outside and finished loading the tuna into her truck.

"All American girls crazy! Why you not date her?" Sashimi asked. "Who?"

"The blond girl, crying!" Sashimi said.

"Karen has no interest in me whatsoever," I said.

"Then why she cries?" Sashimi asked.

"Karen gets upset when other girls are around."

"She save face!" Sashimi said. Tully arrived, and we drove over to the docks. We dipped large live sea bass, eels and blackfish out of the fish pen into Sashimi's holding tank.

"Here your check!" Sashimi said, handing it to Tully. She turned to me and stared.

"Go to blond girl; make big effort to go out, say you really want to, blond girl say no, save face, everybody happy." With that Sashimi jumped back into her truck and sped away.

"What was that all about?" Tully asked.

"Karen's acting weird. Sashimi thought of a way to fix it. I don't know."

"If you want advice about women, don't ask me," Tully said.

"Well, we need to collect our crabs and fill our flounder orders." We headed out drifting from crab pot to crab pot.

"What's a sharpie?" I asked Tully.

"We're sharpies. A sharpie is someone who catches and sells fish on the side, and it puts us at the bottom of the totem pole. At the top are giant Russian and Japanese fishing ships capable of handling hundreds of tons of fish. The second is the tiny local fishing fleet which comes in and out of the harbors. The third is the watermen who crab and fish the bays and inshore waters. On the bottom of the list are sharpies who sell fish and crabs for pocket money."

"Sashimi said Karen needed to save 'face.' What did she mean?"

"It kind of means pride; it means a lot more in Japan, and it's hard to understand. For someone to 'lose face' in Japan means extreme embarrassment, and a sincere apology would be in order. But like I said, son, don't ask me for advice about women."

We caught a fair amount of flounder and made a good haul of crabs.

"Tomorrow we need to fill up with sea bass, eels and tuna for Sashimi's run on Friday," Tully said. "Good luck with Karen."

I went back to the Cave to try to get some sleep.

Should I take Sashimi's advice? Later I got dressed and went across the street to Connie's place.

"Connie, I've thinking about Karen," I said. "I'd like to date her."

"Karen? She doesn't want to date you but can't keep her claws out of your life, either. I'll talk to her."

Later that evening I sat reading a book. Karen and Kathy got ready to go out. Kathy walked forward.

"I'm a little tapped out; can I have some cash?" she asked.

"Karen, here's forty; have a good time." She looked puzzled, but then they left.

Around three in the morning I heard a voice; it turned out to be Karen.

"We need to talk," she said. We walked down to the boardwalk and found a deserted bench.

"Connie told me you wanted to start dating?" she asked.

"No, I just wanted to give you an out to end this thing. You really didn't want to start dating, did you?"

"No."

"Now you have an out. You can tell everyone that I asked to date and that you said no. You can be happy, I'll be happy and we can get on with enjoying our summer." Karen sat staring at the sand.

"I guess I've been overreacting when I see you with other girls. I think the girls you bring around aren't right for you."

"I don't bring girls around at all. I'm almost always alone."

"Except when Godiva's down, or Sunshine, and what's this one, Sashi?"

"Sashimi."

"You should be dating someone nice."

"I've never had much luck finding a girlfriend; that's what shocks me about Godiva."

"Godiva ... your girlfriend who isn't?"

"Karen, I'm too tired to contemplate this. It's almost dawn, and I lost another night of sleep. I've got to go out on the boat soon. The part I don't understand ...."

"What?"

"Most of the guys have an endless stream of girls coming in and out of their rooms. I've never questioned who comes in and out of yours. I'm sleeping in a corner where everyone can see everything thing I do, and you worry about me?"

"You just don't get it."

"What?"

"You're the only one worth worrying about. Let's get home. Maybe you can get an hour's rest before you have to go out."

FIRE IN THE HOLE!

K aren pushed me awake an hour or so later. "The Beachcomber's waiting for you!" she said. "I filled a thermos of coffee and packed a cantaloupe for you."

"You made coffee for me?" I asked.

"Yes, if we're going to be working together, we'd better cooperate, right?"

I grabbed the thermos to head over to the sailboat.

"Ethan?" Karen asked.

"I think she wants a hug good-bye," Tully said. I hugged Karen and headed out.

"Let me guess, you talked to her, right?" Tully asked.

"Yes."

"And you two aren't going to see each other, and now she's all lovey-dovey, right?"

"I don't know ...."

"This is why I told you not to ask my advice about women."

An hour later the sailboat cut through the waves heading south. We pulled in the sea bass pots and sorted out the fish. Later we drifted alongside a wreck and caught some blackfish and porgies to add to the live well.

"Look, son! Breaking fish!" Tully pulled up the sail. "Might be tuna. Get some jigs overboard!" A few moments later Tully trolled the lines past the school. I fought a fish, and Tully gaffed it.

"Yellowfins," I said, "about twenty pounds!" We caught several before the school moved on.

"Maybe if I live line a porgy, we'll pick up a few more," I said. My bait drifted to the bottom, and I felt a fish hit.

"It's fighting hard, but it ain't a tuna," I said.

"Biggest flounder I've ever seen, maybe a ten pounder," Tully said. "Swallowed your porgy whole. We'll keep it for ourselves. If you get some sweet corn and melons, we can grill that flounder at my place. You can even invite that girl over."

"Karen?"

"Any others demanding hugs good-bye?"

"No."

"Well, we need to get in and ice down those tuna."

Later we tied the boat up at the dock, took care of the tuna and placed the live fish in the pens. I walked back to the Cave and asked Karen to dinner. We arrived at Tully's place around five.

"I feel bad," Karen said. "I'm selling all these vegetables and crabs, and you don't want any of the money."

"The vegetables will go bad if we don't sell 'em, and my customers will be upset. You're doing me a favor," Tully explained.

"Okay, but next time I'm making dinner for everyone," Karen said.

"Sounds good to me," Tully said.

"It's hard to imagine it, but Tully's happily married," I said.

"You are?" Karen asked. "Where's your wife?"

"Okinawa," Tully said. He pulled out a scrapbook, and we looked through it after dinner.

"When will you see her again?" Karen asked.

"As soon as I can," Tully said.

"I need to get back to the Cave," Karen said. "Tina's setting something up."

"What's up with Tina?"

"Tina and Connie decided to have a luau tomorrow. We went around collecting money from everyone. I gave her money to buy a ham and pineapples. I also promised her some beer and corn from the cold shed. Can we borrow your car?" I handed her the keys.

The next evening I arrived home to find a luau going full tilt. Tina and Connie wore bikini tops and grass skirts. Sarongs fashioned out of bed sheets covered the rest of the girls. Everyone wore the plastic leis that Godiva won.

"Let me put a flower behind your ear," Connie asked.

"We have lots of beer. Grab one," Jim said. I smelled food cooking. A rotisserie grill sat on our upper deck, probably "borrowed" from one of the neighbors.

"Ethan, help me get the chicken and ham onto platters," Tina said.

Jim started slicing the meat. Tina brought a plate loaded with ham, chicken and pineapple.

"We want to do our own version of a hula," Karen said. "Does anyone have Hawaiian music?"

"I've got some Jimmy Buffet tapes," Jim said.

"I guess that will work," Tina said. The music started, and everyone got up and started gyrating around. I walked out onto the deck to catch my breath. I saw Alice the Goon walking up our steps.

"If this party doesn't stop immediately, I'm hauling everyone in," Alice screamed.

"We're listening to Jimmy Buffet for God's sake, and it isn't even loud," Karen said. "What's the problem?"

"We got a slew of phone calls about the party and drunks leaving the house," Alice said.

"No one left the house, and we only have like twelve people here," Tina said.

"If I hear another peep out of any of you, I'm calling Officer O'Neil and the paddy wagon." She stormed out the door and walked up the street.

"Who would've called the cops?" Tina asked.

"I think she just stopped to hassle us," Jim said.

"Well, I'm turning the music back on. Let's finish the luau," Karen said. We danced until I was too tired to go on.

"I'm heading to bed. I'm going out with Tully at dawn," I explained.

"We should have a campfire," Beth said. I drifted off to sleep.

I woke up sometime during the night to see Karen and Tina doing a hula again. I fell back asleep.

Tully arrived the next morning to go crabbing.

"Your house is on fire!" he screamed, waking me up.

"What?" I pushed aside my sleeping bag. Smoke filled the room, and I could see a blaze glowing red in the center of it.

"We really do have a fire!" I said. "I'll fill pitchers with water; you dump 'em on the deck." Tully dumped the water onto the fire and a god-awful-smelling steam arose.

"What the hell happened?" I asked.

"It looks like someone lit a fire in an aluminum pan. It burned through the pan into the deck."

"I see marshmallows. I guess they made their own campfire and roasted 'em out here."

We stared at the smoldering wooden balcony.

"The water put the fire out, but there's a big hole in the deck," Tully said. "Get your hatchet out of the car and chop the burnt wood away." I did the best I could to remove the charred wood from the deck.

"I know where there's a construction site," Tully said. "We can get some flooring board to cover the hole. You only get so many chances with this stuff before the odds catch up with you! A group of drunks get together, and this is what happens."

We found the flooring, patched the hole and threw a rug over it. Surprisingly no one else at the Cave woke up either for the fire, the sound of chopping burnt wood or the hammering of nails.

"We've done all we can," I said. "Let's head to the dock." Tully and I drove down to the crab boat.

"You know, all summer the routine's been pretty much the same," I said. "Pull in the crab pots. Trade whatever bait we can. Deal with Chicken-neckers robbing our catch."

"Son, we put nothing but sweat into this venture, and we made a lot of money running the lines. The work's been brutal at times, but it's also been fun. I mean there's people sitting in offices wishing to be out on the water like us."

"You're right; I guess this is the life. I keep thinking that I should take a vacation, and it's hard to remember that I'm on vacation. I've put enough away this summer to pay for next year's tuition."

Later I drove Tully home. As we came upon his place, Alice the Goon pulled out from between two parked cars. She made a U-turn and motioned for me to stop.

"You didn't do anything wrong. What's she pullin' you over for?" Tully asked.

"She's been hassling us all summer," I said.

She didn't even ask for my driver's license.

"I told you I didn't want to see you around anymore!" she screamed. "I'm tired of dealing with the whole bunch of you. I want you out of this town! If I see your car parked anywhere in the city, I'm going to ticket it." She got back into her golf cart and took off.

"Has it been like this all summer?" Tully asked.

"Yeah, she's been a real pain."

"Do you have a quarter?" He got out and made a phone call.

"I called the judge; he's a friend of mine. You won't have to worry about Alice any more. People here used to be really laid back."

I got back to the Cave at dinnertime. Karen and Tina walked in.

"Tully woke me up and told me we had a fire last night," I said, showing the repair job.

"Yeah, now there's a hole in the deck," Mickey said. "But we pretty much trashed the place this summer. The carpet's wrecked. Holes are in every wall; even the ceiling has holes in it. And the bedrooms ... someone's gonna pay for all this. I'm glad my name's not on the lease."

"I don't think any of our names are on the lease," Karen said.

"Yeah, but his point is that if the drinking and stupidity continue, someone's gonna get killed."

"I think that's the point. The end's always near," Tom said.

"I hope not," I replied.

The house became quiet for a moment. Karen broke the silence.

"Tina and I are heading to the boardwalk. Will you come with us?"

"Yeah, I'll come."

"If you're going out, can we get some beer?" Ted asked. "There's a ballgame on."

"There's a couple of cases in the shed. Just don't set the house on fire again, okay?" I said.

We headed out to a pizza place on the boardwalk. Tina ordered a large pepperoni pizza. The place was a combination restaurant and bar, and it didn't take long for guys to start hitting on Tina and Karen. Tina got up, danced with some guy and seemed to be having a good time. A couple of guys asked Karen to dance also.

"Go ahead," I said. She danced with someone for a few minutes. Guys began sending drinks to them. Glasses covered our table. A brunette came walking over.

"Hello, Ethan!" she said.

"Hi, Donna, how are you? Would you like to join us?"

"Where do you know her from?" Karen asked.

"She works at a fish house." A song came on the jukebox that Donna liked, and we got up and danced.

We finished the pizza and got up to leave.

"Don't expect us to pay for the drinks we sent," one of the guys screamed to the bartender. "They're cutting out on us."

"We didn't ask for them!" Karen screamed back.

"You thought you could buy us with a couple of drinks?" Tina screamed. A plastic drink cup flew toward her. I dropped a twenty on the table and pushed Karen and Tina toward the door. Tina twisted in my arms to scream at the guys.

"Let's head toward the arcade," I said.

"Let's make sure we're not being followed," Donna commented. She watched, but no one followed us.

"The shots and beers we downed kind of hit me all at once," Karen said.

"Win me a porcelain cat?" Tina slurred. I didn't win the cat but did win some stuffed animals. We stopped and listened to Elvis for a while.

"It's getting late. Let's head back to the Cave while we can still walk," Karen said. I tried to support Tina and Karen as we walked back. It was kind of a clown show with Tina staggering on one side of me and Karen on the other.

"Donna, can you stop by?" I asked.

"I think you have your hands full now."

"I'd like to drop them off and talk a little."

"No, I've got to get up early for work."

"At least come in for a moment."

"Okay."

As we turned the last corner I could sense something wasn't right. Darkness covered the house. No music blared from the balcony. The porch light didn't glow above the steps. I sat Karen and Tina on the lawn chairs.

"What do think happened?" Donna asked. "Do you think the guys from the bar cut your lights?"

"No, I don't think they'd go to the trouble." I called around, but no one was home. I hit the light switch, but they didn't come on.

"I'll get the flashlight from my car," I said. The flashlight shone on beer cans scattered across the floor.

"What a pigsty!" she said. Trash lay everywhere.

"Let's check the breaker," I said. "I wonder where it is." I walked around the Cave a couple of times and finally found the problem. Someone shut off the main electric switch. A wire with a seal held it closed.

"What do we do?" she asked. "The electric company must have shut off the power."

"To me the logical thing would be to cut off the wire loop," I said. I found a pair of pliers in my trunk and did just that. I opened the box and flipped the switch. The lights in the Cave came back on. I led Karen and Tina to the sofa.

"I really do have to go," Donna said. "I'll see you at work."

"Wait, I'll at least walk you to the corner." I walked outside with her and watched her walk up the street. I spotted Mickey standing on the corner.

"Yo, Mickey," I called out.

"Man, am I glad to see you," he said. "The party at the Cave grew to about twenty-five guys, drinking beer and watching the ballgame. The party spilled outside, and more people showed up. Alice the Goon showed up and handcuffed a guy she thought was you. She called for backup, and everyone scattered. To make matters worse, the police spotted the burn marks on the deck. They ordered everyone to leave. Someone showed up and shut off the power."

"I warned the guys not to act like idiots. I guess they didn't understand?"

"Well, we all started drinkin' and ...."

"I feel stupid for having cut the seal and turning the power back on! I guess we still need to sleep somewhere, and I need to keep the cold shed working. I guess if I'm hauled in front of a judge, I can somehow explain the whole thing."

"Yeah, really!"

"Let's just try to go on as if everything's the same. We'll keep things quiet for a while. We'll have to keep the rowdies out and just let the regular crew stay. It's August, and some will be heading back to college soon. The rest of us will somehow have to make it through the summer."

I tried to sleep but couldn't. I thought Alice the Goon would come walking through the door. I kept tossing and turning. I jumped right out of my sleeping bag when Sashimi shook me awake.

"What the hell?" I called out. Karen jumped up from the sofa with a start.

"It's Sashimi," I said. Karen hugged me and staggered toward her own bed.

"You talk to her? She save face?" Sashimi asked.

"Yes, everything is fine between us." Sashimi gave me a thumbs-up sign.

"You have nice tuna?" she asked.

"I'll show you." Tully arrived, and we headed to the dock to unload the live wells.

"I have your check from last week. Soon last haul for summer. I must prepare for school."

"That will be it? I'll miss seeing you!"

"Yes," she said.

"Yes?"

"Yes!" She turned, got into her truck and left.

"What did she mean by yes?"

"She knows you'll miss her," Tully said. "Who wouldn't?"

After Sashimi left, we launched the sailboat and headed out to make our runs for sea bass and blackfish. We caught some nice ones.

"I can convert the sea bass pots into crab pots," Tully explained. "We need to start hauling them in."

"I guess they'll work for that. We'd better head in." We brought two of them back with us.

As we cleaned up the boat Tully brought up his idea about a vacation again.

"We ought to go on vacation, son."

Spend a vacation with a gray-haired old guy? Would that be any stranger than the summer has been?

"Where would we go?"

"I'd like to sail up into Delaware Bay. We'd visit the tiny towns along its shores until we got up to Port Penn. We could then cut over to the Chesapeake Bay where we'd sail from area to area seeing the sights. Along the way we'd camp out. We could cook whatever we caught for dinner. When we got tired of camping, we could sell the sailboat and hitchhike home."

The vacation Tully envisioned was one that I'd dreamed about but never thought possible.

"When would we leave?"

"As soon as we fill Sashimi's truck next Friday. We'll sell the remainder of our catch of crabs and fish also. We'll have to load our crab pots with bait so when we return we'll have crabs to sell."

"We don't have a lot of space on the sailboat. What about our gear?"

"We'll have to take as little as possible and store it in the hollowed-out bow."

"I guess it'll just be my backpacking tent, two sleeping bags and a mess kit. We'll bring some fishing gear, a compass, some extra rope and an army shovel."

I went back to the Cave and got ready to broil some trout for dinner.

"Tully wants me to go on a sailing vacation," I explained to Karen.

"And what about me?"

Does she mean "What about me?" as in, "What about us" or as in...?

"Should I just keep selling the vegetables, or are you expecting me to haul in the crabs or …?"

"The vegetables would be enough."

"I have to head to New York for a couple of days myself. You okay until then?"

"Yes."

"Oh, and Bill, one of Tom's friends, is down for a few days, another football player."

"Oh great!"

"Oh he's cute! He's tall, blond and muscular."

"Someone for you to date!"

"Jealous?"

"No."

Everything had pretty much settled back to normal again at the Cave. Mickey handed out a couple of cases of beer to the neighbors. Karen, Connie and Tina went to lunch with Emma. Maybe things had gotten too quiet, though.

SADIE

Karen asked about Godiva again and I have no easy answers. I don't know where she, or Sadie, is, or even if they're still alive. When I worked at the gas station, they would call on our payphone Wednesday nights at nine forty-five. I hope they're okay.

I'd just left Tully's place when Tina walked up.

"A girl stopped by looking for you!" she said.

"Who?"

"I don't know, some girl. Looked like a runway model. Tall, gaga and brunette. She stepped into the Cave, announced she'd be staying with you a few days, and left. The guys lost their minds! They're cleaning up the trash, vacuuming the carpet and scrubbing the walls. Karen and I couldn't get 'em to pick up their empty beer cans, and she steps in, says she's staying, and they all go nuts over her."

"Sounds like Sadie."

"Let me guess. This one's not your girlfriend either?" Tina asked.

"No, she's Godiva's companion. I took her to the prom, but she's not my girlfriend."

"Okay, I think I heard this story. Godiva said she humiliated the football team?"

"That's her."

"I think I'm going to like her."

"She's easy to like if you understand her; she's holy hell if you don't."

I headed home and found the Cave cleaned like Tina said.

"Do you have dibs on Sadie?" Tom asked. "Everyone wants to know if she's taken."

"Sadie is kinda different," I replied. "My advice would be to treat her nice and stay back. You don't want to make her angry."

"I think I can handle her," Bill said.

"Well, then think again, 'cause you can't. Sadie handles herself."

"She's coming back!" Jim hollered.

A moment later the guys ran to the window to watch her walk up.

"Hello, Ethan," she said wrapping her arms around me. "Is it okay if I stay a few days? I have a concert this weekend in Atlantic City."

"Stay as long as you like, but I don't have a bed to offer you. I'm sleeping in the corner."

"I'm sure I'll find a bed."

"Did you eat dinner yet?" I asked. "We could go out."

"I'd like that, but I need to get cleaned up first. I saw a shower down the hall?"

"Knock yourself out."

We ended up at an Italian restaurant. Sadie ordered shrimp, and I had a salad.

"So what have you been up to?" she asked.

"I've been crabbing and fishing with Tully. We've been catching a lot and selling them."

"Anything I could chip in on?" she asked.

"Yeah, actually there is. We're selling live fish to a Japanese girl, and it's taking us away from our gardens. You could pick the crops and sell them. It's a big job, but I think you can do it. It's Karen's job, but she's away. I'll show you them on the way home."

"I'd like that," Sadie agreed. We got home and found the usual party going on. We sat, talked and tried to relax.

"I'm going out for a walk," she said.

"Can I come with you?" Bill asked.

"No, I need to go alone." Sadie returned around midnight with something rolled up under her arm.

"What is it?" Bill asked.

"A blow-up camping bed. I'll use the air pump in Ethan's car to fill it and lean it against the wall during the daytime." Tom and Sadie went out, and I heard the pump running. Bill downed a couple of shots of tequila.

"She sleeps nude, doesn't she?" he asked.

"That's a really sick thing to even ask!" Kathy said.

"She sleeps however she wishes," I told him.

It was past one when Sadie brought the blown-up bed in. We moved the easy chair and laid the bed down. I unzipped my sleeping bag and spread it out. I found a blanket for her. Bill sat on the sofa drinking and watching Sadie. He finally staggered off to bed.

Sadie undressed under the covers and set her things to the side. I stretched out in my corner. She plastered a kiss goodnight on my forehead.

Sometime during the night I sensed something wasn't right. I heard Sadie giggling. I looked down to see Bill peering under her covers.

"What the hell are you doing?" I asked.

"Just checking," Bill said. He staggered toward his bedroom. Sadie arose and tapped him on the shoulder. He turned in amazement.

"Any questions?" Sadie asked. Bill stood frozen. "Well, sleep tight." Sadie returned to the bed.

"Sleep tight?" I asked. "After seeing you nude, he won't sleep at all."

"Maybe that was my point," Sadie replied.

"By the way, where did you find the bed?"

"Don't ask."

I drifted back to sleep.

The next morning Sadie went to pick her vegetables before it got too hot outside. Around ten in the morning Tully appeared.

"We need to get our catch for Sashimi," he said. A moment later Sadie returned.

"Tully, this is Sadie. She's down for a few days."

"Are you going out on the ocean?" Sadie asked. "Can I come?"

"Sadie, it's messy and hot and …."

"No, let her come, son. I get the sense she knows how to catch fish. Not hard to look at either."

We walked down, took the tarp off the sailboat and gathered our gear.

"It'll be hell getting the lifeguards to let us launch this time of day," Tully said. "We can only launch off this beach when they're not here."

"I'll handle it," Sadie said. She walked up to the first lifeguard, then down to the second, and then returned.

"We're good to go, but we need to go now!" We shoved the boat into the surf. A moment later Tully had the mast up and the sail out. We sailed off to the sound of lifeguards blowing their whistles.

"I thought you fixed it with them," I said.

"It would have taken a presidential order to allow us out," Tully said. "How'd you do it?"

"I explained to our lifeguard that the other lifeguard said we could launch the boat," Sadie said.

"Then what had you asked the second lifeguard?"

"I asked him if I could go in the water, and he said yes."

"He meant to go swimming, not to launch the boat!"

"He didn't specify, so I knew we were good to go."

"I told you she knew what she was doing," Tully said.

We sailed south, and Sadie examined our ropes. She let each one stream behind us in the water and rewound them. She cut any lines that showed frays and spliced together those that she could. She also retied all the knots.

"Were you ever in the Navy?" Tully asked, studying the knots.

"No, but I know knots and ropes."

"I can see that," Tully stated. "I'm guessing it's better not to ask where you learned it."

Sadie pulled a fishing rod out of the hull. She found a diamond jig in the tackle box and tied it on.

"The fish are farther out," I explained.

"Are they?" she asked, casting toward a weed patch. A moment later her rod went double as she fought a fish.

"Ethan, get another rod out," she screamed. I saw Tully grab a rod and throw a white jig into the water.

"As long as we have one on, we can keep catching them," she explained.

"What?"

"Mahi-mahi," Tully stated. "They run in schools near weed patches and drifting debris. They'll keep biting as long as one is in the water." A moment later Sadie hauled a glistening green fish over the side of the boat. Tully did the same a few moments after that. We caught five fish from the school before they moved on.

"Mahi-mahi are supposed to be in warm southern waters, not New Jersey!" I said. "How did you know they'd be there?" She just shrugged. We sailed south and emptied our remaining sea bass pots. Sadie studied a tiny offshore chart that I'd copied from the library.

"You said Sashimi wants tuna?" Sadie asked. "Sail straight east about half a mile."

"East ... what's east?" I asked.

"It's a lump," Tully said. "A small hill underwater. She thinks the tuna will be holding over the lump."

I sorted the catch from the sea bass pots and threw the runts overboard. The rest I put into the live well. Sadie sat tying what looked like hangman's nooses onto lines. She pulled three gunny sacks from the hull and rolled them up. She put heavy diamond jigs on four of our lines and trolled them way out from the boat.

"They're too far out; they'll go way too deep. The tuna would be on top ...." A moment later one of the rods bent double, and its reel began whizzing.

"Fish on!" Tully screamed. The fish ran deep and fought near the bottom.

"I think you hooked a mako shark!" I said. Sadie adjusted the drag and slowly cranked in a little line.

"I'd better reel in the other lines," Tully said. A moment later Tully's rod bent double as he had a fish on.

"Get the other lines in, son!" Tully screamed. "All the lines will tangle." I reeled like crazy and felt a fish slam my line also. Now we had three fish fighting like mad.

"Way they're acting, they could be yellowfins!" Tully screamed.

"No, I think they're all makos; they're staying near the bottom."

"You're both wrong. They're bluefins," Sadie said. I looked to see sweat pouring off Tully as he fought his fish. My arms ached from the fight. Sadie looked relaxed. Her fish came to the surface first.

"Bluefin!" Tully screamed. "Get the gaff!"

"It's okay," Sadie said. I noticed she had one of the ropes in the water, which she drew tight around the tuna's tail. She tied the rope to a cleat. Tully's fish came to the boat next. She stepped next to Tully, pulled his line away from the boat and lassoed the tail of that fish also. A moment later my fish snapped the line.

"You can't horse them in. You need to pace yourself," Sadie advised. I helped her pull the fish onto the deck.

"That's got to be a hundred pounds of fish sitting there!" Tully said. Sadie wetted the gunnysacks and spread them over the fish. "We need to head in." He pulled the sail taut, and we cut through the surf heading west. "We need to sail up to the dock to keep the sea bass alive. We'll have to pack the tuna and mahi-mahi in ice until Sashimi comes."

That evening we placed the sea bass in the live well and drove to the Cave. Tully iced down the tuna and mahi-mahi. Sadie went inside to shower.

"Son, people come and people go, but that girl is extraordinary. How well do you know her?"

"Not very well."

"Well the knots she tied, the splices ... one sailor out of a hundred might know those, but she's never been in the Navy! The one knot she tied, it's called a Chinese Decorator, and it's very rare .... I've only met a few people who have ever learned to tie 'em."

"She's one of a kind," I replied. "She shocked me today with the mahi-mahi and the tuna. She actually tied those slipknots and brought the gunny sacks out before we hooked the tuna. I don't think there's anything she doesn't know how to do."

"Well, she's welcome to come out anytime."

Tully left to head home. Sadie found her shampoo and walked toward the shower.

"Why don't you join her?" Tina said rhetorically.

"You can if you want," Sadie said.

"No, I'll wait." Sadie headed in, and a moment later I heard the shower start up. Tina glared at me.

"Bill told me about last night," Tina said.

"I'm sure. Did he sleep well?" Tina stared for a minute and then finally cracked up laughing.

When Sadie emerged from the bathroom, she was wearing a black silk blouse and matching miniskirt. She looked fantastic. Ted elbowed Bill.

"Sadie would you like to go to the boardwalk?" he asked. "We could get dinner while we're out?"

"Like she'd go out with you!" Tina hissed.

"Do you care?" she asked.

"No. Go and have a good time." They gathered their things and left. Tina sat staring at me.

"Is this a joke? After last night you really don't care if she goes off with them?"

"I told you, she does as she wishes. My guess is she plans on teaching them some kind of lesson."

Around midnight we heard someone coming up the steps. A moment later Bill and Ted walked in. Bill had a garbage bag slung over his shoulder. He dumped an enormous pile on the table.

"Don't ask me for beer money for a while," Bill said. "I'm broke!"

Tina sat staring a pile of stuffed animals, music tapes and gifts.

"Let me guess," Tina said. "You two spent every last dime you had winning these for Sadie? You tried to impress her?"

"Kinda …," Ted said. Tina noticed that Bill's hand looked red and swollen.

"You didn't get into a fight or something did you?" she asked.

"Or something …," Ted said. "Bill and I spent all our money trying to win something for Sadie. We lost every time. Sadie said she'd try and won every game she played."

"And Bill's hand?" Tina asked.

"They had this thing that decided if you were a he-man or not. You rang a bell by smashing a wooden mallet onto a scale. Neither Ted nor I could get it. I finally hurt my hand trying. After that Sadie grabbed the mallet, swung it, and rang the bell."

"You two lose all your money trying to impress her and in the end she, dressed in her mini-skirt, rings the bell?" Tina asked. "What a bunch of losers!" Bill and Ted headed off to bed. Tina sat staring at me.

"They lose every game, and she wins every game?"

"Sadie knows which games she can win and which ones she can't. She only plays the ones she'll win."

"And the mallet?"

"It's probably about rhythm not brawn."

A moment later Sadie walked in.

"I'm glad you put the guys in their place," Tina said. "Ted's been a creep for a while."

"It's not about putting him or Bill in his place. It's about their self respect. They don't bathe, sit drinking all day long, and then they can't figure out why girls won't date them."

"And you expect to change them?" Kathy chimed in.

"They can change if they want."

"I think our guys are hopeless," Tina said.

"If you treat them as hopeless, then they are."

The next morning I forgot to get up early. I lay in my corner staring at Sadie. Godiva always looked sweet and innocent when she slept. Sadie always looked seductive. A moment later I heard footsteps coming up the stairs. Tom walked up to Sadie and me.

"The Beachcomber's here," he said. A moment later Tully appeared in the doorway.

"Son, we need to check our crab pots, and the tide will be right in an hour or so."

"Give me a minute," I asked.

"Could I come?" Sadie asked.

"Yeah, you could really help with the bait sales."

"Tully, why don't you have a cup of coffee," Sadie said. "I need to talk to Bill and Ted."

"You don't mean you're going to go into their room?" Kathy said. "Do you know how disgusting it is in there?"

"I'm sure I've seen worse." She slipped down the hallway and entered their room. An hour later we were out in the boat hauling our crab pots in.

"The crabs are larger than what I'm used to seeing in Florida," Sadie said.

"They bring good prices here," Tully stated. A boat full of guys stopped to buy bait but couldn't keep their eyes off Sadie.

"Do you guys have enough sodas?" she asked. She sold them three six packs before they left.

"I'll set some lines off the stern," Sadie said. "I baited them with squid."

"You'll catch more flounder if you use minnows," I said.

"Trout will bring higher prices than flounder," Sadie said.

"It's been a while since we've seen any trout." I glanced at Tully, but he just shook his head no.

"I told you don't ask me for advice about women."

By the time we'd reached the end of the sound Sadie had filled the cooler with good-sized trout. She'd also sold all the soda and bait.

"I think if we sell the trout on the water, we'll make a lot more than if we sell them at a market," Sadie said. She began waving boats over. As it turned out most of the fishermen had caught little that day. By the time we reached the dock, the trout and the crabs were gone.

"I bet we made over two hundred dollars today!" I said.

"Try over three fifty …," Sadie remarked.

"We couldn't have made that much!" I said.

"Well, we netted three hundred fifty-one dollars in cash and three cases of beer," Tully said, splitting the money up.

"I can't take the money," Sadie said. "It's yours!"

"We wouldn't have made half that much if you hadn't called all those boats over," Tully said. "The girl's a regular cash register!"

"Tully, this is Sadie's last night here. She leaves in the morning. Do you want to come to dinner with us?" I asked.

"No, son, you should spend some time alone, breathe a little." Sadie gave Tully a really long hug.

"Well, it was nice to meet you!" she said.

"Likewise," he said.

"Well, let's get home, get a shower and some rest," I said.

Later that evening we sat on the couch watching TV.

"OH MY GOD, WHAT HAPPENED?" I turned to see Karen standing in the doorway.

"Hello, welcome back!" I said. "How was your trip? Oh, by the way, this is Sadie."

"Don't tell me you cleaned the house?" Karen said.

"Me ... uh ... no," Sadie said. "The guys did it."

"THE GUYS!" Karen blurted out. A moment later Tina walked over to the TV and shut it off.

"OKAY, I'VE HAD ENOUGH!" she said. "Getting Ted and Bill to clean the house was sweet ... but the dates?"

"Dates ... you went on a date with the guys?" Karen asked.

"No, she talked to them," Tina said. "They showered, shaved, and they're both out on dates!"

"Dates ... with who?" Karen asked.

"You know that blond girl that lives next to Connie? Bill asked her out, and she said she'd only do it if they doubled. Ted's taking her friend. They're going to the Bongo Drum Room!"

"They were drifting and looking for a little guidance. Is that so hard?" Sadie asked.

"So, what are we, their moms?" Tina asked.

"No, we're their roommates," Karen said. "She's right."

"Look, we're going out to dinner; do you want to come with us?" I asked. "Sadie loves seafood."

We found a nice restaurant near the boardwalk. Sadie ordered clams, Karen chicken and Tina flounder. I ordered a steak.

"I'll find something on the jukebox," I said. I walked over and began looking at the selection. I guess Tina thought I couldn't hear the conversation, but I could.

"Sadie, what are you doing with him?"

"I love him."

"And Godiva?"

"She loves him, too."

"He says you're not his girlfriend?"

"How could he call me his girlfriend and then drop me off someplace?"

"I don't understand ...," Karen said.

"You don't need to; just accept it. I really can't go into it, but it's not safe for Godiva and me to stay in any one place for long."

"And the boyfriend part?" Tina asked.

"What's a boyfriend to you? To me it's someone that loves and cares for me. That kind is hard to find." Sadie got up and came to the jukebox. She chose two songs from the dollar I'd put in the machine. She stared at Tina and gave me a very long kiss. We walked back to our seats. The table seemed tense, and I tried to break the mood.

"Karen, how was your trip?" I asked.

"Oh, really nice. We went to New York City and toured the Statue of Liberty and Central Park. One night we even went to the Village."

"You're so lucky. I always wanted to go but couldn't!" I said.

"What did you two do while I was gone?" Karen asked.

"Sadie took over the gardens and helped us on the boat."

"You went out on the crab boat with them?" Tina asked.

"And out on the sailboat in the ocean." I said. "Showed us right where the fish were."

"Did you bait the hook yourself and take the fish off?" Tina asked.

"Actually I tied lures on the lines and lassoed the tunas by the tail," Sadie replied.

"Unreal," Tina said.

"Well, we'd better head home," Karen said. "I spent the entire day driving."

We got back late. Sadie and I collapsed around midnight. I fell into a deep sleep. Sadie shook me awake the next morning.

"Were you expecting anyone?" Sadie asked. "A pretty oriental girl?"

I woke up to see Sashimi standing in the kitchen.

"Hello, Sashimi, I have your tuna in the cold shed," I said. Sadie dressed under the covers and then arose.

"Sashimi, this is Sadie," I said as they briefly hugged. "She caught some nice tuna for you."

"We also caught some mahi-mahi," Sadie said. We took her out and showed her the iced-down fish.

"You take her fishing more often!" Sashimi said. "She catch fish, and she beautiful."

I loaded the fish into Sashimi's truck. We followed her to the dock. Tully sat waiting for us.

"We have some nice sea bass and eels this week," Tully said. We loaded the live fish into her tank. Sashimi wrote us a check for last week's catch.

"Next check much bigger," Sashimi explained. "I must go. Get late to Philadelphia." We watched her speed off.

"Tully, I'm taking Sadie to Atlantic City this morning, so this will be it," I said.

"Well, it was really good to have you down, and I hope to see you again soon," he said. Sadie hugged him tightly and plastered a kiss on his cheek.

"I'm going to miss you!" Sadie said. We went back to the Cave, showered and collected our things. An hour later we arrived in Atlantic City.

"Do you want to spend the day together on the boardwalk?" I asked.

"No, it's going to be hard enough as it is. Let's just hug and go on."

We hugged, and I watched her walk off. I drove back to Wildwood.

That afternoon I decided to sit outside on the balcony. The cool ocean breeze drove away the heat and humidity of the day. Two purple finches sat on the edge of the balcony, their cranberry-colored bodies glistened in the setting sun. A moment later they swooped down and landed on a thistle feeder in Emma's yard. Karen came out to find me.

"You look heartbroken. Where's Sadie?"

"I dropped her off in Atlantic City."

"Do you love her?"

"I use the word too much, but in a sense I do."

"I guess I understand. Come on in. I'll make dinner."

LET'S PISS OFF THE NEIGHBORS

I stood on the beach and watched the first pinkish rays of sunlight break over the ocean. The surf lay quiet this morning, and the waves came with hardly a ripple. A pod of bottlenose dolphins broke close to the beach, searching for food.

A line of yellow tractors drove up the beach sifting the sand. They graded it, separating trash from sand, as they headed north. Flocks of least sandpipers, brown bodies with yellow legs, ran ahead of the tractors. Their raucous cries filled the air.

I hope Sadie is okay ....

I walked back to the Cave and made my pot of coffee. About halfway through the pot Bruce walked in.

"Did some of the guys head back to school already?" he asked.

"It's the tail end of summer now," I said. "In a few weeks the place will be empty."

"Why don't you come with me to Ocean City? My mom's making dinner. We can come back here to stay the night."

"I could use a regular meal," I replied.

Bruce's mom made a dinner of chicken, corn, mashed potatoes and gravy.

"Ethan, have you been catching any fish lately?" Bruce's dad asked.

"Yes, quite a few," I said. "Why don't we take my boat out tomorrow? You and Bruce might catch some flounder."

"I'd like that," his dad said.

Later Bruce and I returned to the Cave. Mickey joined us; we went to the boardwalk and walked along the shops.

"Who's the guy with the guitar?" Bruce asked.

"That's Elvis. Come on. I'll introduce you." We listened to Elvis for a while, and Mickey started talking to some girl. He decided to take off with her. We told him we would meet him back at the Cave.

The next morning Mickey still hadn't shown up. Bruce's dad arrived, and we drove down to the dock. It seemed strange that after fishing for a living all summer I would enjoy doing the same thing for fun. We drifted the channels for flounder, caught quite a few and had a good time.

"Want a beer?" Bruce's dad called.

"No, I'm okay."

"You've really cut back on drinking this summer," Bruce said.

"When I first came to the beach, I drank a lot. During the summer,

I traded bait, fish, crabs and fishing tackle for beer. Now that it's August I can't remember the last time I drank one. I just lost the impulse."

"You don't seem to like hitting the bars anymore, either," Bruce said.

"The whole bar scene bothers me a lot. Usually the music's so loud and it's so crowded that I can't talk to anyone. The guys from the Cave use any excuse to get drunk and cause problems."

"So, being down here all summer's been a positive influence?" Bruce's dad asked.

"The only positive thing this summer is Tully. He even convinced me to go to church with him a couple of times."

I gave all the fish I caught to Bruce's dad. He headed back to Ocean City that afternoon.

Later that day Tully and I tended our crab pots. We made the last preparations for our vacation. Everything on the sailboat was set.

"How much cash should I take?" I asked.

"It'll be best just to play it by ear," Tully said. "I think two hundred will be more than enough, though." I stowed the tent, camping gear, fishing rods, nets and extra clothes into the bow of the sailboat.

"All that's left is to sell Sashimi her fish in the morning, and we're off," Tully said.

I headed back to the Cave and found Karen standing in the kitchen. I'd forgotten that they planned an end of season party tonight.

"It will be a western party with cowboy hats and boots," Karen said. "Tina went shopping for food. I found a straw hat and army boots for you."

"That should work fine."

The guys constructed a pit out back to barbecue chicken. Someone brought country music tapes to go with the barbecue. As usual I supplied most of the beer from the cold shed. A few hours after dark the beer was gone.

"You know, we've really behaved ourselves this last week. We should do something radical," Tina said.

"Let's build a bonfire and dance around it," Mickey said.

"Let's find a baby pool and do belly flops off the roof," Bruce said.

"No, we ought to do something to piss off the neighbors," Beth said.

"We ought to strip nude, walk down the street, cross the main drag, and go skinny-dipping," Tina said. "When we're done, we can turn around, cross the main drag again, and walk home." The thought that we'd be spotted as soon as we left the house, or that we'd cross the main drag clogged with people, didn't faze anyone.

"The beach is closed at night and heavily patrolled by jeeps with spotlights," I said. None of this seemed to bother anyone. Maybe the reason

I had second thoughts was that I was the only one sober.

"I'll count down from ten to one, and then we'll all start stripping," Tina said.

Soon everyone stood naked and high-fiving. I grabbed a pair of gym shorts just in case. We all walked up the street toward the traffic light and the main drag. As surprising as it seems we didn't make a big commotion. The intersection lay deserted. We walked across the main drag and down to the ocean without incident.

"I can't believe we had made it to the beach unnoticed," I said to Karen. "Twelve of us, seven of them cute girls, march nude down the street and cross one of the busiest areas in town without incident. It's unreal." We went into the ocean and swam for hours.

"I'm getting cold!" Tina finally said.

"We should head back before we're caught," Karen said. I think everyone was starting to sober up. We walked toward the traffic light. A police car sat at the intersection.

"It's Buckwheat!" Beth said. Tina, Connie, Kathy and her ran to his squad car and began jumping up and down. I started to pull my gym shorts on. The officer in the car lost it, disbelieving what he saw. It wasn't Buckwheat, though; it was Officer O'Neil. Just as I pulled my shorts on he hit his flashing red lights. Everyone paused for a moment as if time stood still. Alice the Goon pulled out from behind a parked car. The parking ticket she'd been writing blew away. Everyone scattered, with nude bodies running everywhere. I followed Mickey as he tore through a backyard. One moment he was running forward and the next moment he was thrown back. I helped him get up.

"What happened?" I asked.

"I ran full speed into a chain link fence!" he screamed.

"I can image the bruises that will leave," I said. He found a pair of shorts hanging on a wash line and pulled them on. We heard cars beeping and turned to look.

"That's something you don't see every day!" Mickey said. I turned to see Bruce running nude up the main drag, Alice the Goon's spotlight focused on him.

"Let's head back to the Cave," I said.

"Can't," Mickey said, "O'Neil's sitting outside."

We cut around the neighborhood and went the back way to Connie's house. We found all seven girls inside.

"I'm sorry, Ethan, but you're on your own," she said. "I have to find clothes for everyone, luckily you already found some."

We knew that eventually Officer O'Neil would get tired, go home, and the whole thing would blow over.

"Mickey, we'll have to sneak over to Tully's place," I said.

"Sounds good," he said. We met Tully halfway.

"What are you doing up so early?" I asked.

"Did you forget about Sashimi?" he asked. I explained what happened.

"I thought you guys learned your lesson with the fire?" Still dressed in our shorts, we walked with Tully to the Cave. We arrived to find Sashimi getting the third degree from Officer O'Neil. Emma stood to the side aghast.

"I saw that officer attack her!" Emma screamed. "I called the police!"

"Leave her alone!" Tully screamed. Sashimi didn't seem to understand what was going on.

"All Americans crazy!" she screamed. A sergeant pulled up and started hollering at O'Neil. Karen, Connie and Tina came from across the street.

"What happened?" the sergeant asked.

"I was watering my roses and heard the poor girl screaming," Emma stated. "That man walked up to that pretty girl and started rubbing his hands all over her! We can't have that here!"

"I come to get fish; he want me to take clothes off!" Sashimi stated.

"I knew she was swimming nude with the rest of 'em, so I thought her clothes would be wet," O'Neil said. He pointed toward Tina. "She was swimming with them, too!" He walked toward Tina.

"Now he's going to try and feel us up!" she screamed.

"They're dressed, their hair's dry, and they came from across the street," the sergeant said. He looked at O'Neil as if he were crazy.

"Look, head back to the station. I'll take over here." Everyone started heading home.

Sashimi finally calmed down. We drove over to the dock and got the live fish, eels and crabs. She sorted through it, taking the ones she wanted and rejecting others.

"Here's your check," she said. "I mail you the next one." Sashimi hugged Tully and me good-bye. I saw a tear in her eye.

"Are you okay?" I asked. She smiled, got into her truck and left. "I'm surprised because she usually shows no emotion at all," I said.

"Japanese women are taught from birth to keep all emotions inside."

"Well, what do we do with the rest of the fish?"

"Net 'em out of the pen. We'll sell them to the local markets. Anything we get is gravy." I noticed Mickey running up the street.

"Ethan," he said, "Alice the Goon caught Bruce, and they're bringing him up on some weird charge."

"Oh, perfect, she'll probably charge him as being a flasher or something!"

"We'll take care of it," Tully said. "We'll head over to court after we sell our fish."

We walked into court at 10:00 AM. After almost an hour of nonsense and ridiculous ramblings, the door finally opened. The bailiff shuttled fifteen guys into the courtroom. Bruce wore some kind of orange jumpsuit.

"Stay here, son," Tully said. "I'm going to talk to the court clerk." Fifteen minutes later Tully came out and tapped me on the shoulder. We walked over together and sat down next to Bruce.

"I worked it out with the judge," Tully said. "You'll plead guilty to pissing in public and pay a twenty-five dollar fine."

"Okay, let's get this over with; my head's killing me," Bruce said.

About an hour later Alice the Goon walked into the courtroom, glared at me, and sat down. The judge called for Bruce's case. Alice the Goon got Bruce and escorted him up. The judge sat scowling.

"I understand you're pleading guilty to urinating in public?" the judge asked.

Alice the Goon turned purple. "Your honor those charges are wrong! He was running nude all over town!"

"Is that correct?"

"If you saw her coming, you'd run, too!" Bruce said. The judge nodded in agreement, and the courtroom exploded in laughter.

"But, your honor!" Alice told the judge. "I didn't see the defendant urinating in public; I saw him running nude."

"Did you see him pissing in public or not?" the judge screamed.

"No, sir, I didn't," Alice stated.

The judge seemed irritated. "The charge I have in front of me is urinating in public. You're the arresting officer, and now you say it didn't happen. I have no choice but to throw out the complaint! You're free to go!" We could see Alice the Goon's hands tremble with anger as she removed Bruce's handcuffs.

"He's taking the clothes we gave him!" Alice called out.

"Stop wasting my time!" the judge called back. "If you have no other cases, I suggest you leave my courtroom."

"Let's get something to eat," Bruce said. "I'm starved." Tully and I went with Bruce, ate lunch and then said good-bye to everyone. The sailboat awaited us.

A SAILING VACATION

"I'd hoped we'd get an early start, but it didn't happen," I told Tully.

"Life's like that, son; you do the best you can."

We'd already packed everything we would need on the boat. All we had to carry onboard was a small duffel sack each. We shoved off and headed south. When we got to the inlet, Tully steered the sailboat straight out.

"Tully, I figured we'd head up the sheltered waterway. Are you heading out into the ocean?"

"We head southeast into the ocean and tack west into the mouth of the bay," Tully said. "It works out better that way."

"How far out we got to go?"

"Not so far." He steered through the first large waves.

"Wouldn't it be better if we'd taken the motor?" I asked.

"No, we travel by sail only on this trip."

We ran with the wind straight out into the ocean. He took a heading of east-southeast into the blue water. The wind picked up, and we raced along at a good clip. The little sailboat cut through the waves, and all seemed well with the world.

"Which way is the bay?" I asked.

Tully pointed toward the setting sun. I looked back as the shoreline disappeared from view.

"Are we something like ten miles out?"

"About that."

"The sun's setting. Are we gonna be okay with no lights on the boat? Huge freighters, oil tankers and fishing boats regularly use this area. They could run right over us in the dark."

"We'll be fine."

We continued cutting through the waves as we slipped into complete darkness. Here and there a star would shine briefly and then be covered by clouds.

"How far out to sea will we have to go before we tack back toward the bay? I think we're heading toward the Bahamas."

"We won't have to go too far out." The wind picked up, and far ahead I saw a little light. I scanned the horizon and briefly saw it again, a lightning storm far off.

The wind picked up and came straight out of the east.

"Do we have to worry about those storms?" I asked.

"No, they're too far away to bother us much," he said. An instant later one engulfed us.

Tully held onto the tiller for dear life. The waves suddenly swelled to huge heights. The wind picked up, blowing in all directions at once. Everything loose started sliding around. I lashed everything down. The storm brought waves, lighting and driving rain.

"Here's a life vest," I screamed. I put one on also. "The thunder sounds like cannons going off!"

Tully held the boat on a forty-five-degree angle to the waves, which made it easier to handle. Waves filled the boat with water one moment and drained out as we climbed the next one. Lightning lit the black sky here and there. The flashes of light revealed giant waves about to crash on us.

The storm intensified, and the waves grew even larger.

"I'm tying myself to a cleat," I said. "I'm not getting swept out to sea." The boat slowly rose on a giant wave until it seemed to hit the clouds. We surfed down it at breakneck speed. When we hit the wave's bottom, we held our breath as the water surrounded us. Then the boat broke free and began climbing the next wave.

"What are we, fifteen miles out at sea in a car-top sailboat?" I asked Tully. "No radio, no lights, and no one even knows we're here?" I looked back and saw ... Tully smiling. He seemed thrilled.

"Let go and just enjoy the ride!" he screamed.

"What?"

"JUST LET GO!"

He's making sense! When I ride a roller coaster I close my eyes and wait for it to end. What fear am I trying to avoid? I fear dying and nobody knowing what happened to me. If I die and no one knows about it, what does it matter?

"Yeehaaa!" Tully screamed as the next wave hit. I braced myself.

I need to conquer the fear! I need to just let go. I'll untie myself and let go of the sides of the boat ....

"Look at this wave!" Tully hollered. The boat began climbing it.

"Yeehaaa!" we both screamed out as we rode the wave down. It took me a few minutes to comprehend all of it. Now when I held my breath underwater, it was exhilarating.

"If the wind catches us right at the crest, we fly right out of the water!" I said. We spent the next fifteen minutes whooping it up and enjoying the ride. Out of the darkness a wave rose up.

"This one's gonna be bad, son," Tully said. When the boat hit the wave, it was like hitting a brick wall. We shot straight up into the air and turned sideways. I dove out, jumping through the lines and cables. When I landed I went straight under. I popped to the surface a moment later. Another wave crashed over me.

Where's the boat? Where's Tully? As I rose up with the next wave I could see the boat half underwater, drifting about fifty yards away.

I've got to make it to the boat! Thank God I wasn't tied down! I can't swim while wearing a life vest. I'll take it off.

I struggled toward the boat. A wave pushed it toward me. I crawled back on. The sunken sail held the boat sideways. I tried to put my weight on the gunwale. At the top of the next wave the sail broke free from the water, the wind caught it, and the boat took off.

Okay, now I have the boat, but where's Tully? I swung the tiller around trying to turn the boat. I could see nothing in the darkness. The giant swells made things worse. The boat rode up another giant wave. Lightning flashed, and for a moment I thought I saw something. I turned the tiller toward it and hoped for another flash of lightning. Between the waves and the gullies, I could barely see something. I pulled the sail down and held onto the mast looking but could no longer see whatever it was.

I hear a weird hacking moan. What's that? I just heard it again! It's Tully laughing his ass off! At the peak of the next wave I saw him about ten feet from the boat, still whooping it up and laughing. I found a paddle and pulled him in.

"You don't get rides like this at Disneyland, son!" Tully said. He sat catching his breath and looking around. "Raise the sail back up, put the boat at a forty-five-degree angle to the waves." I did as he instructed.

"What happened? One minute we were fine and the next I was flying through the air!" I asked.

"A rogue wave. They come up every now and then. They cause grief for everyone."

"I remember the wave rising and stopping. When we hit, it felt like solid rock."

"It jolted me right out of the boat."

"When do we turn back toward shore?"

"We did that about an hour ago."

"How far out are we?"

"Does it really matter?" Tully asked. "We're having the time of our lives; that's what matters."

"Well, I'm glad we're heading toward shore."

The storm passed, and we skimmed across the waves. Wet and cold, I fell asleep against the side of the boat. I dreamt about a truck. I could hear its motor getting louder and louder. I bumped my head against the side of the boat, and it woke me up. I looked back to see Tully asleep with the tiller under his arm. I could still hear the truck motor sound. I looked and saw a giant freighter off to our side.

"Tully, look out!" I screamed.

He awoke but did not seem disturbed.

"It'll miss us, son," he said. The freighter continued on and passed out of sight. A moment later we encountered its swell, but it wasn't too bad.

"Where are we?" I asked.

"I think we're in the bay now," Tully said. "When the fog lifts, we should see the shoreline." Long before dawn I could see the lights of the Delaware coast.

We followed the coastline to a river. Tully sailed upriver until an old dock appeared, almost hidden by huge pine trees. He tied up to the dock and stepped out.

"Our duffle bags are sealed in the bow. Pull 'em out," Tully said. "I think they'll still be dry."

"Should I set up the tent?"

"There's a house up the hill. We'll stay there."

"How far is it?"

"I don't know. I've never been here before."

"You never fail to amaze me! We just traveled through a horrible storm, got swamped by a rogue wave and almost got chopped to bits by a freighter. We traveled to exactly where you wanted to land, and you've never been here before?"

I grabbed my duffel bag and followed him up the trail. As we topped the bank a woman came running out to greet us.

"I heard you were coming!" she called. "I'm Sara."

"How could she possibly know we're coming?" I whispered. "Things are getting stranger as we go."

"Come on in. The shower is to the right," she said. "Once you're cleaned up, come into the kitchen. Breakfast is ready."

"Thank you," Tully said.

"Michael told me so much about you two!" she said. "He really thinks highly of both of you."

"I followed the directions he gave and sailed right in," Tully explained.

Who's Michael? Is he one of the guys from the Cave? A high school picture hung on the wall. There was no mistaking the photograph; it was Elvis. Michael was Elvis.

After breakfast she invited us to church. All I wanted to do was collapse in bed, but Tully insisted we go. It was a Pentecostal church with lots of singing, praise and dancing.

"I'm making fried chicken and mashed potatoes for dinner," she said as we drove home. "I hope you'll be hungry."

"Little doubt of that," Tully replied. "We're always hungry."

We arrived and ate a fantastic dinner. Afterwards I finally collapsed in bed, the first real bed in a long time.

The next morning I awoke to the sound of someone chopping wood. I went outside and found Tully.

"Need any help?" I asked.

"You could help stack it," he said. A moment later Sara appeared.

"You didn't have to cut wood for me!" she said.

"Least we could do, ma'am," Tully said. After lunch we said good-bye to Sara.

"Thank you so much for letting us stay," Tully said.

"Thank you for being such a good friend to Michael and supporting his ministry," Sara said.

His ministry? I'll talk to Tully about it later. We loaded our gear onto the boat. Tully hoisted the sail, and we took off. Sara waved to us as we sailed away.

We sailed up the bay to an area Tully called "the Anchorage." Huge ships sat side by side.

"Why are all these boats here?" I asked.

"The tankers and freighters wait here until they're told to proceed forward." We sailed on until we came upon a lighthouse.

"During the war Navy sailors were stationed on the tiny rock island," Tully said. "The local people would sail to the island to bring them food, drinks, comics and newspapers. It's been vacant for a long time. The lighthouse is rundown and decaying." Later that day we sailed north across the bay to the New Jersey side. We fished near the concrete ship, catching several nice trout.

We sailed toward Fortescue and set up our tent on a deserted beach for the night.

"We have the trout for dinner, but I'm sure we can also catch some clams," Tully said.

A creek entered the bay, and we walked up it looking for clams. We found two dozen round ones and a large coffee can to cook them in. We went back to the tent and made a campfire from driftwood. Once the coals had burned down, we broiled the trout over the coals. We also had steamed clams for dinner.

"The night's quiet, the bay calm. Let's take the sailboat out on a moonlight ride," I said.

"The evening thermals are starting up. Let's go," Tully agreed. We headed west for several miles. We stopped to look at the lights from the houses on the opposite shore. To the south we could see a large vessel all lit up.

"Look at that freighter, son," Tully said. "It's in the ship channel about five miles south of us."

"Its lights and size, even at this distance, are unbelievable. I can imagine all the sailors and workers onboard getting ready for their first night on shore after being at sea for so long," I said.

Tully sailed back to our campsite.

"What time is it?" I asked.

"I'd guess around one in the morning," Tully said.

"I bet those sailors are just stepping off that ship right now," I said.

"If I had my way, I'd be onboard when it sails off again," Tully said.

I woke up the next morning, and Tully, and the boat, were gone. I looked up the bay and saw him sailing toward camp.

"I sailed into town and traded some trout for eggs, butter and bread for breakfast," he explained. "They'll take all the trout we can get them."

"I hadn't really thought about working to pay our way on this trip, but it makes sense," I said. "We can dig clams for bait and search the rocks for shedder crabs." We looked for both and got quite a few. Tully sailed to an area known as the Oyster Stakes.

"This is a weird-looking place," I said. "It looks like someone tried to make a flooded forest out in the bay. It's like the trees are growing out of the water."

"Let's try drifting and see what we catch," Tully said. Almost immediately we began catching good-sized trout. By noontime the tide had changed, and we decided to give up fishing for the day.

"Let's sail into Fortescue and sell the bigger trout," Tully said. "We can cook the smaller ones on the beach."

After lunch we sailed west up the bay to a point of land on the Delaware side not too far from Dover, Delaware. We set up camp for the night and made a bonfire on the beach. Two surf fishermen came walking down the beach with a bluefish each.

"The blues were hitting pretty good," one said.

"Why don't you stay, and we'll broil those for dinner," Tully said. We made a dinner of broiled trout, bluefish, American fried potatoes and lots of coffee.

"Where do you live?" Tully asked.

"Smyrna."

"Could you give me ride into Dover? I need to buy some things."

"Sure, we can even drive you back if you want," the guys said.

"Do you want to come into town with me?" Tully asked.

"I'd rather stay and just relax," I said. Tully got back late.

The next morning I got up early to try and catch some fish for breakfast. I found a box of doughnuts. I made coffee.

"Tully, you're gonna spoil me! All summer I've been eating nothing but fruit for breakfast." Together we finished off all the doughnuts and the coffee.

"We heading up the bay to Port Penn?" I asked.

"Yeah, and then across the canal to the Chesapeake," Tully replied. "Any problem?"

"It's where I spent one of the most frightening nights of my life," I said. "A year ago I had a powerboat on the Chesapeake Bay side of the Chesapeake-Delaware Bay canal. We often took the boat up and down the bay fishing, water skiing, swimming and just goofing around. Huge freighters and oil tankers use the canal regularly, and it's no place to be in a boat when they're passing through. The huge ships steam up the canal, and the current changes direction as their props churn water. Everything in their way is in trouble as they go up and down the canal."

"That's how it is," Tully admitted.

"Bobby and I had decided to take my boat through the canal to fish near Villas during the gas shortage. We fished the bay and did well. We found gas and filled up for the return trip, and we should have made it back without any problem. Things have a way of going bad on the water, and that's what happened."

"Things do tend to go bad. What happened?"

"A storm came up right before we entered the canal. The water flooded the boat and the engine sputtered and died. Boats passed nearby, and we blasted our horn but no one stopped. Night fell, and the tide would have taken the boat out to sea, so we threw the anchor out and waited."

"Sounds awful," Tully said.

"About 11 PM that night a weird series of lights lit up the sky to the west of us, a set of giant barges pushed by a tugboat. The barges and the tugboat cleared the canal and headed straight toward us. We set off flares, turned our running lights on and blasted the horn. The tugboat couldn't see us. The barges passed so close we could have hit them with our oar. We heard cursing, and a giant spotlight lit up our boat. We jumped up and down and screamed for help. The barges and the tugboat kept on going south down the bay."

"Did someone come and get you?" Tully asked.

"About a half hour later a rescue boat from the Port Penn volunteer fire company towed us in. It's been almost a year to the day since the incident."

"Well, you need to get over it, and the easiest way is to sail up there again," Tully said. "Don't worry; we won't sail close to any freighters or barges."

Tully walked off to check on the boat. As I began to break camp I noticed a flock of terns turning and cavorting in the air.

"What ya thinking about?" Tully asked.

"I was watching the terns diving into the water and sweeping through the air. The birds are such delicate things with tiny bones and thin wings. They go so far out to sea without caring. If the birds aren't worried, should I be?"

"That's the spirit!"

The next day we sailed past the canal. We camped for the night at a place known as Baha. It's a chunk of river sand on the New Jersey side that actually belongs to Delaware due to some quirk of the law.

"It doesn't seem like any roads lead in or out of here," I said.

"It's a weird spot," Tully agreed. "Let's see what we can scrounge for dinner."

We treaded for clams, feeling for them with our bare feet, and found quite a few.

"We'll keep the smaller ones to eat and use the larger for bait,"

Tully said. We set our lines out and waited. We caught three large catfish. I was admiring the catfish when Tully started hollering.

"What's going on?" I asked.

"It's a turtle!" Tully called back. "Get in front and grab it!" I saw its beak snapping at me.

"I'm not getting in front of that thing!" I replied. I grabbed one of its back feet. We dragged it onto the sand. Tully studied it for a moment.

"We have more than enough for dinner," he said. "We'll let the turtle go."

I made a campfire out of driftwood, waited for the coals to burn down and made a pot of coffee. Tully made a small pit, filled it with hot coals, seaweed, the catfish, clams and a few potatoes. He then added some more wet seaweed and left them to cook.

"While they're cooking let's walk up the beach and see where we are." A large complex sat nearby. It seemed to be some kind of power station. Every few hours a huge freighter would come up the bay heading for Philadelphia, Camden or Wilmington. Tully would look fondly at the ships, and sometimes tears would well up in his eyes.

"Those clams and potatoes are done now," he said. We returned and ate.

"This is one of the best meals I've ever," I said. "The potatoes are soft, the clams perfectly steamed."

As we sat that night by the dying campfire, Tully said something I didn't expect to hear.

"I'm going to go out to sea."

"What do you mean?" I asked.

"I'm signing on to a freighter and going out to sea. I grew up near the ocean, and I've loved boats my whole life. I fished and worked these waters and know them well. I worked as a deck hand on a fishing boat when World War II broke out. I, like everyone else I know, enlisted in the Navy when it did. I asked for forward duty and fought the Japanese in the Coral Sea and a lot of other places. Shrapnel wounded me during Kamikaze raids. I hated the fighting and the waste it caused, but I loved being on the sea."

"Is that when you met your wife?"

"When the fighting ended, I was first stationed in Japan and then later in Okinawa. That's where I met my wife. I loved her, but I also loved ships. She needed to stay in Okinawa, so I worked the freighters and returned when I could. I need to go back soon."

"How did you end up back here?" I asked.

"I'm the last of my family and inherited the building I live in now. I just sold it; the deal will be done at the end of August. I'm a Seaman, and I need to go out." We talked long into the night. I watched the campfire's embers glow as I fell asleep.

The next morning we sailed back down the bay. The area looked familiar, but I couldn't place it. A moment later the canal reappeared.

The sight of my near doom! I need to get my courage up!

"The canal looks safe with its flat water and grass-covered banks. Are we even allowed to sail up it, or is it restricted to power boats only?" I asked.

"Well, we didn't bring the motor with us, so I guess it's by sail only," Tully said.

He swung wide, caught the wind and headed straight into the canal. Spray blew off the bow. As we began the track up the canal I could see boaters shaking their heads in disbelief. Powerboats sped by and gawked at us.

"I wonder if they think we've lost our minds," I said.

"We *have* lost our minds; only a fool would try to sail the fourteen miles of the canal," Tully said smiling.

"Will they arrest us if we catch us here?" I asked.

"I'm not sure we're doing anything illegal," Tully said. "Just foolish. The danger isn't the police; it's the chance that a freighter might suddenly appear. A ship like that would crush us like a bug before churning us up in its giant props."

"Oh, I feel better now," I said.

Tully waved at everyone as if he didn't have a care in the world.

"We're making good headway up the canal," he said. "I hope we can continue these long gradual tacks the whole way. The tide's been working in our favor also."

"Tully, look at this place; it's beautiful!" Lush, green farm fields lay on each side. Large oak and maple trees grew along the banks, and in some places they were already beginning to change color. "I can't believe the luck we had. We haven't seen any Marine police boats, no Coast Guard boats, and no one's bothered us the whole way," I said. "How far have we gone?"

"I think about halfway."

A gentle, constant wind blew us west toward the Chesapeake Bay.

"Should we stop for lunch?" I asked.

"No, let's try to clear the canal and then worry about lunch," Tully said. The sun shone bright, and the air was warm. Tully made another long tack using the whole width of the canal. As we turned back toward open water the current violently changed from west to east, spinning us around.

"What the hell!" I grabbed the gunwale to keep from going overboard. Tully tried to straighten out the boat and looked puzzled. The boat righted itself and slowly began making its way toward open water.

"Oh no!" Tully cried. I turned to see a huge ship coming up behind us. Its massive props changing the current from west to east.

It's my nightmare from Port Penn all over again. A ship about to grind us into splinters.

"We're not going to make it on this tack; we've got to spin around,"

Tully screamed.

The ship blasted its horn, and I could see men running on deck. It rose higher and higher above us as it came on.

"It's gonna' hit us broadside!" I said.

"Pray for a miracle, son!" Tully screamed. A small breeze filled our sails for a moment, but it still looked hopeless.

At the last moment a swell arose in the water, the forward wake of the ship, just before it would have hit. The little sailboat rode it like a surfer on a wave. Now we were about to crash into the rocks on the shoreline. Just as we would have hit, Tully thrust the tiller around. We spun in a tight circle. Up ahead lay a cove and we sailed into it. The ship sped on. Sailors onboard shook their heads.

We pulled the sail down and hoisted the boat up over the rocks onto a grass-covered bank. The cove contained a marina and a small restaurant. I felt exhausted and collapsed on the grass. Tully and I didn't say a word to each other. The near collision had been way too close.

It seemed an eternity before I got up. When I did I saw Marine police boats speeding up and down the canal. A small Coast Guard boat went by.

"Tully," I called, "come and see this."

"They're looking for us, but I don't think they'll find us here," he said. "Let's get something to eat at that restaurant, son." I hadn't eaten all day and ordered a huge meal of chicken and crab.

"It's dark now. Let's just camp on the grass bank," Tully said. "We don't need a fire."

"Tully, the incident with the tanker was way too close, and it brought back the memories of the giant barges off Port Penn. I don't think I'll get much sleep tonight."

"Yeah, it was close, but that's not the thing," he said. "We're here on the vacation of our lives. No one can tell us what to do or where to go. We can sail off tomorrow and head wherever we want; north, south, west, it doesn't matter. Right now we're probably the two luckiest guys in the world. That's what really matters."

"I guess you're right. I lived rent-free all summer at a nice beach house. Instead of partying the entire summer away, I spent most of my time working at one venture or another. We traded bait, fish, tackle and whatever else. To cap off the whole summer we traveled over a hundred miles on a car-top sailboat. Now we're in a rocky cove on the eastern shore of Maryland trying to avoid being caught by the cops, the Marine police and the Coast Guard. Life does have its moments of lunacy, but it's been fun. You know, I can't remember the last time I had a beer."

"The point is that everything changes quickly. The guys in your house that are drunk every night, do they really enjoy themselves? Alcohol is addicting. It sneaks up on you. What they don't realize is that one morning they'll wake up and realize they're drunks."

"I guess that's what happened to my uncles and my aunts. Almost every time we'd get together they'd be smashed. My boss at the gas station tried to quit drinking quite a few times but couldn't."

"That's what I mean. You can spend your life enjoying yourself or in misery. As far as enjoying yourself, this is as good as it gets." Tully settled into his sleeping bag.

"I can't complain about the summer. I enjoyed the beach. Godiva and Sadie visited. The really great find of the summer is the grizzled old geezer I met." I heard Tully snoring. I turned in also and fell asleep almost immediately.

Somewhere around three in the morning Tully shook me awake.

"We need to clear this canal before dawn so we're not spotted." We pushed the sailboat back into the water, got the sail up, and a light breeze quickly filled it. Lights shown on the water, and we found our way west toward the Chesapeake Bay. At about 5 AM all the lights seemed to go out at once.

"It's not dawn yet, and I can't see a thing," I said.

"The current just changed again," Tully said. "You don't think another ship's coming, do you?"

"I think we sailed into a fog bank because I can't see much at all," I said. "It's strange because the wind's still blowing west, so maybe the fog is floating with us."

"Let's just listen, and maybe we can hear if a ship's coming," Tully said. "I'm going to land at the first shore I can see." We could hear motors, tinkling sounds from masts and the far off sounds of cars driving on roads. We couldn't see anything.

"Look, an island!" Tully hollered. He steered straight for it. We pulled the sailboat onto the bank and got off on dry land.

"Just in time, son!" Tully said. The faint form of a freighter passed us in the fog. A moment later it blew its horn, nearly scaring me to death.

"Do you have any idea where we are?" I asked.

"No, but we're on dry land, so how bad can it be?" The fog slowly lifted as the dawn came.

"Son, we're not in the canal any longer; we're on the Elk River. We made it to the bay. We're not on an island either but on a wooded riverbank."

"Are you sure?"

"The Chesapeake Bay is a whole series of rivers, which really aren't rivers at all but arms of the bay that go up different small creek beds. If we'd follow this river up to its source, we'll find a small rocky creek that we could cross without getting our feet wet. No, we made it to the bay."

We sailed south down the river and stopped near Turkey Point. We set up camp early since we hadn't gotten much sleep the night before.

"I checked the food supply," I said. "We're getting low, but we still have a canned ham and some potatoes."

"I'll make a campfire. We'll have them for a late lunch," Tully said. We ate and rested for part of the afternoon.

"We need to find a town and get some supplies," Tully said. "We'll have to climb this hill and find a road."

"Turkey Point's a long finger of land that sticks out into the bay," I said. "Elk River lays on one side and the Northeast on the other."

"Then let's go son." The climb from the beach to the top was steep and rugged. As we crested the hill I noticed the road ahead.

"Look, son!"

I turned to see three deer standing in a grassy area.

"They're beautiful!" I said. One of the deer snorted, and they all ran off. "Well, maybe someone will give us a ride into town." We flagged down a guy in a pickup truck.

"Any place up ahead where we can get some groceries?" Tully asked.

"Yeah, there's a small place outside of Northeast," the guy said. "It should still be open." He gave us a ride into the town. We bought groceries as well as some fresh fruit.

"Tully, they have fried chicken and rolls also; let's get a box!" We ate outside on a picnic table.

After dinner we started walking and hitchhiking back toward our camp. No one picked us up. We went to cross a bridge, and I felt the hair on my arm stand on end. Tully stopped walking and looked perplexed.

"Come on, son," he said. "A bad storm's coming."

"We should just keep walking," I said.

"No, we need to get under the bridge." I followed him down.

The storm hit with great ferocity. The wind howled. Rain came down in buckets, and lightning lit up the sky. Hail tore leaves from trees. It gathered in piles along the road. We huddled underneath the bridge to keep dry. The sky lit up with bright bluish-white lightning, which spread in giant strings. The thunder boomed so loudly that the earth seemed to shake. The storm continued on well into the night, and it put on a good show.

"Where will we stay the night?" I asked.

"Right here. Where the road joins the bridge there's a soft dry bench." We found some dry branches under the bridge and made a small fire.

"I guess the storm drove the bugs away because they're not out," I said. I tried lying down and found the sand comfortable. The storm seemed to be getting worse, but I was too tired to care. I fell asleep quickly.

The next morning broke bright and sunny.

"It looks like we got a nice day," I said. We hitched a ride with two guys who were going out for rockfish.

"You guys wanna stop and get something on the way?" the guy asked.

"We'd like that," Tully said. "We have no idea what our camp will look like after that storm." Tully and I climbed into the truck's bed, and the guy took off. A few miles later he pulled into a small gas station. I bought doughnuts and coffee for everyone.

"We got caught under that bridge by the storm last night," Tully explained to the guys. "We're camped on the shoreline down the road a ways."

After breakfast we drove toward Turkey Point.

"I think this is our place," Tully said. He tapped on the rear window. The driver pulled over and let us out.

"Thanks for the ride," Tully called.

"Good luck," the guy called back.

We walked downhill to where our camp should have been but couldn't find it. I walked down the beach but found nothing.

"Son, it was here!!" Tully said pointing. The tent stakes stood in the sand, but everything else was gone. The sailboat, tent, sleeping bags and gear could not be found.

"Did someone steal our stuff?" I asked.

"No, I think the storm and tides washed everything away." I searched and found our mess kit out in the water.

"At least we have the groceries we bought," I said.

"Well, let's get some lunch going, and we'll try and figure this out," Tully said. He found some squaw wood to start a fire. I used my jack knife to open a can of stew.

"You know, it's not as bad as it seems," I said. "The road's right above us. We could be home in a few hours."

Tully sat scratching in the sand with a stick. "Way the current ran, our boat probably drifted with the tide north toward the flats. Between the storm and the tides, it would be on the other side of the peninsula somewhere on the Northeast River."

"The boat would be wrecked, wouldn't it?"

"Could be, but you never know."

"And our gear?"

"The tent would be a mess, but the rest should still be sealed in the hull. It would be wet but usable."

"If we're going to climb that hill again, let's go now before it gets any hotter," I said.

"Sooner the better."

We walked up the hill huffing and puffing. We crested it and stood catching our breath.

"Well, at least it's all downhill from here," I said. "But the woods are too thick to see to the bottom." We started walking down. We hiked over a small rise and saw the Northeast River below. A rocky beach appeared to our left and a swimming beach to our right. Tully stopped to ponder the situation.

"The boat should be here," he said.

"There's a bunch of boats anchored near the swimming beach. Maybe they've seen it." The walk to the boats exhausted us. A tree lay washed up on the beach. We sat down on it to catch our breath.

"There's our boat, son!" Tully pointed out into the river. About a quarter mile away I could see the white hull of a boat, partially sunk in the water.

"This river is shallow," Tully said. "We can walk all the way out." I found the walking difficult because sharp rocks covered the first fifty yards or so out. After that, the bottom was sand. Tully and I waded out to the boat.

"How do we right it?" I asked.

"I think if we put our weight on the gunwale, it will come around." We tried, and the boat turned upright.

"Well, the mast is still attached," Tully said, "and the sail's still tied down."

"The centerboard is missing."

"Let's pull it closer to the beach," Tully said. We pulled the boat onto the sand, and he opened the bow compartment.

"Everything's wet but still here." We bailed the water out of the bow.

"Let's see if she'll still sail," Tully said.

"Without the centerboard? Are you sure? It looks pretty beat up?"

"How else will we know?"

We pushed the boat out into the river and climbed aboard. The boat seemed to float okay, even without the centerboard. We looked at the soaking-wet sail.

"The sail's okay, but some of the hardware and lines are gone," Tully said. "I'll jury rig it until we can get some new ones." Tully worked with some of the ropes and gear. He lifted the sail and tied it off. A good breeze blew and the boat started gliding across the water. He ran the boat almost to the opposite shore and then tacked back toward Turkey Point.

"It's beat up but it'll sail until we can make the repairs," he said. As we rounded Turkey Point I noticed what looked like a big blue trash bag rolling in the water.

"What's that?" I asked.

"It's our tent!" Tully said. As we pulled alongside I grabbed it. We struggled to pull it onboard. We found our centerboard, all beat up, tangled in the tent. We decided to sail back to our original campsite on the Elk River.

"Let's try and sort out the mess," Tully said. "I'll make a clothesline of sorts that we can hang everything on." We removed all the wet and filthy items from the boat. We squeezed what water we could from our sleeping bags and hung them up.

"It could be worse, but almost everything's here," Tully said. "Yesterday morning we passed a big marina, didn't we?"

"Yeah, lots of sailboats and power cruisers, why?"

"We need to sail there. Can't spend the night here." We did our best to put everything back in the bow. We sailed north up the river and arrived at the marina in the late afternoon.

"If we don't make a big scene, the marina operators will just assume we're members and not hassle us," Tully said. We landed on a small beach near a store.

"What's the big building?" I asked.

"A clubhouse to accommodate sloop and cabin cruiser patrons. Sometimes they just like a real bed instead of their boat's bunks. Let's go take a look." The clubhouse had showers, vending machines, pool tables and a lounge area. A woman stood behind a counter.

"Do you need anything?" she asked.

Tully nudged me. "Look, washers and dryers!"

"Thank God!" I said.

"We need to wash some things; we've been sailing quite a bit," Tully told the woman.

"Help yourself," she replied. "You'll be staying for the party, won't you?"

"The party?" I asked.

"Yes, we've invited the club from Still Pond over," she said.

"Of course we'll stay," Tully replied. We dragged everything in and loaded the giant washers.

"You're not really supposed to machine wash sleeping bags, but ours are the cheap kind," Tully said. "After what they've been through, it really doesn't matter. We may as well wash the tent also."

We found a hose and washed most of the muck out of our nylon tent. We threw it in with the rest. We opened up the bow of our boat, got everything out and used the hose to wash everything down. We oiled our fishing reels and checked our rods. Everything seemed undamaged.

"I found someone who's driving into town," Tully said. "He says there's a Kmart there. We could spend a hundred dollars purchasing the hardware we needed at a boat shop or less than ten dollars there."

We drove into town, crossing over the canal again. The thought of sailing it put chills down my spine. Tully didn't say anything, but I knew he felt the same because he kept his eyes shut until we passed.

"I'm heading back in an hour if you need a ride," the guy said.

"We'll be ready," Tully said.

We went in and began shopping.

"Where do we begin?" I asked.

"Auto parts. Most of what we need they'll have for tying down luggage and such." We went over, and he picked up rope, tie-downs and other gear. We found a paddle in sporting goods. We also stopped by the hardware section, and Tully bought some adjustable gadgets. We paid for our things and sat out front awaiting our ride.

The Beachcomber

When we arrived back at the marina, a full-fledged party was underway. Dinghies ran people back and forth from sloops anchored in the river.

"We picked the right night to be here," Tully said. "No one knows who's a guest or who the members are. Let's get some food." I noticed a long table filled with fried chicken, potato salad, snacks and drinks. A woman began filling plates for us as we walked up. We pigged out since we hadn't eaten dinner.

Afterwards we sat talking with the other boaters.

"Where ya from?" one asked.

"Wildwood," Tully replied. "We sailed the whole way."

"Up the bay?" he asked.

"No, through the canal," Tully admitted.

"You're braver than me," he said. I nodded in agreement.

After eating, we made the repairs needed on our boat.

"The only thing we can't fix is the centerboard," I said. "It's beaten up but usable."

"We'll think of something," Tully said. "Let's check our wash." Everything had dried and, for the first time in a while, was clean.

"The sleeping bags seem all right even after the seawater dunking and mud. The tent's cleaner than when we left."

We loaded everything back onto our boat. Tully noticed lights shining in one of the garages.

"Let me go look," he said. He went to investigate and later returned. "It's actually a shop, a shop with tools! I think I can fix the centerboard."

"I'll help you," I said.

"It'll be better if you head to the lounge."

"Okay." I walked over and entered it.

"Let me guess, you're stuck here, too!" a girl said. "I'm Cheryl. My parents are playing cards somewhere. Do you play pool?"

"I can't think of a better way to pass the time."

Cheryl and I played pool for almost two hours. Finally she left to go find her parents. I sat watching TV.

Somewhere around one in the morning Tully walked in. He held a new centerboard in his hand.

"I found a guy working with wood," he said. "He said to help myself from the pile. I cut this one out and spread resin on it."

"It looks better than the original."

"It did turn out nice. Well, it's late. Let's turn in."

"Where will we stay tonight?"

Tully walked to a door and opened it. It held rollaway beds. "Let's camp here by the TV."

The next morning I felt much better, even jovial.

"We survived the storm, lost our boat, gear and camping equipment, but it all came back to us," I said.

161

"God's been good to us. I saw they have free doughnuts in the marina. Let's get some."

A guy pulled up towing a cabin cruiser. Tully held the door for the guy, and we went in for the doughnuts. A dairy truck sat outside, and man in a white suit loaded their freezer with ice cream.

"Does anyone know how to launch a boat?" the guy asked. No one volunteered.

"I do," the ice cream man said.

"I just bought a boat, but I've never launched one," the guy said.

"I've launched lots of 'em," the ice cream man replied. "Back your boat down the ramp, and I'll meet you at the dock." Tully and I followed them outside. The guy backed his boat down the ramp as instructed. The ice cream man, dressed in a snow-white uniform, guided him.

"Tie a rope to the back cleat," he stated, "then hand me the rope." The guy did as instructed. The ice cream guy wrapped the rope around his hand.

"Now what?" the guy asked.

"Release the lever on your winch," he instructed.

"What?" Tully said aloud. The guy released the lever, but the boat sat there.

"Rock your boat a little," the ice cream man instructed.

"No, don't!" Tully said, but he was too late. The guy jolted it. The boat shot out into the water. The ice cream guy saw the boat go and realized that the rope was wound around his hand. The boat yanked him off the dock in a perfect swan dive. The ice cream man climbed out of the water cursing, his white uniform now a chocolate color. Tully and I laughed so hard that I had trouble breathing.

"Hey, my boat!" the guy screamed, watching it drift away.

"Go get his boat, son," Tully finally said. I managed to swim over and climb aboard. I steered the boat toward shore and waited for the owner to walk down.

"Thanks!" the guy said.

"Wouldn't have missed that for the world."

I showered and found some clean clothes. Tully finally calmed down.

"We need to get going," he said.

We sailed down the river until it opened into the bay.

"Seeing that ice cream guy flying off the dock was something I'll never forget," I said.

"Nor I."

"What do we do tonight?"

"If we set up camp early, we might be able to try and catch some giant rockfish."

"At least our sleeping bags will be clean and dry." We set up camp for the night near Tolchester. We decided to put together a seafood feast from what we could find around the area.

Tully discovered a clam bar not far from where we were camped. He gathered about four dozen. I decided to hand line for crabs.

"Let's try and see if we can catch some rockfish on the clams," Tully said. We didn't catch any rockfish but did catch some nice pan fish for dinner.

Tully added a certain kind of seaweed to the clams, crabs and fish. He steamed them over our fire.

"Tully, these are unreal!" I said, eating them later.

"Better than in the finest restaurant."

"The water's warm enough. I'm going swimming." I swam as Tully snoozed.

The next day we sailed into Rock Hall before turning west and sailing into Baltimore.

"It's strange being in the harbor with so many large ships," I said.

"Yeah, it's kinda overwhelming." Tully found a dock owner who allowed him to tie up. We left the boat with all our gear stored in the bow.

"Baltimore's not the kind of town you want to camp out in," Tully said. "Why don't we rent a room for a day or so? I've got business to do here."

We found a cheap room near the water. Tully left that morning. I watched a couple of movies.

Late that afternoon I went to see the restoration of Baltimore's Inner Harbor. New shops lined the port. Ships lay in the harbor, and you could board them. Some of the sections were pretty rough, so you had to watch where you went. I ate dinner at a Chinese place.

"Are you visiting the town?" a girl asked.

"Yeah, came in on a tiny sailboat."

"Would you like to see Edgar Allen Poe's grave?" she asked.

"Yeah, I would."

"Good 'cause I wouldn't want to go down alone. By the way, I'm Steph."

"Ethan." We walked a few blocks to an old church with an iron gate.

"This is it!" she said, staring at a map.

"Looks creepy!"

"Yeah ...."

We walked in, and I saw a tomb to our right. Roses, coins and booze bottles lay on it. Another girl stood to the side.

"I didn't expect this!" Steph said. "These guys are buried above ground like they do in New Orleans's."

"It's a creepy place, and the sun's beginning to set," I said.

"Well, Poe was a creepy guy," the other girl blurted out. "This wasn't his first grave."

"What do you mean it wasn't his first grave?" Steph said.

"I mean they moved his body here. I can show you his first grave," the girl said.

"Okay," Steph said. She led us behind the church where things seemed even creepier. She pointed at a tombstone.

"That's where he was originally buried."

"I'm ready to go," Steph said. "I've had enough." We walked up the street, avoiding vagrants as we went. We ended up at her hotel, an old brownstone building.

"Look, I'm kinda freaked out right now," she said. "You want to catch a movie or something? Something not scary?" We found a theater showing a movie called 'The Front Page.'

"At least it won't be scary," she said. We both enjoyed the movie. I walked her back to her hotel around midnight.

The next day I began contemplating the whole summer. It began when I spotted myself in the mirror. I didn't recognize myself. My skin had gone from pale to an orange-brown. I used to be a strawberry blond, but now the sun had bleached my hair almost white. I somehow seemed taller.

The strangeness of this summer cannot be described. How did I end up here? The summer is almost over, and I'm sitting in a room in Baltimore? I sailed all over New Jersey, Delaware and Maryland with a guy fifty years older than me? We made the journey in a car-top sailboat? If all that isn't weird enough, can I add that I left a house full of cute girls to be out on the water with Tully?

Speaking of Tully, where is he? He said he had business but didn't explain. These old guys are like that, though. I figured he would be back by now. If he doesn't show up by tonight I'll probably abandon the sailboat and hitchhike back to Wildwood.

I walked down to the docks to check the boat. I found it tethered exactly as we had left it. I felt some kind of bond with it. We caught fish for Sashimi and sailed all over creation in it. Something remarkable since we got it for free.

I walked over to the Inner Harbor. Everything seemed perfect. The sun shone off the water. People milled about. Children played.

When I returned to the room I found Tully sound asleep on one of the beds. I let him sleep and watched TV. Later I heard him stir.

"We ought to get some dinner, son," he said. We found a seafood place. I ordered a surf and turf, and Tully ordered prime rib. We hadn't eaten this fancy all summer, and it was quite a treat.

"I'm heading for Okinawa," Tully said. "I'm going to see my wife."

"You gonna fly out?" I asked.

"No, I don't do that. I'm a Seaman. I signed onto a freighter. In a few weeks I'll be home."

"When do you leave?"

"September. It'll work well because you need get back to school also."

"Well, I wish you luck," I said.

"I decided something else also," he stated. "The sailing, these little towns...."

"Yes."

"I'm buying a sloop when I get to Okinawa; I want to spend the rest of my years sailing around with my wife." I sat dumbfounded, trying to take it all in.

"I can see how you'd like that."

"Son, what are you going to do? The summer's almost over."

"I'd originally enrolled at Temple University for the fall but ...."

"But what?"

"I don't know. It just kinda fell to the wayside. The beach somehow changed that."

"The house you're living in, the people you know, they're really an illusion. In a week or two they'll be gone. All this will end like a puff of smoke, and you need to be ready for it. College seems right. What are you going for?"

"Business. But that doesn't seem right either. It seems ... I don't know, wrong."

"Wrong?"

"Like a nasty occupation."

"Really? What have we been doing all summer? I thought we've been running one business after another? Maybe you need to learn business and then get into the right one? One you'd really enjoy?"

"I guess you're right."

"Well, it's late. Let's get back. We sail south tomorrow."

The next day we sailed out of the harbor.

"This is where the National Anthem was written," Tully said. "A man named Key was held by the British. He saw the huge flag still flying at Fort McHenry."

The wind blew strong and constant all day. We sailed south until we approached a wildlife refuge. A bridge stood in the bay.

"They say you can catch giant rockfish under that bridge," Tully said. "You catch 'em on eels here. We can catch the eels near the creek's mouth, maybe even sell a few."

We tried different spots before catching about three dozen eels. We sailed out into the bay. A flotilla of boats sat under the bridge.

We rigged our lines with the eels and began drifting with the tide. Most of the boats were anchored. Using our paddle and our rudder we swerved through all the others. As I paddled around a large cabin cruiser my rod bent in half.

"I got one!" I screamed. The fish took out my drag and pulled our boat around in circles. I finally began to gain some line on the fish. Tully got the net.

"You don't have a rockfish; you've got a giant ray," Tully said. "Rather than deal with it, I'll just shake it off." He grabbed a pair of pliers and pulled the hook free.

About the time Tully freed my ray his rod started humming. Tully fought the fish, and it pulled our boat all around the bay again. I got the net and waited in front. An enormous rockfish surfaced next to our boat.

"Look at the size of it!" Tully stated.

"I'll get it," I said.

"No, it's a cow, and it will have lots of babies. Let me get it." A moment later the fish was free.

Later that evening I caught a bluefish, which we saved for dinner. We sold the rest of our eels to the fishermen around us.

"Let's call it a night," Tully said. "Tomorrow we sail into Annapolis, the end of our sailing trip."

The next morning we broke camp and sailed south. We reached Annapolis that afternoon.

"Keep your eye open for a marina or dealer who'd want the boat," Tully said.

We went to three different marinas before we could find anyone interested in our sailboat. The operator wanted to buy our boat and rent it out to his customers. He needed a title to the boat, which we didn't have. We decided to sail on to the next dealer.

I paddled the boat out of the marina. Tully spotted a guy in a pickup truck waving at us. I paddled over to meet him.

"Are you guys trying to sell that boat?"

"Yes, we are," replied Tully.

"I own a cottage, and I'm looking for something we can launch from shore. I don't have much money, but I could offer you three hundred."

"We don't have a title," Tully said.

"Why would I care?"

"We only want a hundred dollars," Tully replied. "Come on. I'll show you how it sails." The guy climbed aboard, and Tully sailed out into open water.

"I love this boat. It's a lot faster than I would've dreamed!" the guy said. "Could we sail it right to my cottage?" Tully gave up the rudder, and the guy took over. Half an hour later we beached the boat at his place.

"What about your truck?" Tully asked.

"My wife will drive me over. I'll bring the money back also." We unloaded our backpacks and gear. We took our fishing rods apart and tied them onto our packs. We left the rest.

"I'm gonna miss that boat!" Tully said.

"Yeah, but look!" Two girls walked up and stared at the boat.

"My dad bought a boat?" one asked.

"I can't wait to get out on the water," the other said. After a short wait the man returned with his pick-up truck. He paid Tully and gave us a ride to a McDonald's.

"This might be the first hamburger I've eaten this summer," I noted to Tully.

"Yeah, but …."

"But what?"

"I'm just not ready to head home yet."

"I'm not ready, either. Where would we want to go?" I asked. "Washington and Richmond are close, but I really don't want to go to them."

"I'd really like to visit Norfolk, Virginia, but that's too far," Tully said.

"No, it's not too far because I'd like to hit the Outer Banks, and Norfolk's on the way." A huge grin spread across Tully's face.

"The Outer Banks … I've always wanted to go but never had a way. You really wouldn't mind?" he asked.

"We got our camping gear, money, time …."

The Outer Banks of North Carolina is a long series of barrier islands, which stretch out from the coast into the Atlantic Ocean. Some of the islands are tourist areas; others are not. Some are not even inhabited.

The history of the islands includes Native Americans, lost colonies, German U-boats, lots of shipwrecks and daring sailors. It's where the Wright brothers flew the first airplane. It's a special place on earth.

A few hours later we rode in an eighteen-wheeler toward Williamsburg, Virginia. The trucker left us alongside the road.

"Where will we camp?" I asked.

"Lots of woods around; I don't know who owns it, but we'll be all right. We don't need a fire."

"I'll set up the tent." Tully took a walk as I made camp. He returned just as I spread out my sleeping bag.

"Steakhouse right up the road," he said.

"Sounds great!" We went, ate and then returned to our camp.

The next morning we explored the town. Colonial Williamsburg is restored as it was during the late 1700s. It contains churches, shops, taverns, stores, houses and barns. The workers dress in colonial garb and use primitive tools and methods.

"Look at the wagon!" I said to Tully. "Cows are pulling it."

"Oxen," Tully said. Later we talked with a man dressed as a revolutionary soldier.

"Well, this was nice, but we need to get going," Tully said. "We need to get to Norfolk before dark."

We arrived in Norfolk at dusk and rented a motel room.

"Do you mind if I go into the Naval Base alone tomorrow?" Tully asked. "I served here during the war, and … some memories are good, some bad."

"Will they just let you in?" I asked.

"Tomorrow's Sunday, and that means the base should be open to visitors."

"I'll just stay at the room and watch some TV," I said.

He must have bad memories of seamen who never returned from the war. Hopefully the visit will bring closure for him.

The next morning Tully seemed quiet and solemn. I could tell a lot was going on in his head.

"Son, I changed my mind. I don't want to go through those gates alone. Will you come with me?"

"Sure, I'd like that."

"Let's get some breakfast first." We crossed the road and ate alongside sailors on their way into the base.

"Could you give us a ride onto the base?" Tully asked.

"Sure. You going to visit one of the ships?"

"You mean they'd let us on?" Tully asked.

"Yeah, one of the destroyers has an open house today. I'll drop you off at it." We climbed into his car. He drove past a series of enormous ships. He stopped by the smallest one.

"This one's open today," he explained. Tully seemed dumbfounded.

"I served aboard a ship very similar to this," Tully said. "Thanks for the ride."

"No problem."

"Let's go aboard, son." We walked up, and an officer welcomed us.

"You can roam the ship at will," he said.

As we walked the ship, Tully seemed to be in another world. He would stop and gaze at the ship and the sailors onboard. It was clear he was recounting scenes of war.

"What do you see?" I asked. Tully said nothing. "Tully?"

"Kamikaze raids and slain friends. Each section of the ship brings back memories of shooting, torpedo bombers, submarine attacks and … fires. I dreaded fires the most."

We spent a good part of the day onboard the ship and touring the base. Tully showed me where he had lived and the areas of the base where he had worked.

We returned to our room late in the day. Tully still looked stunned.

"Tully, you okay?" I asked.

For several moments he said nothing and then finally spoke. "The sailors we saw today looked exactly like my friends. I could put names to half of them. I need some time alone."

"I'll go out and get some dinner; I'll bring you something back." I took my time with dinner. I brought back a doggie bag for Tully. I found him asleep when I returned.

The next morning Tully shook me awake early.

"Time to go, son. We need to clear out of here." We hitched a ride with a sailor who was going on leave. He gave us a ride into North Carolina. Next two surf fishermen picked us up. We rode with them all the way into Buxton, a part of the National Seashore.

"Where will we camp?" I asked.

"We'll set up camp in the last line of dunes before the beach. We want to be far enough from the road so we don't get caught." We ate a canned ham for dinner that night. I fell asleep listening to the pounding of the surf.

The next morning I put my rod together, found some sand crabs, and went fishing. Tully joined me a little later.

"Any luck?" he asked.

"Nothing yet."

"Well, let me try." He cast out and almost immediately hooked something.

"Nice croaker," I said. We caught a number of whiting also and fried them for breakfast.

"We need to pack our things and hitch a ride to Ocracoke Island. That's as far south as I want to go."

A middle-aged couple picked us up that morning.

"I hope the ferry isn't backed up," the woman said. We drove onto the car deck just before it left.

"This sound we're crossing is about as shallow as anything I've ever seen," Tully said. "I can see the bottom, and it's as flat and calm as a millpond." We drove with the couple to the end of Ocracoke Island. They went to visit the shops.

"Let's look around," Tully said. I found a map of the area.

"Blackbeard the pirate met his fate here," I said. "Let's go look." We walked down and read the accounts of his last battle.

"There's a cemetery close to here," Tully said. "It's for the British sailors who died serving during World War Two. Let's go see it." We walked over.

"The British flag flying was sent by the Queen herself," I said. "These men died trying to stop German U-boats from destroying Allied shipping." Tully seemed moved. Later we spent a lot of time visiting the shops and seeing the sights.

"Do we want to camp here tonight?" I asked Tully.

"No, bugs will drive us nuts here. Let's head back to Buxton." We hitched a ride back and camped for the night at the same spot as before.

The next morning we had a surprise.

"You need to come out!" someone called. I emerged from the tent; a Park Ranger had found us.

"I know the campgrounds are full, but you must pack up and go," he said.

"Any that aren't full?" Tully asked.

"Try Oregon Inlet," he said.

We hitched a ride north and found the campground. Just as we set up camp Tully spied a line of fishing boats coming in from the ocean.

"Let's go see what they caught," he said.

We watched crews unloading marlin, tuna, wahoo and mahi-mahi as well as other fish.

"I always wanted to go out for the big ones, but the cost was outrageous," I said.

"From here the Gulf stream isn't too far," Tully said. "Might be worthwhile." The boat's captain walked over to us.

"We'd like to go out, but we ain't got that kind of money," Tully said.

"You may not need much," the captain said. "Stop at the office. Sometimes groups of guys get together and make up a party. It could be a lot less than you think." We followed the captain into the office and met four guys from Richmond. A charter would cost us eighty dollars each.

"We'll never get a chance like this again. Let's go," Tully said. "Ship sails at dawn tomorrow."

We arrived back at our camp before nightfall and surf fished the beach. We lobbed our bait out about twenty yards from shore and waited. We caught flounder, pompano and lots of small trout. We caught more than we could use and gave away quite a few.

The next morning we arrived at the boat very early. The crew arrived and began stocking the boat.

"Do you need any help?" Tully asked.

"No," the deckhand said. Tully helped him drag the gear aboard anyway.

The captain arrived and shook hands with Tully.

"Captain Bowers," he stated.

"Tully."

"Well, Tully, come on up. I'll show you and your friend the helm." We climbed a ladder to the cabin, and he started the boat's engine. Tully stared at the equipment. One piece fascinated him.

"Fish finder," the captain said. "Uses sonar. Locates schools of fish."

"We used them to find submarines," Tully said. "But we just got pings and blips."

"You were in the Navy?" the captain asked.

"Destroyer ... Pacific," Tully replied.

"My father said it was hell," the captain replied.

"Yes, sir."

The captain showed us all around. The other fishermen arrived. The captain blew his horn, and we sailed off.

"How far out do we go?" I asked a deckhand.

"We start trolling about twelve miles out," he replied. Offshore, the water became a deep blue. The deckhand tied flashing spoons onto lines and put them out.

"Fish on!" Tully cried as one of the reels began screaming. A moment later another line bent over. The guys from Richmond grabbed these lines and reeled as hard as they could. Tully stared into the water as they fought the fish.

"Bonito!" Tully hollered, and the deckhand gaffed the first fish. The second was a bonito also.

"Well, it's our turn now," Tully said. The captain trolled along some weed lines. All four lines screamed at once. Tully, I, and two other guys all fought fish at the same time.

"Mahi-mahi," Tully said. Somehow we got all four fish aboard without tangling the lines.

Early in the afternoon the captain located a school of tuna, and we all caught several. A crewman climbed a ladder and looked around. He spotted several marlin to the east. The captain headed toward them.

"Tully, you're up," the captain stated. The crewman teased the fish, finally grabbing the rod and jerking it to set the hook. He handed the rod to Tully. He fought the fish long and hard until it finally appeared behind the boat. I could see the fish beautifully lit up in blue, silver and turquoise.

"Can we release the fish?" Tully asked.

"Yes, we'll tag and release him," the captain said.

We arrived back at dock in the late afternoon.

"If we sell our fish, it'll help replenish our wallets," Tully said. "We can keep a small mahi-mahi for dinner."

We sold the other fish and broiled the mahi-mahi over our campfire.

The next morning we hitchhiked north to Kitty Hawk.

"Tully, I stayed here as a child. I remember a cheap motel near here. It's actually two motels. One is nice and one rundown, but they have a pool."

"Sounds good." We checked in to stay overnight. We swam in the ocean and later in the pool. As night came, we walked down to an ocean pier.

"The ocean's calm and beautiful," Tully said. "Look at the sun setting over the sound."

Two mechanics showed up that evening to fish for sharks. They brought heavy specialized fishing rigs with huge reels.

"How do you cast out with those?" Tully asked.

"We don't; we float our baits out," one guy said. We watched as the guys blew up trash bags. These acted as floats and allowed the wind to carry their bait several hundred yards out to an area they called the "honey hole." When the bait reached the spot, they ran backwards deflating the trash bags and allowing the bait to sink to the bottom.

Tully and I caught a few Spanish mackerel that evening. We were ready to walk back to our room when we heard a lot of commotion at the end of the pier.

"One of the mechanics hooked a shark," Tully said.

We watched as the guy fought the big shark for almost an hour. Finally it could be seen in the lights.

"Tiger shark," Tully proclaimed.

"I'm going to try and beach it," the guy explained. A moment later the shark swerved, brushed the pier and snapped the line. A groan went up from the crowd, but the mechanic seemed relieved.

"I don't know what I would have done with something that big," he said.

Tully and I decided to call it a night. I stopped for a moment to watch the moon rising over the water.

"Anywhere else we want to go on this trip?" I asked.

"No. Let's head home tomorrow. I've had enough."

The next morning we stood wearing clean clothes and carrying our backpacks. Our first ride took us across the Chesapeake Bay bridge/tunnel. He left us at a McDonald's near Salisbury, Maryland. Next Tully found a ride in a delivery wagon heading for the ferry to Cape May, New Jersey. We got into Wildwood around one in the morning and walked up to the Cave where I said good-bye to Tully.

"Get some sleep. We have crab pots to check tomorrow," he said. I crept into the Cave, found my corner, and fell asleep.

LIANA

The next morning I sat on the balcony drinking coffee. Beer cans blew around my feet. I realized the guys hadn't made much of an attempt at cleaning the place since I left.

A dark green spruce tree sat in Connie's yard and I noticed a mottled, yellow bird in it. The bird looked this way and that. It flew down and picked at some of the hard waxy berries in her yard.

It's a warbler... I thought they ate bugs only?

Karen joined me on the balcony a moment later.

"We need to talk. I made you some breakfast," she said.

"Thank you," I said. I stumbled over to the table. She handed me a plate of pancakes.

"How was your ...?"

"My trip ... it was really nice."

"Tonight's the last party; tomorrow everyone leaves."

"Well, I'm not ready to head to school yet."

"But you'll be going, right?" she asked. "Look, I don't know how to say this, but I wouldn't want to be the last guy here when the owners come. I mean this place got destroyed this summer, and someone's going to have to pay." A moment later Tina walked in.

"Hey, Ethan, you're back!" she said. "Do you have any idea where your car is?"

"My car? I just assumed it's wherever I left it, but I can't remember right now ... why?"

"Kathy borrowed it a few days ago, and no one's seen it since."

"Great, my car's lost again!"

"Oh, and Godiva dropped in while you were gone," Karen said. "She'll be staying for a day or two next week."

I helped Karen with the dishes, and Tully came by.

"Let's go check on the boat," he said.

"I think my car's lost again," I said.

"We'll be all right."

"I'm still in on this, right?" Karen said. "You have a lot of frozen bait and drinks to get rid of?"

"Of course," Tully assured her. We loaded the bait and soda onto the wagon and walked down to the dock. The boat looked fine. The motor started and ran. All the gear we needed was onboard.

We found our pots overloaded with huge crabs.

"I really didn't expect this many crabs," Tully said. "And the size of 'em!"

Karen attracted a lot of customers to our boat. She sold all the drinks and bait. Several boats stopped and bought crabs.

When we arrived at the dock, Karen took a bushel of crabs to deliver to her customers. The remainder we dragged over to the fish dealers. All in all, it was one of our best days crabbing ever.

I arrived back at the Cave late. Tina stopped me in the kitchen.

"Can you contribute some beer for the party?"

"If there's anything left in the shed, you can have it." Karen walked in and stared for a moment.

"A girl stopped me today and asked if you were back," she said.

"A girl?"

"Yeah, really homely and I don't know ... straight-looking? Said her name was Liana and that you knew her from the library?"

"I do remember a blond girl. Horn-rimmed glasses and no make-up. Talks with a really cute lisp?"

"So you're coming to the final party, right?" Karen asked.

"No, I'm not sitting around here. I'll go to the library tonight."

I walked to the library and found a book. I heard someone tapping on the window. It was the girl, and she came in.

"You're back!" she said.

"Yeah, Tully and I took a long trip and ...."

"Tully? You know Tully?"

"I hung around with him all summer. Where do you know Tully from?"

"Church?"

"And he would know you as ...?"

"Miss Liana? Most people just call me Liana."

"You got something to read?" I asked.

"Yeah, I do." She sat in the cubicle next to me, and we both quietly read until closing.

"You need to walk me home," she said.

That seemed strange, almost like it was expected.

"Why?"

"There are some rough characters that hang around these streets at night." We began walking toward her house.

"Are you heading to school soon?" she asked.

"Tully convinced me to begin school. I'll be at Temple."

"Temple? I'm going to Temple University also," she said. "Maybe we'll see each other at the library."

We walked past the Cave on our way.

"Do you want to come inside?" I asked.

"In there? Are you crazy? Why in God's name would I want to step into there?" As we passed, empty beer cans rolled off the deck. Six or seven intoxicated guys stood on it screaming down at her.

"What a bunch of drunken losers! How can you stand to live with them? You can do better than this! You really can! Come on."

The house where Liana lived was about two blocks from ours.

"You're welcome to come in," she said. "I live with two other girls. I'll room with them at Temple University." We walked into a very neat house and found her roommates quietly reading.

"Laura, Ellen, this is Ethan," Liana explained. "He works with Tully." Laura, the short brunette, stood and shook my hand. Ellen, the taller blond, set her book aside and took off her reading glasses.

"What courses are you taking at Temple?" I asked.

"Education," Laura said.

"Music," Ellen stated.

"Have you been down here all summer?" I asked.

"Yes, we've really enjoyed the beach," Liana said. Artwork seemed to adorn all their walls.

"Do either of you paint?" I asked.

"I paint, Liana cross stitches, and Ellen sings," Laura said.

"Ellen do you sing at church or …?"

"Classical," she explained. "I do opera in English and Italian." We talked until they decided to turn in for the night.

The walk back to the Cave was difficult. I really didn't want to leave Liana.

They have a neat quiet house; everything seems at ease there. Liana seems so … gentle.

That night when I walked into the Cave, I noticed the depravity that had gone on all summer.

It's a pigsty, a broken, destroyed and smashed pigsty. Someone owns this place, and they're going to walk in and have a heart attack. The big burned hole in the deck could be seen from the outside. The ruined kitchen, furniture and carpet greeted you as you came in. All the torn-off interior doors lay in one spot or another.

Why not just torch the place and be done with it.

I pulled my sleeping bag up over my head to drown out the noise of the party. I woke up around four in the morning. I walked out onto the upper deck and sat thinking.

Where had the summer gone? What am I doing here?

The next morning everyone packed up to go home. I hugged Tina good-bye and helped a few of the guys pack their things. By noontime Karen, the last to leave, loaded her things.

"You're staying?" she asked.

"Yes."

"What's up?"

"Remember Liana?"

"That weird girl?"

"I went over her house and it was so … homey. I think I'm going through a transition. I think I never want to do this again."

"Well, I'm going to miss you!" she said.

"I'm going to miss you, too; I think I'm just totally confused." I kissed her good-bye and watched her drive off.

The whole summer came rushing past me as I walked around the Cave alone. I relived every detail of it in my mind. I sat down in a chair and fought back tears.

"Ethan ... Ethan, are you up there?" a voice called. I looked outside and saw Liana.

"Come on up," I called.

"No way!"

I walked down to meet her. "Everyone's left; it's just me here now."

"I'm still not ready to go in. Why don't you come over? I'll make lunch."

We walked over to her house and talked. Later she made a giant tossed salad.

"This okay?" she asked. "I know it's not what you're used to."

"What do you think I've been eating all summer?"

"You've probably been living on pizza and beer."

"I usually eat fruit, soup and fish. I don't remember the last beer I had."

"At that house!" Liana asked. "Emma Henry always described that house as a hellhole."

"You know Emma?"

"She goes to my church."

"Along with Tully?"

"Yes."

"Well, I should get going."

"I'm really glad we got a chance to talk," Liana said. I turned and kissed her good-bye. She froze and stood blushing.

"Liana?" I asked.

"I'm sorry ... that was really embarrassing ...." I headed down the street, bought trash bags and walked into the Cave.

I've got a lot of cleaning up to do. I kicked and pushed the trash into piles. I found a broom and swept everything together. I went into the kitchen and did the same.

"Hi!" I looked up to see Liana watching me. Stunned, I walked toward her. She stepped back.

"You look like you need some help," she said. She grabbed the broom and began sweeping the floor.

"I know you're uncomfortable being here, but just relax," I said.

"I'll make you a deal," Liana said. "I'll help you clean up if you promise to come to church with me."

"Tully's church? Yeah, I'll go. Hun, do you have a boyfriend?"

"Do you think I have a boyfriend?"

"I wouldn't know."

"Actually I never had a boyfriend. Do you have a girlfriend?"

"Godiva's the closest thing I have to a girlfriend."

"Godiva?" Liana listened, flabbergasted, as I told her about Godiva.

"I'd like to meet her sometime," she said.

"She's supposed to stop by any day now."

"Why don't you just call her and ask her to come to church with us?"

"I don't know where she is or how to get in touch with her. If she wants to stop by, she will." Liana and I continued working and filled fifteen trash bags.

"Look, I feel bad about you helping me so much," I said. "I want to take you out to dinner."

"Not until you apologize."

"For the kiss?" I asked.

"You should have asked first."

"What, I should have said something like, 'Liana can I kiss you good-bye?'"

"Yes!"

"Yes, I should have asked, or, yes, it's okay to kiss you?" She blushed, grabbed her purse, and we walked off.

We went to a small restaurant and placed our order.

"Are you okay about the kiss now?" I asked.

"It wasn't how I imagined my first kiss being!" she said.

"How did you imagine … your first kiss? No one's ever kissed you before?"

"I thought my first kiss would be something special. Someone would sweep me off my feet."

"In Wildwood?"

"Anywhere."

"It meant I was leaving."

"The blond girl that lived here, you kissed her good-bye?"

"Sometimes … and in a week she probably won't remember my name."

"Is that how you want things to be?"

"That's how things are."

"If you see me at school in a couple of weeks, will you pretend you don't know me?

"No. I want to visit with you and do things."

"And if I did have a boyfriend?"

"I'd still want to do things with you." Our meal came; she had Italian wedding soup, and I had clam chowder.

"I'll walk you home," I said. We headed toward her house. About halfway she turned and stared.

"You promised!"

Now what did I do wrong! I didn't even brush up against her.

"I didn't try and kiss you!"

"You promised to come to church with me!"

"I thought you meant on Sunday. Let me get changed."

"No, you're fine as you are. It's really casual."

We arrive at church and went in.

"Son, I didn't expect to see you tonight!" I turned to see Tully standing to the side. We talked with him for a few minutes and then walked on. Emma walked over.

"You know Emma," Liana said.

"Do you know Miss Liana?" she asked. "She's such a sweet young girl! Are you her boyfriend?"

Liana blushed so badly I thought she'd pass out.

"I'm helping him clean up that nasty house near yours," Liana said.

"Well, it needs cleaning!" Emma said. Liana walked me into another room.

"Have you ever heard of Elvis? He runs his ministry out of our church." I turned and saw him surrounded by young girls.

"H-e-l-l-o, E-t-h-a-n," he called in his usual stammer. "H-o-w a-r-e y-o-u?"

Everyone knew Liana and talked to her. Afterwards I walked her home and we sat on her porch talking.

"You said Elvis ran a ministry out of your church?" I asked. "His mom said the same thing. What … how?"

"I understand your confusion, and it's not easy to describe. Elvis has his own room at the church; it's small but comfortable. I know it seems weird, but he's one of the best counselors I've ever seen. I think it's his ability to listen and not be judgmental."

"And he counsels … who?"

"Everyone who's screwed up and can't decide what to do! A month ago a guy showed up who was suicidal, lost all his money at the slots. Elvis talked to him, and he's back with his wife. And he's talked more runaway girls into going to shelters than I know of!"

Late that night I headed back to the Cave and, out of habit, fell asleep in my usual corner.

The next morning Tully let himself in.

"Son, we need to check our crab pots!" I looked up, the sun was shining and it was morning.

"I'll make some coffee," he said. "Did someone leave a brown backpack when they left?"

"A brown backpack? Liana and I threw away everything not nailed down." Tully held up the backpack to show me. I looked into the side bedroom.

"Godiva's here," I said. "She's asleep in the back."

"The brunette?" Tully asked.

"No, the blonde." I draped my sleeping bag over her.

"Hi," she said, opening one eye. I left a ten-dollar bill on the kitchen table for her.

"I still didn't find my car," I complained to Tully.

"We'll be all right; it's not a long walk. Bring the wagon for our crabs and fish." We walked out and made it to the end of our block.

"Look who's coming!" Tully said. Liana and Laura walked up.

"What are you doing up so early?" I asked.

"We're out for our morning walk," Liana said.

"Godiva showed up at the Cave this morning."

"Is she awake?" she asked.

"No, she looked exhausted to me."

"I'll stop by later and check on her," Liana said.

We pulled our crab pots and made out well. We drove the boat to the fish house and sold everything.

I arrived back at the Cave around one in the afternoon. Liana and Godiva sat at the kitchen table.

"We've been waiting for you to come back," Godiva said. "We wanted to make you a late lunch."

"I need to get a shower," I said. When I returned, Liana stood over a pot in the kitchen. Godiva sat at the table cutting up vegetables.

"What are you two making?" I asked.

"Vegetable soup," Godiva said. We spent the time together eating lunch and talking.

"I'm heading to Texas for a while," Godiva said. "I got an offer to work with horses, and I can't turn that down. I'll be living at a ranch."

"A ranch! That sounds neat!" Liana said.

"You've always loved horses, and it's far enough away that you should be safe," I said.

"It's more than that; I want to straighten my life out."

"When are you leaving?" I asked.

"In the morning. A guy'll drive me all the way; he's heading to Mexico."

"Do you feel safe driving with a guy all the way to Texas?" Liana asked. Godiva just smiled.

"Well, I know you want to lay down roots somewhere, but I'm going to miss you!" I said. "Maybe we could go somewhere tonight?"

"I'd rather just spend a quiet night indoors," Godiva said.

"Why not play a board game?" Liana said. "We've got a lot at our house."

"I have a letter to show you before we go," I said to Godiva.

"A letter? From who?" she asked.

"Remember Clair the Mormon girl from our trip out west? I've been writing to her, and she sent a letter addressed to you."

"You didn't open it?"

"No." Godiva took the letter into the back bedroom to read it.

"Clair?" Liana asked.

"When we traveled out west, we met a girl who was thrown out of her community. Her Elders told her that her marriage was annulled and she wasn't allowed to see her husband again. She didn't know why they ordered her to leave; they just did."

"That's awful!" Liana said. A few moments later Godiva came back to the table.

"Clair's back with her husband in Colorado; evidently it was some kind of punishment against him. He did something the church didn't like, and they retaliated by sending his wife away."

"They can't do that!" Liana said.

"Trust me, it's their community; they can do whatever they wish," Godiva said.

"But you said she was back?" I said.

"Evidently her husband made amends with the church, they flew her back home, and she thinks she's expecting!" Godiva said.

"Well, it sounds like she's home and happy," I said. "Let's head over to Liana's and pick out a game." We walked over; Laura greeted us at the door.

"Godiva, this is Laura," Liana said. Godiva looked through the stack of games.

"I like Trouble," Godiva said.

"Well, have a good time," Liana stated.

"Don't think you're not invited!" Godiva said. "I want you and Laura over at seven for dinner, and then we'll play."

"Okay," Liana said.

Godiva and I headed back toward the Cave.

"I didn't mention it, but Clair hopes we have children soon also," Godiva said. "I couldn't give you that, but Liana could."

"Kids? Let's not even go there. It's not like Liana's my girlfriend."

"She could be," Godiva said. "I need to buy some groceries. Why don't you go home and get some sleep?"

"Do you need any cash?" I asked.

Godiva held up the ten I'd left for her. "I'll be okay," she said. "Get some rest; you're exhausted."

That evening I woke up to the sound of girls laughing. I walked in to the kitchen to find Godiva, Liana and Laura sitting at the table.

"Look at his hair; it's standing straight up!" Laura said. I pushed my hair down with my hands.

"Godiva made roast chicken, wild rice stuffing, homemade biscuits and fresh corn," Liana said.

"Godiva did?"

"Laura brought a salad, and I brought iced tea. Can I say grace?"

"Well, that will be two firsts here: someone using the oven and someone saying grace."

Liana said grace, and we all ate. It was excellent.

"We had a chance to talk while you were asleep," Liana said. "I think I'm beginning to understand all this."

"Godiva, Laura and you talked while I was asleep?" I asked. "About what?"

"EVERYTHING!" Godiva joked.

"Anything I should be worried about?" I asked.

"She said really nice things about you," Liana said. "I can see you two are close." Liana kept staring at Godiva and me, attempting to understand our relationship.

"Let's play Trouble and let Ethan get out of trouble," Godiva said. We played well into the night.

Later Liana asked if we would walk them home. It seemed strange to me that two girls would feel unsafe walking home, even though the area can be unsafe. When we arrived at Liana's house she hugged Godiva goodnight.

"If I don't see you again, have a safe trip," Liana said.

Godiva and I walked back to the Cave.

"Ethan, don't let this one get away," she said, staring into my eyes.

"Don't let what get away?"

"Who do you think? You and Liana make a really cute couple."

"Liana? She has no interest in me, and it's you I'm going to be hurting over."

"She's smart, innocent and fragile. I'd give anything to trade places with her. I've got to go where I can be safe and do something I enjoy."

"I'm so confused now, I don't know what's up. I mean I kissed her on the spot the other day, and she almost freaked out. As it turns out she'd never even been kissed!" Godiva walked over and gave me a really long hug.

"I know this is hard, but I think it's all for the best. You need to go one way and I the other."

The next morning I woke up to find Liana staring at me.

Where's Godiva?

"I let myself in. I hope you're not mad. I wanted to surprise you. I brought a cantaloupe for breakfast." Coffee brewed on the stove, and steam rose from the teapot.

A few minutes later Godiva walked out of a back bedroom wearing jeans and a white tee shirt. She giggled and nudged me with her foot.

"Can you help me for a moment?" she asked. We walked to the back room.

"No interest in you, huh? What do you call this?"

"She wanted to surprise you!" I said.

"She came early to see if we were in bed together, you idiot! I think she really likes you!"

We went back to the kitchen and ate breakfast. The mood felt uncomfortable, and I really didn't know what to say.

"You two will be together at school?" Godiva asked.

"Yes," Liana answered.

"Promise me you'll look after him?" Godiva asked. Liana looked stunned and didn't know what to say. Someone blasted a car's horn out front. Godiva grasped Liana hand.

"I've always loved Ethan," she said.

"I can see that."

We carried Godiva's things out to the car. Liana and I watched as she drove away.

WHAT WOULD HAPPEN IF?

It's early morning, and here I am walking the beach again. I shouldn't be out, the sky is dark with rain pelting down. Flashes of lightning cut across the sky, but I really don't care. Godiva left for Texas, and I doubt I'll ever see her again.

I walked back to the Cave, soaked to the skin. I found a wet umbrella sitting in the kitchen. Liana stood making breakfast.

"You loved her didn't you?" she asked. "I can understand that; she's beautiful."

"I've always tried to hold back my feelings for her. Sometimes it worked, and sometimes it didn't."

"Why would you have held back your feelings?"

"Godiva and Sadie have had to keep moving since I met them. They both worry that people are looking for them. I don't understand all of it, but I think both have families that are utter nightmares. They worried that if I kept them for more than a few days at a time they'd be found. That's why I could never keep them and why I always had to let go. Seeing them leave has never been easy. I worry about them a lot."

"So you couldn't love them because they had to keep leaving?"

"Yes."

"You mentioned another girl, Sadie? Is she still around? Could she show up at any time, too?"

"Yes, she's Godiva's companion. Sadie's the stronger, worldlier, of the two. If you can believe it, she's also prettier. She's tall and brunette."

"But she's not your girlfriend?"

"I think we just covered that. I haven't had a lot of girlfriends." The mood seemed tense, and once again I didn't know what to say.

"Well, there's still a lot to clean up around here. Mind if I help you?"

"I really should spend some time alone."

"No, you really need someone here with you!"

"I guess you're right. Well, I wanted to put the doors back on their hinges."

"What stopped you?"

"I couldn't do it alone."

"Then you really do need someone here with you."

I took wooden pencils and hammered them into the worn-out screw holes. We then took new screws and attached the hinges to the doorframes. Lastly we adjusted the doors so they would close right.

"I really do like working with you," Liana said. "Why don't you hang around with other guys?"

"I always seem to get into trouble when I'm with other guys. I grew up with a lot of destructive people. Lots of low-lifes, drunks, druggies, creeps. It's more than that, though; it's that I can't do the things I need to do with guys around. Take Sadie and Godiva. I've really enjoyed the time we've spent together, but if I had other guys around, all they would want to do is hit on them."

Liana seemed hesitant as if there was something on her mind.

"Hun, is there something you want to ask me?" I asked. "If it's something about Godiva or Sadie or anything, it's okay to ask. I won't jump down your throat or get angry." Liana said nothing and went back to sweeping.

"I really care about you, but I don't want you to get the wrong impression," Liana finally said. "I don't want you to think that I'm here to take Godiva's place. I don't need a boyfriend."

"I didn't think you did." Liana still seemed troubled. I took her by the hand, and we sat down on the sofa. She pulled her hand away, seemed torn and then grasped mine. I could see her eyes tearing up.

"Would you like to get something to eat?" I asked.

"No, I need to go home." I went to hug her good-bye, but she pulled away and left.

I decided to make a bowl of soup. I found a can in the cupboard and pulled a pot out. When I turned I saw Liana standing, staring at me. Tears ran down her face. She started to speak but stopped.

"Are you upset about Godiva?" I asked.

"No, this is something important."

"Do you want to go for a walk or sit on the sofa?"

"The sofa." As I walked past her, she grasped my arm.

"If you die tonight, do you know for sure you'll go to heaven?" she asked.

"I never really thought about it."

"Let's go for a walk and talk."

We talked about God well into the afternoon.

"Would you consider making a decision at church?" she asked.

"I'll think about it." Liana and I walked toward her house, and a police cruiser pulled alongside. It was Officer Buckwheat.

"Ethan, we found your car in a cornfield. Do have any idea why it would be there?"

"Tina said someone borrowed it, but I had no idea where it was."

"Come on. I'll drive you to where it's at."

"Can I come, too?" Liana asked.

"Yes," Officer Buckwheat said. We climbed into the back of his cruiser, and he headed out of town.

"I'm finished here on September fifteenth," he said. "I got a real job in the suburbs."

"I'm happy for you; I'm just about ready to leave also."

He drove to a farm field. "It's in there," he said.

Liana and I followed the car's trail through the cornfield into a blackberry thicket.

"There's my car!" I said. "How did it get here?" When we opened the door, we found the interior full of beer cans, trash and spilled French fries.

"Look, a tiny hairbrush," Liana said.

"I recognize it. It's Kathy's."

"What would her hairbrush be doing in your car?" Liana asked.

"While Tully and I were sailing, her and her friends must have taken my car for a joyride."

"That's really wicked! Do you really think she could have done this?"

"I'm sure it was her and a few others." I tried my key, found that the car started, and looked for a path out.

"Get in," I said. I drove the Pinto back through the cornfield to the road.

"Will your car make it home?" Officer Buckwheat asked. I checked the car, and everything seemed in working order.

"I think we're in good shape," I said. Liana and I drove off.

"What time is it?" I asked.

"Almost two in the afternoon," Liana said. "Why?"

"Tully and I need to make our last run for crabs." He sat waiting for us when we arrived back at the Cave.

"I see you found your car," Tully said. "Well, this is it, son. The last darn crab run of the year."

"Can I come out with you two?" Liana asked.

"Tully and I should do this …."

"No, son, have her come." Tully joined us in my car, and we drove over to the docks. We all climbed into the boat and went out.

"I talked with Ethan today about God and faith and heaven," Liana said.

"Everything's going so fast," I said.

"I warned you that it would be like that," Tully said. "Things change in an instant."

"But I'm not ready to finish this yet," I said.

"Well, this is it, son; our crabbing season's done."

"No, I mean I'm not ready to see you go."

"Well, go I must. My work here's done. It's time for me to get back to my wife."

"It just seems too soon."

"What she talked about is right," Tully said. "Things don't always go well. When things don't, it's faith that gets us through. It's God who protects us."

I tried to keep my composure as we pulled the crab pots in and dumped them. I stood on each of the crab pots to flatten them.

"It's a lot of changes all at once." I said. We hauled our crabs to a dealer and got paid in cash for them. We threw the flattened crab pots into a dumpster.

"Do you want either of the boats or the motor?" Tully asked. "If not, I know someone who'll buy them."

"No, get rid of them."

"Can you give me a ride to Camden on Saturday night?" Tully asked.

"Saturday? I thought you sailed in two weeks?"

"We have a ship to prepare for sea." We dropped Tully off at his place and drove back to the Cave.

"We didn't leave the door open, did we?" Liana asked. "I saw a tall blond kid sitting on the top deck." Liana and I walked up.

"Bobby, this is Liana." Bobby kind of scowled when he saw her.

"I thought we could go out for night blues," he said. "But it looks like you got company."

"I'm about to take her home."

"Then we could go?"

"Yeah, I think I'd like that." I drove Liana home in silence.

"Are you upset?" I asked her. "Did you want me to hang around with you tonight?"

"No, I told you I don't need a boyfriend."

"I understand."

"Please?" she asked.

"Please what?"

"Please don't go out with Bobby?"

"Bluefishing is safe. I'll be fine." Liana whirled, wrapped her arms around me, and her fingernails dug into my sides.

"Hun, I thought you didn't want a boyfriend?" I said.

"It's not about that. I've got a really bad feeling about tonight. Please don't go!"

"I'll be okay." I left her and went to meet Bobby.

"She's a strange chick," Bobby said. "Why you fooling with her?"

"I can't describe it, but there's something really special about her." We loaded our gear into his blue Mustang and headed to the docks.

"You won't believe what Tully and I did," I said to Bobby.

"What?" he asked.

"Sailed a car-top sailboat up the canal from Port Penn."

"Port Penn where the barges almost took us out?" he asked.

"Yeah, sailed it through the canal all the way to Annapolis."

We drove down to the party boat GAMER and paid twenty dollars each to go out. The captain searched an area about ten miles offshore before finding a school of large bluefish. Bobby and I caught fish until our arms tired. The fun intensified when a school of giant trout moved in. I struggled with a trout, finally dragging it over the side.

"That's the largest trout I've ever seen," the captain said.

"I might get it mounted," I replied.

At three in the morning we returned to the dock. We loaded up Bobby's car with our fish and gear.

"Do you know where we are?" Bobby asked over his blaring radio.

"It's part of Wildwood I've never been in." We drove through a series of four-way stop signs.

As we came upon the next stop sign everything went wrong. I saw a flash of a car skidding out of control.

"Look out!" I screamed. Blinding lights approached, brakes squealed, and a car slammed into my door. The sound of metal tearing and glass shattering filled my ears. Bobby's car flipped over and spun like a top before stopping. I felt something in my neck, a piece of the side window. I pulled it out and we both slid through what was left of our doors.

"Bobby, what happened!"

"Look out!" he screamed. Four furious drunks ran at us from their wrecked car. One held a tire iron. He hit me on the side with a sickening thud. I wrenched it away from the guy and threw it as far as I could. Then fists flew everywhere. A girl in a car behind us laid on her horn. The guys ran for their car. One grabbed a bag and tried to hide it in a culvert. The police showed up. Ambulances arrived. The police handcuffed the other guys and took them away.

"Are you hurt?" an EMT asked later.

"I'll live."

"Let me clean you up at least; you're covered in blood."

"No, just leave me alone. I feel stupid enough as it is." They checked Bobby out and decided to take him to the hospital.

"You coming?" he asked. "I'm sure my car is totaled."

"I'm walking out of here as fast as I can."

"You sure?"

"I've had enough. I'm leaving."

I walked until I was in a part of Wildwood that I recognized. I passed Liana's place. I stood outside more in a stupor than anything else. I found her door unlocked.

I didn't know which bedroom was hers, but I took a chance and got it right. Liana and Laura slept in two twin-sized beds. I tried to shake Liana awake. Laura woke up and screamed. Liana woke up and stared.

"I warned you not to go," she said.

"I know."

"What was it?"

"A car full of drunks hit us. Terrifying."

"Are you ready?" she asked.

"Yes."

Laura returned with a towel and washed the blood off me.

"We'll meet you in the kitchen," Liana said.

Liana and Laura came into the kitchen dressed in pajamas. The three of us prayed together. I made my peace with God.

"It's early. Why don't you sleep on the couch?" Laura asked.

"No, I'm going home." I left, walked back to the Cave, and collapsed in my corner.

Around noontime I woke up to see Tully standing over me.

"You all right, son? I heard about last night."

"I guess I'm okay."

"We need to go to the impound and get your things." As I got up I felt sore and shaky.

"I guess I'm hurting a little more than I thought."

Climbing into my Pinto was harder than I thought it would be. I sat in the driver's seat unable to turn the key.

"I'm not ready to drive yet."

"I'll drive," Tully said.

"Can we pick up Liana and Laura on the way?" I asked.

"Sure." We switched sides, and he drove over to Liana's place.

"Are you still hurting?" Laura asked.

"Yes." We all drove over to the impound lot together. Bobby's car sat twisted and barely recognizable.

"Is that the car?" Laura asked. "God was watching over you! That's the only way you could have survived that wreck!"

"Their car struck right where you were sitting?" Tully asked. "The impact bent the car into a U shape."

"And flipped it over," I said.

"I don't see how you climbed out through the window?" Liana said. "I doubt a cat could slide through it now."

"Somehow I got out."

"I don't see how you two escaped death," Laura said.

"Well, Liana warned me not to go; I should have listened to her. And after we got out, the other guys attacked, but I don't know why."

"The guys that hit you are in jail," Tully said. "The driver's being charged with drunk driving, the others with public intoxication. They're all being charged with assault. They found a bag full of drugs nearby, but they haven't charged them with that yet."

"What do you want to do?" Liana asked.

"I just want to go home and think things through."

"We need to get your things out of the trunk," Tully said. He pried it open and retrieved my fish and gear.

"I've never seen a trout that big," Tully said.

"I'm going to get it mounted; it'll remind me not to be an idiot."

The Beachcomber

Tully dropped the girls off. He drove me back and walked home from the Cave. I went inside to think. I tried to concentrate, but the sound of the squealing tires and twisting metal kept ringing in my ears. After sitting for over an hour I heard footsteps coming up the stairs. Liana walked in.

"I know you wanted to be alone, but this isn't a good time for that," she said.

"I think I realized that while sitting here."

"Do you want to talk?"

"There's issues in my life that I need to resolve. The first issue is alcohol. All summer I've drunk less and less, but I need to decide to either continue casual drinking or quit altogether. I've seen the effects it has on people, and I don't like it at all. It's been around me my entire life. Every family gathering, every party, every social event boasted alcohol. Every gathering someone asks, "Where's your drink?" People would seem upset if you didn't have one in your hand at all times. And last night a drunk almost killed me, again."

"I understand."

"The second issue is destructive friends. I think I need to drop them."

"It's hard."

"Do you or Laura drink at all?"

"Oh my gosh, no!"

"And your friends?"

"That's harder … we all know people, including family members, that can pull us down."

I heard a knock at the door and looked out to see Laura's smiling face.

"We're talking about drinking and destructive friends," Liana said.

"I've found that choosing the wrong boyfriend can be destructive," Laura said.

"And booze?"

"I tried communion wine and didn't like it," she explained.

"Do you have any booze left around here?" Liana asked.

"I'm sure I have some beer left in the cold shed."

"Why not just pour it out?" Liana asked.

"I wouldn't fool with it," Laura said. A moment later we heard footsteps coming up the stairs.

"Anyone home?" I looked and saw Sadie standing at the door.

"Come on in!" I called. A moment later she stood in the room with us.

"Liana, Laura, this is Sadie!" They stared at her wide-eyed not knowing what to say.

"I heard you were in a really bad accident!" Sadie said. "What were you doing fooling with your f-r-i-e-n-d anyway?"

"We spent the night fishing."

"I warned you he was bad news!" Sadie said.

"I told him the same," Liana said.

"So you're Liana?" Sadie asked. "Godiva called and told me about you! You're even cuter than she described." Liana blushed. The mood seemed awkward.

"Well, I haven't eaten yet. You want to go out?" I asked. We drove over to a diner and ordered. The waitress brought us our food as we talked. Laura and Liana seemed awestruck by Sadie and kept staring.

"I need to clean up my life," I explained to Sadie.

"I know ...."

"It's nice that you cared enough for Ethan to come and make sure he was okay," Liana said.

"Godiva and I can only list one person in the world that we love, and it's him. Do me a favor? Watch over him?"

"Where are you staying?" I asked.

"I got a ride in from Philly when I heard about the accident," Sadie said. "But I'll have to leave soon."

"How did you hear about the accident?" Liana asked. Sadie just smiled.

"Sadie knows everything," I said.

"You can stay with us," Laura said. Sadie smiled and nodded.

"I'd like to, but I have to go." She gathered her things and left.

"She leaves that quickly?" Liana asked.

"They come and go at will."

She seemed perplexed. "I can't compete with this!" she blurted out.

Laura seemed shaken. "Liana!" she said.

"Hun, you didn't hear what Godiva said. What Sadie insisted! They'd both trade places with you in a minute just to lead a normal life. You don't need to compete with them. You're the lucky one."

HAS ANYONE SEEN MY BEER?

I stood at a bulkhead, staring out at the salt marsh on the opposite shoreline. Brown reeds grew out of the green, grass-covered banks. Red-winged blackbirds perched on the reeds, bending them in half. The high tide flooded the area, covering the mud banks and giving a peaceful look to everything.

So many changes in my life so fast. My bumps and bruises are healing. I have to call Bobby's insurance company and give a report....

One morning Bruce walked into the Cave.

"I heard about your accident. It's best to face these things and get them over with. You ready to go fishing again? I heard that big trout are hitting at Villa's."

"I need a break. Fishing sounds good."

"Well, I've got a small boat at Villa's. We can launch it off the beach. Do you have any beer left?"

"In the cold shed. Take all that's left and keep what you want." An hour later Bruce and I arrived at Villa's on Delaware Bay. We walked down the narrow beach to check it out.

"It's really shallow for quite a ways out," I said. "I can see every rock on the bottom."

"We'll just walk the boat out and climb in. I filled the cooler with the sixteen-ounce bottles from your cold shed."

"I'm kinda at an impasse on the beer. I'm thinking of giving up drinking. I think God doesn't want me to drink anymore."

"That sounds kind of radical," Bruce said. "If God doesn't want you to drink, then he'll give you a lousy day and we won't catch any fish."

"That sounds right," I said. We shoved off and began drifting. Almost immediately we began catching big, beautiful trout. We also caught flounder.

"Well, we're catching fish like crazy, so have another beer," Bruce said. The sun was bright, the water calm, and it wasn't too hot. We caught fish all day long.

"We had a fantastic day, and nothing could have gone any better," I said. "Let's head in." He drove the boat back toward the shore.

"We'll have to drag the boat the last ten yards or so; it's just too shallow here," Bruce said.

"At least we won't end up stepping on something. The water's clear as glass."

We pulled the boat to the water's edge and began unloading it.

"The cooler's a two man job; it's full of fish and beer," I said. I grabbed one side of the cooler and Bruce the other.

"See I was right," he said. "If God didn't want you to have the beer, he wouldn't have given you such a perfect day." At that moment we heard a crashing sound as the bottom fell out of the cooler. Bruce and I looked into the clear water. Nothing was there. No fish, no full beer bottles, no empty beer bottles, nothing. Bruce grabbed the net and walked around the area.

"Could they have swum away?" he asked.

"The dead fish? Beer bottles, full and empty, should be floating. Even the ice is gone!"

"I don't understand," Bruce said.

"Well, do you want the sky to light up with ETHAN, DON'T DRINK? That's the last drink I'm gonna take."

"You almost got me convinced. This one takes the cake."

We packed up everything and drove back to Wildwood.

"Look," Bruce said, "this is just another of the freaky things that happens when we're out drinkin' together."

"No, it's the last freaky thing that's going to happen when we're out drinkin' together."

When we drove up, Liana sat waiting on the porch.

"You need to get cleaned up!" she said. "Tonight's the night we drop Tully off at his ship."

"Tully?" Bruce asked. "Oh, she means the Beachcomber? He's leaving?"

"Going out to sea."

"Well, I'm heading home," Bruce said, climbing into his car. "It's been real."

"That it has!" I watched as he drove off.

I turned to Liana. "Hun, I'm not ready to see Tully off. It just seems too soon! So many changes have taken place so quickly, and I can't deal with this!"

"I know."

"I've learned so much, and to see him just walk onboard a ship seems … wrong."

"Remember Godiva and Sadie?" Liana asked. "You had to let them go, and now you have to let Tully go."

"I'll get a shower."

Later Laura, Liana and I picked Tully up. Surprisingly, the only thing he had to take with him was a large duffle bag. He climbed in, and we took off for Camden.

"It looks like you got some sun today!" Tully said.

"Bruce and I drove over to Villa's and went out."

"You didn't spend the day drinking beer on his boat, did you?" Laura asked. "I warned you not to fool with this!"

"You don't have to ask. I know he did," Tully said.

"We did, and Laura was right."

"What happened?" Liana asked.

"We caught lots of fish, drank lots of beer and …."

"And WHAT?" Liana asked.

"God took them all back."

"Sounds right," Tully said laughing.

"Tully, there's something else. I don't know how to say it, but I'm grateful for all you've done with me this summer. I don't think I'll ever forget you. I …."

"It's okay, son. We've had a good time and got to do things most people couldn't."

We got to the shipyard much faster than I ever would have imagined. I pulled Tully's duffle bag out of the trunk.

"At least give me a hug good-bye," I asked. We hugged tightly.

"I'll try and write, but sometimes it's weeks until we can get mail off these ships," Tully explained. He hugged Liana and Laura good-bye also. A moment later the ship blew its horn.

"The night watch is beginning. I've got to go, son," Tully said. "Like I said, my work here is done. You'll be okay." We all waved until he walked through a doorway. Then he was gone.

"Laura, can you drive home? I really shouldn't drive right now."

"Of course." I gave her the keys and climbed in back. She turned out of the shipyard and headed home. I just couldn't hold back anymore and burst into tears.

Later that evening Laura pulled up to the Cave.

"Do you want me to stay awhile?" Liana asked.

"No, I think I'm okay now." I went inside. Liana and Laura stood out front.

I can't believe how jaded I've become this summer; they want me to walk them home!

We headed up the street toward their place.

"Ethan," Laura said, "a lot's been going on. Don't do anything stupid, okay?"

"Like what?"

"She means that you've had emotion after emotion hit you this week. Take some time to breathe. Don't do anything silly."

"I won't."

DISASTER BY ANY OTHER NAME

*F*irst Godiva left and then Tully. I don't even know what to do without him around! I can't call Bruce or Bobby... I may as well try and fix the Cave. I hope Liana will stop by. I could use a friend. I can fix the burnt deck boards.

I pulled the old boards off and purchased new ones. I started fixing the bathroom, which was all but destroyed this summer. I heard footsteps.

I hope it's Liana. Kathy walked in.

"Kathy, what are you doing here? Everyone's gone home."

"So now it's your private house?"

"No, I just didn't expect anyone to show up."

"Are you actually going to try and fix up this wreck?"

"Something like that."

Kathy took her things into one of the back bedrooms. She reappeared wearing a bikini. "I'm going to the beach; you coming?"

"No, I'm going to just hang around."

"You're acting weird. Is your girlfriend down?"

"Godiva? No, she's in Texas."

"Well, I'm heading out."

After Kathy left I started to think about why I wanted to fix the Cave. The work seemed therapeutic but expensive. Around noontime Liana stopped by.

"Whose stuff is in the back room?" she asked.

"Kathy stopped by. She went to the beach."

"I don't remember her."

"She's got brunette hair and usually wears a mini-skirt."

"Oh, the wild one, I remember her now. She gave me a really nasty look the last time I saw her. Isn't she one of those who abandoned you car in the farm field?"

"I guess. I can't deal with that now."

"What are you trying to do today?"

"I want to fix the house, but it's expensive."

"Call the realtor who manages the place and explain your dilemma to him," she said.

"Oh, like he won't call the cops or something."

"Maybe he will, but what's wrong with addressing this head on? Maybe it will work out."

"How would I find out who manages the place?"

"Did you look in the drawers and cupboards? They usually leave

194

their card around."

Liana searched the drawers and found the realtor's card.

"His office is two blocks away. Let's walk over," she said. We walked down to explain the situation to him. He didn't seem upset.

"You mean the house got the hell kicked out of it this summer? What a surprise. All the houses that college kids rent get wrecked. Well, let's drive over and take a look."

We arrived a few minutes later.

"Well, at least someone swept the trash away," he said. "That's encouraging."

"I'm trying to fix the place up. I guess I feel guilty. I hung the doors and fixed the deck. The toilet's cracked, so we'll need a new one."

"Actually the place is in better shape than what I expected. Look, if you two want to fix the place, I'll pay you three dollars an hour to do it."

"That's fair," Liana said.

"You've made a good start. I've got an account at the building supply place as you head out of town. I'll give you my business card, and he'll ask the address."

"Sounds good." We watched him get into his car and leave.

"Well, he didn't call the cops, did he?" Liana joked.

"I'm sorry. You were right, and I was wrong."

"Well, if he's going to pay us, I'd better make a ledger to track our hours." She found a notebook and began writing.

"I'd better get to work," I said. I disconnected the commode and dragged it out. Liana joined me, and we disconnected the faucet also. We drove over to the supply place and bought a cheap commode and faucet. We also rented a carpet cleaner.

"We might have to scrub the carpets over and over again, but I think they'll come clean."

"We can try our best," she said. Later Liana made an impromptu dinner for us.

"I really like working with you," I told Liana.

"I've had fun also," she replied. A moment later Kathy returned from the beach.

"Who's she!" Kathy demanded.

"This is Liana; she's helping me fix the house." Kathy shook her head in disgust and went in back.

"Ethan, come back here!" Kathy called. I didn't move.

"Go!" Liana breathed out. I found her in the back bedroom.

"WHAT ARE YOU DOING WITH HER?" Kathy screamed. "She isn't for you! Have you looked at her? You need to get your head examined!"

"Don't scream. Liana will hear, and I care about her. She's my friend, and she's welcome any time!" I said.

"I'm not trying to fight; I guess I'm trying to look out for you.

I'm heading to the Sand Dunes tonight, and I need a ride. I've waited all summer to date Jimmy, and now I have my chance. We're getting together. Maybe you'll find someone?"

"I don't want to go to the Sand Dunes! I don't want to ever have another drink!"

"Look, we've lived together all summer, and have I even asked you for a favor? I'm begging now, and you're saying no?"

"Look, I'll drive you over to the Sand Dunes. I'll drink a diet Coke. If your guy shows up, he can take you home. I'll stay one hour, and then I'm leaving with or without you."

"If that's the way you want it."

I walked back to the kitchen to find that Liana had left. I caught up with her halfway to her house. She'd been crying.

"I can't deal with this!" she said.

"I know, people can be cruel."

"So are you going to this bar with her?"

"I feel obligated."

"Listen to me … DON'T GO!"

"I promised."

"Look, I can understand why you'd want to go out with her. What I can't understand is why you won't listen to me."

"I'm not going out with her, but I promised I'd take her."

"I'm not your girlfriend, so what does it matter?"

I returned to find Kathy wearing a black mini-skirt and boots.

"Maybe you'll find someone more your type at the Sand Dunes tonight," Kathy said. "I can't believe you're fooling around with her."

"I'm not dating Liana, but I'd rather date her than anyone I'd find at the Sand Dunes. You just don't understand."

"Understand? I walk in and see her sitting at the table wearing a white sunhat, a blouse with sailboats on it and knee-length Bermudas? Give me a break!"

"She looked nice to me."

"Well, wait till you see the girls at the Sand Dunes."

"Look, remember what I said? I'm not paying your cover charges or your drinks. I stay one hour, and then I leave. If you're not ready, then you can find a ride home. Got it?"

"Fine."

I changed, and then we left.

"Look, I'm sorry I was rude to that girl," Kathy said. "She's just not your kind. You don't need to be so uptight. This is a special night for me. I'll finally get to spend some time with Jimmy!" Kathy slid over and put her arm around me.

"Why won't you relax?" she asked.

"Because you're scaring the hell out of me."

"Would cookies help?" she asked.

"Are you kidding me?"

"No, cookies are supposed to calm you down. Stop and let me buy you some cookies!" We stopped and bought a bag of chocolate chip cookies. We ate the cookies while driving to the Sand Dunes.

"We're here!" I said. We each paid our cover charges, got our hands stamped and went in. Kathy brought the cookies in with her.

"One hour!" I said to Kathy. The stamp allowed us to go in and out of the club if we wished.

I hate bars; the music is always booming, and I can't hear enough to talk to anyone. I went outside and started talking to a girl from Vermont.

"It's so loud and crowded that I couldn't stand it in there," she said.

"I didn't like it, either."

A few minutes later Kathy appeared with some guy. "Can we use your car?" she asked.

"If you mean to have sex in it, then no."

"I mean to just talk," she said. They went to my car and returned a few minutes later.

"Is my hour up?" she asked.

"Fifteen minutes," I said. I sat outside talking, and Kathy returned sometime later.

"Jimmy had to leave. I'm ready to head home," she said.

"Thank God!" I said. We walked to my car and got in. Kathy clenched the bag of cookies.

"Can I have some? I'm starved," I said.

"There's really nothing left. Why don't you stop and buy some more?"

"No, I'll wait."

"You're way too uptight. Can't you relax?" she asked. We turned onto the highway and began the drive home. I looked in my rearview mirror and saw flashing red lights coming toward us. I pulled over.

"I wasn't speeding!" I said to Kathy. A moment later two New Jersey State patrolmen approached my car. One was a sergeant, and one was very young, a rookie being broken in.

"Was I speeding, Officer?" I asked. Kathy lit a cigarette and tossed the smoking match out the window. The patrolman stood looking at the smoking match.

"Put out your cigarette!" he ordered. She flung her lit cigarette at him and stuffed her cookies under her seat.

"Get out of the car!" he ordered. We did.

"Why did she fling her cigarette at me?" he asked me.

"I don't know."

"What did she stuff under the seat?"

"Cookies."

The patrolman pulled out the cookies out and dumped them on

the car. Half a dozen cookies fell out as well as four bags of drugs. They handcuffed us and put us into the patrol car.

They took us to a police station and chained us to a bar on a wall.

"Don't talk," he ordered. He sat typing up charges. They later drove us over to Atlantic County prison for processing.

When we arrived, they gave us jumpsuits to put on. They also gave us a mug and a tablespoon. A changing room sat to the side, but Kathy decided to strip down in front of the guards and jeering prisoners.

"I'm ready to go," she said. They marched her away. They put me in a cell with nine others to await my bail hearing.

They passed around a jug of milk for breakfast. I decided not to have any. A mixture of runny mashed potatoes and undercooked liver greeted us for lunch. I decided not to eat that, either.

"Your case is next," a guard called. They walked me into the adjoining courtroom. Kathy sat in the second row, and I sat in the fourth. They charged her with simple possession. She made bail and left. Next it was my turn.

"The county has no charges against you, but you may be called as a witness," the judge explained. "You're free to go."

"My car?" I asked.

"The clerk will explain how to get it out of impound."

I paid a small fortune, and they released my car. I bought a new door lock for the Cave since I never wanted to see Kathy again. When I arrived, I found that she'd beat me home. Her things and one hundred and fifty dollars of my money were gone.

I found some bread and ate half a loaf before passing out in the front room. Someone pounded on the door, and it awakened me. Liana peered through the window. I let her in.

"I've been worried sick about you!" she said. "I thought the worst had happened."

"The worst did happen. I ...."

"Don't be an idiot, you could have been killed or maimed or something."

"I got arrested with Kathy; she was dealing drugs. I wasn't charged."

"Look, you learned a lesson on trusting destructive people. Now don't do it again!"

"Will you just hug me for a long time and say nothing?" She hugged me very gently, holding the sides of my arms.

"No, a real hug?" I grasped her tightly, and I felt her arms wrap around me. Her tears fell on my chest.

"What are you going to do about Kathy?" she asked.

"I've been plotting all kinds of things against her."

"You need to let go of your anger against Kathy. It's hard, but you need to do it."

"I'll try."

I like Liana a lot. She has a will and strength I've never known."

"Can we …?"

She put her finger to my lips. "I think we've had enough emotion for one day?"

"Okay."

"In two days I head back to school," she said. "We'll be attending classes. We won't have much time for each other."

"We won't?"

"Let's just take things slow and see what happens. I'll need to study. I mean, I don't know what to do."

"To do?"

"I've never had a boyfriend, and I won't know what to do."

"Hun, can I kiss you?"

"No! ... I guess."

"Yes or no?"

"Yes, you can kiss me!" She stood with her eyes squinted shut and her lips puckered up.

"Hun, relax?" She did, blushing. I lightly kissed her and stared. "Was that so hard?"

"Yes, and I feel … stupid! Well, we have work to do!" She began sweeping. She stopped and stared. "You're going to help, right?" I went to work on the bathroom door. A moment later she came to get me. The realtor had returned.

"It looks like you got a lot done," he said.

"We have more to do yet, but it's coming."

"I meant to ask. You're the kid who hung around with the Beachcomber, aren't you?"

"Yes."

"I sold his boardwalk property for him. He had me wire the money to Okinawa."

"Yeah, we fished and crabbed together. I'm going to miss him!"

"I think everyone will," Liana added.

THE ANGEL

We finished all the work we could at the Cave. I would be driving Liana to Philadelphia.

"Well, this is it," Liana said. "You can say good-bye to this house. It's time we headed to school."

"Good-bye, you miserable house!" I said. "We just need to stop by the realtor and get paid. Then I'll be ready to hit the road." We stopped, and the realtor paid us for our time.

"The money will help a lot," Liana said. "It might be enough to cover my books. Will you have enough for the fall?"

"I put a small fortune in the bank this summer. I don't know what I would've done without Tully. I guess he kept me busy. We had a lot of fun earning what we did."

"And your friends? Have you decided which are destructive?"

"I think it's a sifting process and not like what you'd think."

"Like what?"

"Well, like Sadie and Godiva--they've always been helpful and ... loving. Karen was here all summer and ... nice. Tina, Kathy, Jamie either did me in or borrowed my car and abandoned it. Some of the guys were decent, some the pits."

"Well, I can't condone how Godiva and Sadie live their lives, but they did care for you."

"But they're gone, and you're here."

Liana just smiled. "I need to reflect on this entire summer," she said.

"I do also. Do you mind if I stop by the boardwalk on the way out of town?"

"I don't see why not." We drove to the boardwalk and parked.

"I'll just wait," she said.

A few minutes later I walked past the black door where Tully had lived on the boardwalk.

"Hey, kid," a stand holder called out. "What happened to the Beachcomber? I ain't seen him around lately." I didn't answer him. I did my best to hold back the tears. The whole summer came rushing past again. I thought of everyone I met and knew. I continued on and came upon the benches. I saw three girls smiling at me.

"E-t-h-a-n," someone called. I turned to see Elvis sitting to the side. "E-t-h-a-n, your angel's ... not ... here."

"Liana? She's waiting in my car. She's heading home."

"No … not her … your a-n-g-e-l isn't here!"

"I don't understand." He motioned to the bench, and I sat down.

"W-h-e-n you first came," he stammered, "I said to myself that b-o-y needs an a-n-g-e-l. You lived with all those d-r-u-n-k-s, and it was bad."

"You mean at the Cave?"

"Yes. It was bad, and that first day when you went out to f-i-s-h, I said to myself 'That boy needs an a-n-g-e-l.' I prayed and saw you catch a fish. I closed my eyes and saw your a-n-g-e-l appear. The Beachcomber was standing next to you."

"Tully?"

"He was your a-n-g-e-l to keep you safe while you were here."

"Are you saying Tully was an angel sent here to protect me?"

"Yes, to make sure bad things didn't h-a-p-p-e-n to you."

"Well, he went home to his wife."

"Yes, his work was done, and he went home. You should go home now also before something bad h-a-p-p-e-n-s to you."

"It's time I headed to school." Elvis looked confused and stared at the ground. Liana walked up.

"I was wondering what was taking you so long," she said.

"Elvis and I were just talking. He says Tully was an angel sent to watch over me."

Liana seemed perplexed. She walked over and sat next to Elvis.

"Some have entertained Angels unaware …," Liana said. "Elvis, you always see the things that none of us notice. I think you're right."

"Well, let me take one last look around," I said.

I stared out at the beach and noticed a flock of snow-white birds, wings extended, soaring on the ocean's breeze. Each bird seemed to follow the other on cue, descending and ascending in unison behind the other.

"Mom, what are those?" A child nearby asked.

"They're white pelicans, but I've never seen them here before," she said. My eyes stayed glued to the flock until they soared out of sight. I noticed Liana and Elvis staring at me.

"Whether Tully's an angel or not I can't say; all I know is that he was heaven sent. I'm going to miss him," I said.

I stared at the white-tipped waves crashing on the beach. The surf pounded the shoreline, and I wondered if a storm lay offshore. I looked to the horizon and noticed a tiny black speck of a freighter heading east. Somewhere out on that blue water Tully stood on the deck of a freighter just like that one. I knew from his love of ships that he would be happy.

"It's time to go," I said.

About the Author

Walt is an avid hunter, fisherman and gatherer who has journeyed to the remotest regions of the country. He began traveling around the country at the age of fourteen, often hitchhiking to his destination.

Walt's travels, encounters, and memories are often the inspiration for his writing. His novels THE BEACHCOMBER, AND THE CABIN relate to portions of his life and the people he interacted with. His novel THE BLUE OCEAN'S PEACE describes a Muslim Chechen girl who grew up fighting the Russians before being sent on an assignment in the United States. Tiny, blond haired and blue eyed she will raise no suspicions.

Walt lives in Lancaster, Pa. with his wife and two children. He still loves to travel and spends his free time hunting, fishing and writing.

Breinigsville, PA USA
12 December 2010
251187BV00002B/2/P